SOLSTICE

jane redd

W0006412

Mirror Press

Edited by Haley Swan and Jaime Theler

Cover art by Claudia McKinney: PhatPuppyArt.com
Cover model Amliel: Amliel.Deviantart.com
Cover design by Rachael Anderson
Typeset by Rachael Anderson

Published by Mirror Press, LLC
ISBN-10:1-941145-69-8
ISBN-13:978-1-941145-69-2

In loving memory of Estee Wood,
Who lost her battle against cancer before this
book could be published,
But who gave me valuable feedback on Solstice
that I'll always treasure.

Other Books by H.B. Moore
Finding Sheba
Lost King
Slave Queen
Beneath
Esther the Queen

Other Books by Heather B. Moore
Heart of the Ocean
Power of the Matchmaker
Love is Come
The Aliso Creek Series
The Fortune Café
The Boardwalk Antiques Shop
The Mariposa Hotel

It is unnatural for a majority to rule, for a majority can seldom be organized and united for specific action, and a minority can.

—Jean-Jacques Rousseau

CHAPTER 1

*J*ezebel, you must not laugh.

My caretaker had warned me about this day, though I didn't believe her at the time.

Don't let them see your tears.

I hadn't cried for years, and even when I was a child I had done it alone, in the dark haven of my bedroom. My heart beat harder with each second as I waited for Sol to come into the classroom. The other students were already scrolling through assignments on their desk consoles, oblivious to the warmth spreading to my cheeks. Their uniformly pale faces, dull eyes, and drab blue-and-gray clothing matched the endless rain outside. We were all the same inside as well—at least we were supposed to be.

You must not show any emotion. Ever. They will find out who you really are.

The door slid open with a whoosh, and I felt Sol's presence before I actually saw him, my heartbeat changing to

1

match the rhythm of his step. No one else looked up or even seemed to notice as he walked across the room and took his seat next to mine. Lately I noticed everything about him.

His hair was a black mess today, which probably explained why he was so late—he must have overslept and run here in the rain. And he must have crossed the schoolyard with no umbrella, since water droplets trickled from his hair. I didn't dare meet his eyes because I knew they'd be on me, and it was getting harder to suppress the urge to touch him. He'd passed so close to my desk that I imagined the brush of his hand on my arm. It was all that I was allowed. Imagining.

Jezebel, you are the Carrier, but no one can ever know.

I tugged my gaze from Sol, feeling the heat creeping through my body, knowing that if anyone in this room could read my thoughts, they'd report me at once. If anyone knew I was *immune,* that the Harmony implant didn't work on me, I would be imprisoned . . . or worse.

Sol settled in the desk next to mine and leaned over. I caught his earthy scent, a mixture of rain and leaves.

"Jez," he whispered.

I had to meet his eyes now, and the way he looked at me made me feel like he could read my soul. His eyes were murky gray, like the early morning sky. *You have no idea what you're doing to me, Sol,* I wanted to say. Instead, I said, "Yes?"

"Sit by me at assembly?"

"Sure," I said. *How does he know there will be an assembly today?* I wanted to smile at him, but didn't—I'd save that reaction for later, once I was alone in my dorm room, remembering every detail of our conversation.

I knew Sol was different the moment he was moved up

to our sixteen-year-old A Level class a few months ago. He was younger than the rest of us, barely sixteen, but that wasn't why I noticed him. He *knew* things. Things about the world Before . . . before the rain started and before the world began to die. Before America and Europe and Africa started to slip into the ocean. But we were forbidden to talk about the Before, and our instructors were forbidden to teach it.

By the third year of nonstop rain, the US government announced that surviving in the weather conditions was far beyond their technological expertise, and that's when the fortifications began. The Constitution gave way to martial law as entire cities flooded, mountains slid into the oceans, and governing bodies were fractured. By the fifth year of the rains, every able child began training in science and technology.

If we wanted the next generation to survive, and the one after that, we had to create a new world. We were now in the thirty-seventh year of the rain, cut off from any civilization outside of Sawatch, the former mountain range in a place named Colorado that was home to our settlement. Now it was only five hundred feet above the ocean.

The countdown to the beginning of class flashed on our screens: *4-3-2-1-start.* I pressed my hand against the upper right corner of the transparent desktop, and my ID transferred. I was logged in. I popped in wireless earbuds just in time to hear an androgynous voice announce, "An assembly has been called. Please exit in an orderly fashion to the assembly hall."

I glanced over at Sol, and his eyes met mine, as if to ask if I was surprised. It was hard not to smile at him, or laugh, but I'd been trained well. I gave him the barest of nods and saw the satisfaction in his gaze.

How he knew the things he did was a mystery—his brilliance was seemingly effortless. Before he'd advanced, I'd been the top of the class, but now I felt like I was scrambling just to keep up with him.

It took everything I had not to tell him how I felt about him.

I stood from my console; half the students had already filed out of the room.

My roommate, Chalice, stepped in front of me, her hand lifted in greeting before she turned and headed for the door. She wore her hair "Chalice-style." Instead of a long ponytail or braid, her cropped hair was as black as night, never tamed, with silver streaks throughout—like carefully arranged chaos. I was more average looking, with long brown hair, dark brows over dark brown eyes. The only thing that set me apart was the barest tint of olive coloring in my skin. Chalice was smart, too, usually second only to me and Sol in her scores. She would definitely make it to the University.

The too-large auditorium, oval in shape, had once been a government building. It felt cold as usual, and I suppressed a shiver as I took a seat next to Sol. There were about thirty students in the A Level, and we spread out among the beat-up metal chairs.

The lights dimmed, save for one focused on the stage. With water-powered machines harvesting energy from the rain, we had no shortage of electricity. The school director, Dr. Wells, stepped onto the stage, his freckled face muted into a dull pink from where I sat near the back.

No one spoke, but the tension practically crackled around the room; an assembly more than once a month was unusual. On my right, Sol whispered, "He must have a big announcement."

I stared ahead, although I sensed every part of Sol next to me.

"Repeat the Covenants with me," the director ordered.

We all stood, and Sol's voice washed over me as we spoke together:

"We unite together to honor the Legislature and respect all judgments. It is our duty to preserve our resources and work toward a secure future. We will sacrifice as one with the single goal in mind . . ."

Sol's arm brushed mine, and the heat crept along my skin. He probably didn't even notice the contact.

When we finished reciting the Covenants, Dr. Wells held up his hand. "With the Separation in one week, we have been asked to do some recruiting among our numbers. You are the elite class of 2099. The A Level courses groom our future scientists and leaders."

I looked forward to the Separation of boys and girls at the University—I wouldn't have to constantly battle my emotions around Sol. Then again I dreaded not being around him, too. I would miss our secretive conversations and always knowing that he'd be there for me to talk to. But while other students would be working on new flavors of processed foods, or developing cement that wouldn't crack in cold temperatures, I would bury myself in a science lab. I already knew what I had to do—my caretaker had made sure of that.

You will infiltrate the Science Commission and become one of them. That way, when the time comes, you'll have the security clearance we need.

Joining the A Level had been the first step in the process. A Level students were meant for greater things than raising families—a small sacrifice that would result in finding ways to save humanity. As long as I avoided any profession in the Legislature, I'd be able to hide my Carrier identity.

Civilization cannot last much longer in this rain, Jezebel. We can't wait for another generation. It must happen through you.

It had been raining for thirty-seven years. When Naomi hadn't been able to achieve A Level, she passed the role of Carrier onto me.

Wells's voice echoed through the auditorium, his face taking on a red tinge. "Members of the Legislature are here to begin the recruiting process."

CHAPTER 2

I f all the lights had been on, it would have been impossible to conceal the apprehension on my face.

Do not let the Legislature know who you really are. Avoid them at all costs.

Naomi's words seemed to echo through my head until I wanted to scream. *They must never know you're a Carrier.* I had known this as a young child. Every baby had a Harmony implanted in their right shoulder to suppress violent emotions that could lead to a rebellion and ultimately undo all of the Legislature's carefully constructed programs to save our civilization.

I had been no different.

When I received my Harmony, Naomi removed the stitches and added a small chip into my shoulder—a Carrier key that I could use to start the generators. Built by the government in the second year of the rains, they could give civilization a second chance, but not without catastrophic risks, and that was my job as the Carrier of the key: to get all of the information necessary before taking those risks.

I realized that Sol was speaking to me—whispering. "They haven't done this in a long time. It's been at least ten years since the Legislature recruited anyone."

Words tried to form around my dry mouth. "What does Wells mean by recruiting?" I asked the question, but it was easy enough to guess.

"Specialized training at the University," Sol said. "You'll be separated from the rest and undergo rigorous testing. If you pass, you're recruited." His gray eyes held mine, and his breath brushed my face.

I absolutely could not go through any testing. Naomi was Taken soon after I reached A Level, but she had warned me plenty about recruiting.

From your first class, you must make your intentions clear. You must excel in your science courses so they'll steer you toward those vocations.

Naomi's caretaker had passed the chip to her before surrendering her own life. If there were any other Carriers, Naomi didn't know them, which meant I was on my own.

Doors slid open behind us, and the recruiters entered the room, their steps almost silent as they walked. They didn't look any different than other government officials— they all wore the sun badge as a sign of the Solstice—but somehow that made them all the more frightening. Often what looked harmless on the outside was anything but on the inside.

Sol's fingers wrapped around mine, and I flinched. He had not touched me like this before. He must have noticed me shaking—something I should have never allowed. His gaze was curious, burning through me.

"I—I must be cold," I said. I could never let him know that it was fear. I couldn't allow myself to touch him for fear that my feelings for him would become plain.

"It's a great honor to be recruited," he whispered.

I nodded, but my eyes stung. As I tried to follow what one of the men was saying about privileges and training, I wondered if this would be the last time Sol and I would sit in a dark auditorium together.

His fingers were strong and steady around my cold and trembling ones. I closed my eyes, grateful that the lights were dim so that no one would know I wasn't paying attention. I'd rather think about Sol's warm hand and the sound of his breathing and the way his leg nearly touched mine. Nearly.

"Solstice is only a few days away," he whispered. "Your hands will be plenty warm then."

Was it possible to hear a smile in a voice when no one was smiling? The next Solstice was one day before the Separation. We only had two Solstice days a year: one during the warm rains, and the other during the cold rains.

My lips tried to curve as I thought about the sun on my skin, but I kept them straight. Seeing and feeling the sun was an experience unparalleled by anything else, the heat more powerful than anything I'd ever felt. The entire city stopped all activity during the Solstice so everyone could bask in the rare sunlight. The closer Solstice grew, the more my skin seemed to desire it.

Dr. Wells introduced each recruiter and his or her credentials and accomplishments, his voice blending into a dull drone.

"Tell me about the Before," I whispered to Sol.

His breath puffed. "You want to get me sent to Detention again?"

"No . . . I'm not asking you to tell me about a cult or a rebellion." Although I did want to ask him about *how* he knew so much, I was afraid he would put himself in danger if he answered.

He squeezed my hand, and I could almost imagine him smiling at me, but when I opened my eyes his expression was as serious as ever. The top two ways to earn Banishment from our city were:

Join a religious cult

Rebel against the Legislature

"In the Before, the sun shone nearly every day." Sol's voice radiated through me. "It was called summer."

"Sum-mer," I repeated. "How long did it last?" I wanted to talk about anything other than what was happening on stage. Naomi had warned me about asking too many questions, but the more I knew about the Before, the more I could find out about the generators. That was the difference between Naomi and me. She was afraid of knowledge, while I thirsted for it.

"Summer was four months of a year," Sol said.

Months of sun. Nearly impossible to comprehend.

The world had been completely different back then, at least from what I could piece together. It was hard to imagine a time before Harmony implants, when people governed their own emotions and kids didn't have to worry about student informers.

Sol's method for identifying informers was to look for those with small, beady eyes. He said they always looked like they were scheming about something. I laughed at his reasoning—well, laughed inside—and said he was ridiculous, but we were very careful. And when he'd tell me things, it was never above a whisper and usually in the school yard where no one could hear us over the rain.

In front of us, Chalice turned. She'd heard us whispering. Although Chalice was my roommate, I wasn't entirely sure whether she was an informer. Seeing my gaze, Chalice quickly fumbled with something in her hand, hiding it from view. But it was too late—I'd seen the metal ring she was wearing, and the strange symbol embossed on it.

A deep cold rushed through me. Chalice had worn the same ring a few days before. I made her leave it in the dorm when she tried to wear it to class, not sure if she'd been testing me. I glanced at Sol, but he was listening to the recruiter's speech.

"Chalice," I whispered. I didn't want to get her into trouble, and I didn't want to draw Sol's attention to it, either.

I shook my head slightly, sending her my disapproval, which really masked my growing fear. Was she an informer, trying to draw me out, or was she rebelling? She turned back around, shutting out my warning.

I was about to tap her shoulder when light flooded the auditorium. The metal doors automatically locked behind us, and a voice came over the speakers, overpowering whatever Dr. Wells was saying.

"Inspection in progress. Please remain seated."

CHAPTER 3

nspection at an *assembly?*

Sol's hand slipped away from mine, and we sat rigid in our seats.

"Stand and walk to the aisle," boomed the voice on the speakers. "Put your backs against the wall and face outward."

I stood, hands clenched by my side, and looked over at Sol. He met my gaze, his eyes calm and steady. Somehow it made me feel better.

Then I looked at Chalice. Her hands were balled into fists as she walked to the aisle. Had someone seen the ring and turned her in?

I watched as the other students took their places, looking for any hint of triumph. I had grown adept at picking out the slightest nuance of emotion—even in the most stoic. I looked for subtle physical signs: the shaking leg, clenched fingers, eyes too wide. Inspections happened once a month, but never in an assembly.

Even the recruiters seemed at a loss. They stood on the stage with the director, watching and waiting. When the doors slid open seconds later, everyone's heads turned. Two inspectors entered, carrying agitator rods. My stomach knotted as I glimpsed into the corridor where several more inspectors had lined up.

Chalice looked at me from across the room. Her hands were clasped in front of her, her ring turned around, exposed. There was no mistaking it now. My mouth went dry, and I tried to think of some excuse I could offer for Chalice. Nothing came.

As the inspectors reached her, she held out her wrists.

My stomach clenched with anger at Chalice for breaking the rules. Then at whoever had turned her in. "No," I croaked out, at the same moment feeling Sol's hand on my arm, as if he'd anticipated my movement.

I wanted to race across the aisle and defend Chalice, but it wouldn't help her and would only get me into trouble. Despite the sharp anger building inside me, I knew it was futile to resist the inspectors, especially with the recruiters present. They'd know instantly that I was different.

As an inspector clamped cuffs on Chalice's thin wrists, I wanted to shout, *It's only a ring!*

The pressure of Sol's hand increased on my arm, and not even his nearness could distract me. But I managed to keep my mouth shut.

Chalice's narrow shoulders sagged as if a large weight had just been piled on top of her. The inspectors escorted her out of the room and into the pristine hallway.

"What will happen to her?" I whispered.

"Detention." The word brushed against my hair. "Hopefully."

"Hopefully?" I had avoided Detention at all costs, since I couldn't afford to miss lessons.

"It's better than Demotion."

Demotion meant she'd be kicked out of A Level, and her chance at a University education, and subsequent career, would be lost forever. Sol's hand had dropped from my arm. I glanced at him—his eyes were trained on the metal door that had closed behind Chalice, but I could still feel the touch of his fingers. It meant nothing to him, I knew, to touch me, but I had felt it all the way to my heart.

Dr. Wells told us to retake our seats. My entire body trembled now, and I worried that Sol would see my fear. In fact, the recruiters could probably see it from the stage.

But it was too late to sit apart from him. Sol followed and sat right next to me as the lights dimmed around us again.

The head recruiter spoke loudly, and I jumped in my seat. "You will now return to your schedules, and in the next two days, you'll be interviewed individually."

Cold flushed through me like I had fallen into a deep pond. Before I knew it, we were all shuffling out of the auditorium, through the echoing hall, and just as we reached our classrooms, the intercom came on again, announcing lunch period.

My heart rate slowed a notch as I turned toward the school yard. I had no appetite for boiled sweet potatoes, and I was only too thankful to be away from the recruiters' eyes. I needed time to process the fact that my roommate had just been sent to Detention and tomorrow I might be facing recruitment testing.

For once, I regretted being at the top of my class.

I walked into the cement yard, which was basically a broad pad of sloping concrete that kept the rain running off.

A high iron fence surrounded the area, intended more to keep others out than to keep us in. The rain had picked up from its morning drizzle, and I hadn't brought my umbrella. I might be cold and wet, but thoughts of Chalice suffering in Detention chased away my complaints.

I should have known Sol would follow me, which made me want to hide in my room so I wouldn't have to keep fighting so hard against my emotions. When he came to stand next to me, the rain stopped pattering on my head. We had to stand close to fit under an umbrella he'd found— standing close was both a good thing and a not-so-good thing.

"Jez," he said, his voice low. "Where did Chalice get that ring?"

"She won't tell me where she found the metal." I couldn't look at him now; I had to wait until his voice stopped vibrating through me. "But I think she carved it herself."

"How did she learn to make those symbols?"

I forced my breath out. He had seen the ring clearly, then. "We saw them in the museum a year ago, before the exhibit was removed."

Sol went quiet, and even though I felt upset about Chalice, having Sol next to me was comforting. *Don't focus on that,* I told myself. *Don't listen to his breathing or look at the way his fingers curve around the umbrella.*

Sol grasped my hand. "Are *you* wearing one of those rings?"

My breath fled again. "Of course not." I knew I should pull away, but his hand was so warm.

"You're still freezing," he whispered, slowly rubbing my hand.

A warm shiver shot through me, and my hand tightened around his for a second before I reluctantly drew it away. I didn't want him to sense anything; as it was, my face felt much too hot for having such cold hands.

But he was watching me closely, and I wished I knew exactly what he was thinking. I'd never had a friend like him—one I couldn't stop thinking about even when we weren't together. One where I had to close my eyes and bury my face into a pillow to shut out all thoughts of him so that I could fall asleep.

Thinking about the Separation made my chest hurt.

"Promise me you won't do something stupid," Sol said.

Another focused breath, and I dared to look at him. His longish hair was black against the backdrop of gray, matching his murky eyes.

"When have I ever done anything stupid?" I asked.

"I guess that's a yes?" he said.

My eyes flitted away, and I hid a smile. "Correct."

A few kids came into the courtyard. They hardly looked in our direction, moving on past toward the tree line. They had a couple of umbrellas between them and huddled in a group, most likely talking about Chalice.

"This may not be the best place to talk," Sol said, pulling my attention from the other students.

"About what?" Curiosity pushed away thoughts of Chalice shivering in some cold Detention room.

"We don't have much time left together now," he said. "I want to tell you some things."

My chest constricted more, if that were even possible, and I shoved my hands into the pockets of my royal blue jacket as I peered up at him through the gloomy afternoon rain. He was nearly a head taller than me, something that made me feel safe when I was with him.

16

"What things?" I asked. *And how do you know them?*

His voice dropped to a whisper. "About the past."

Normally I would have been excited to hear something new—about the Before or the Burning. But not right now, not after what had just happened with Chalice. "No," I said, perhaps too quickly. His eyes flickered with something I couldn't quite describe. Disappointment? Did he . . . I wondered . . . did he feel something, too?

I broke eye contact. If I could read any emotion in his eyes, he could read far more in mine. I looked around at the other kids in the school yard, standing in their groups, clustered together. They were still too far away to hear anything we said, yet I worried.

"Please." Sol leaned toward me, his voice just audible.

I wanted to close my eyes and lean against him, let my cheek rest against his chest—just once. Instead, I pulled away so that I was barely beneath his umbrella, also keeping my voice low. "Why?"

"After the Separation, I won't be able to share my memories with you." His gray eyes absorbed mine, and I felt my resistance weakening. "We don't have much more time."

"All right," I whispered back, my pulse racing.

He seemed to relax, and his body bent toward mine.

"My caretaker had a book filled with pictures," he said. "I found it before he was Taken."

"Pictures?" Pictures were images of people and places from the Before. Now, pictures could only be seen on the WorldNet. "Real ones?"

He nodded.

I thought about having an image—a picture—to carry around. Would I have kept them all together in a book? "Do you still have any?"

"I destroyed them when my caretaker left. I didn't want his name to be blotted out from society records, and I didn't want to get cited."

I nodded, understanding. Had his caretaker broken more rules and told Sol about the Before? If so, how did his caretaker know so much? The forbidden "pictures" were destroyed, and that was a relief, but my heart hammered to think of what could happen if our instructors or, even worse, the Legislature, discovered what Sol had seen, and that he hadn't turned in his caretaker for breaking the rules. The Legislature was afraid that we'd rebel, remove the Harmony implants, and civilization would regress into a rebellious society and become extinct.

I knew I should shut him up now, before it was too late. Before his memories became my memories. I fought against the curiosity bubbling up. Naomi's words echoed in my mind: *Jezebel, don't ask so many questions.* I had almost conquered my questions when Sol said, "My caretaker had pictures of flowers that blossomed in the sun."

Thirty-seven years of rain had put a stop to all blossoming. "Tell me what they looked like." I had seen images of flowers on the WorldNet, but I wanted to hear it from Sol.

He hesitated, and the color of his face warmed. I watched him closely. Was he fighting an emotion?

"Are you sure you want to hear this?" he finally asked.

I realized that I did want to know more—so that when we were separated, I had more of Sol to remember. The time left between us was sliding away with each moment. "Whisper in my ear," I said.

Sol's eyes clouded as if he were seeing something from long ago. A bead of water dropped onto his face, and I clenched my hands to keep from brushing it away.

He leaned closer, his breath soft against my skin. "The flowers had bright colors, like red and pink. Some were white or yellow."

Inside, I smiled. "Like the sun."

He nodded. "They weren't grown for food, like our plants, but for beauty. Some of them grew wild beneath the sun and blue skies—fields and fields of them."

Naomi had told me much of this, but I couldn't admit it. It would be incredible to see an entire field of flowers. I wondered how long it had been since Sol saw the pictures. "How old were you when your caretaker was Taken?" I asked.

"Ten." His voice sounded odd, and I looked up at him. His eyes looked moist, as if he were actually sad, but there was no way he could feel sad like me. Being Taken was simply the cycle of life.

"And you still remember the pictures?" I asked, digging myself deeper. I glanced around, checking to make sure none of the other kids had moved closer to us. I couldn't afford Detention so close to the Separation. I wasn't like Sol, or even Chalice. I had to stay at the top of my class. I had to get chosen for the science program.

Sol bent close enough that his breath warmed my cheek. I ignored my racing heart as he spoke. "They were impossible to forget—they were so beautiful. The pictures were old and fragile. They were given to my caretaker by his own caretaker, who he called 'grandfather.' He was over sixty."

Now I was surprised. Sixty-year-old people only existed in the O Level society. Others, like Naomi, were Taken when their duties were accomplished.

The rain came down harder now, and Sol's voice penetrated the din. "He told me the sky was blue almost every day, not just at Solstice. In the summer it stayed blue from dawn to dusk." His dark gray eyes traveled from my face to my shoulders. "Blue like your jacket."

I hunched my shoulders as if to pull the jacket closer and tried to imagine the color splashed across the sky, replacing the low gray clouds and the ever-present rain. I remembered Sol talking about summer in assembly. I leaned closer to him, stealing some of his warmth. Even during the day of Solstice, the clouds remained, parting just enough to allow the brilliant sunlight through.

"A year was divided into four seasons of weather patterns," he continued.

"Seasons?"

"Spring, summer, fall, and winter." A hint of a smile touched his lips. But it was gone so quickly, I wasn't sure if I'd imagined it. "It rained a lot in the spring."

I shuddered. I knew rain.

"In summer, the sun shone from early morning to late evening," he said.

How would it feel to have several days of sunshine in a row—even weeks? Did they cancel school and work so everyone could stay outside and feel the sun all day?

"In the fall," Sol continued, "the rain came back, but the sun still shone most days."

"So it was gradual . . . a cycle." I urged him on despite knowing some of the answers already from pestering Naomi. I didn't want Sol to stop talking.

"Exactly," he said.

"And the fourth season?"

"Winter. That's when it snowed."

I'd heard about snow in whispered corners from other students who were no longer with us—some who'd been

Demoted for breaking serious rules. I didn't realize that snow was a part of the winter season. I could never trust anyone to ask more about snow. Those students I'd heard the whispers from had been Demoted and never returned to school. They were imprisoned or reassigned to C Level to do menial tasks the remainder of their life cycles.

"Have you seen pictures of snow?"

"No." Sol shifted the umbrella and his hand brushed against my back.

His touch warmed me. As hot as the sun. I breathed out, slowly, letting the heat subside. All I knew was that the snow was colder than rain. "Tell me about the snow."

"My caretaker's grandfather said the snow was as cold as ice. It made you shiver all over. But it wasn't hard; it was soft somehow, and white." He made a noise that was almost a laugh and grasped my hand. "You're still freezing—this is probably what snow feels like."

"Tell me about the summer," I said. Could he feel the pulse in my hand throbbing like mad?

"In the summer, the sun became so hot that whole forests dried up and sometimes caught fire." He kept his voice soft and his head close to mine so I could hear his words.

I casually pulled my hand away as I tried to imagine a fire so big that it covered a whole forest. "Is that what started . . ." my voice dropped to a whisper ". . . the Burning?"

"No, Jez. Do you want to talk about the Burning, too?" He was teasing me now. We were taught to focus on the world as it was now, and how the Legislature had restored it to order. The earlier civilization had destroyed the world with poor choices long before the rain came.

"Of course not," I said. But something inside me broke, and I blamed it on the extra exertion I was making, standing with Sol and trying not to feel anything. "I don't understand why man would destroy his own beautiful world."

Sol raised his eyebrows—my statement had bordered on argumentative. *Jezebel, do not argue.* He leaned in, his dark hair falling across his forehead. "To make it better, of course."

I thought I saw confusion in his gaze just for an instant. Maybe he *was* like me. But even as I thought it, I knew it wasn't true. I had watched him carefully enough over the past months—his calmness and control—to know he was not fighting against strong emotions like I was.

I wanted to agree, like a good citizen, but my stomach twisted at the thought.

The civilization that came before us had mired itself in thievery, child abuse, prostitution, murder, and government corruption. It had allowed pedophiles to live a street away from elementary schools, built strip bars at the edge of decent neighborhoods . . . The List went on. Every child over the age of five had the List of Failures memorized.

The world Before was a black stain on humanity. Our world—our gray world of Order—was faultless.

But still. I wanted to hear more. I glanced around the yard again. Lunch must be almost over, but no one had made a move to go inside yet, despite the heavy rain. My heart thumped and seconds slipped away.

"What else did your caretaker tell you?" I asked as casually as possible as I shifted away from him, hoping he wouldn't notice. There was only so far I could move and not remain under the umbrella. The class bell rang, and the other students broke up their groups of umbrellas and started heading for the doors.

We watched them pass by, then Sol said, "We should go, Jez—"

"Tell me more about the flowers, then we'll go in." I didn't want to be late, either, but we could spare one minute more.

His breath swept my face in a sigh. "Flowers were grown only for their beautiful colors. Golden sunflowers that were dark yellow with black centers."

I nodded, closing my eyes and becoming lost in the image he created. Remembering this would help me when I was isolated in my own science lab, separated from Sol and Chalice.

"They had oval petals and stems growing as high as your shoulders. Red flowers called peonies—so red it looked like the color of blood—with long green stems. Thousands of them grew in the same field. There were violet and pink flowers called roses that had small circular petals all grouped together. My caretaker said they smelled like the most expensive perfume."

I exhaled, imagining a perfume-scented plant. "They must have been beautiful."

He nodded and looked at me with an almost-smile. It wasn't a true smile, but I pretended it was, and it melted something inside me.

"Now we have the same memories."

"Promise to tell me more tomorrow," I whispered before I could monitor myself. I didn't mention the recruiters—maybe if I pretended they didn't exist, it would all go away. We hurried into the building. When we stepped onto the thick mat just inside the school and removed our raincoats, my stomach coiled into a knot. Another morning had faded, another day half-over. Another hour closer to the Separation.

The pale green floors seemed to extend a mile, forming a wide corridor lined with tall metal doors. Sol and I stopped in front of one, and he raised his palm to the small ID kiosk on the right. The door swooshed open, and we both entered the square classroom containing twenty-two desks and chairs, the same pale green on the walls as on the floor. Twenty pair of eyes turned to look at us.

We were late after all.

CHAPTER 4

There were no flashing lights, no sudden appearance of the school director. But those twenty pairs of eyes had all witnessed our late entry. I wondered which one would report us. I couldn't mess anything up—not so close to the Separation. I kept my eyes on the ground as I hurried to my desk, completely avoiding even a glance at Sol when he sat next to me.

The lesson was already in progress as I slipped in my earbuds: "The claim of free agency is what criminals use to justify their crimes."

I stared at the screen, trying to digest the words so I could regurgitate the lesson later on the final test. The voice thumped on. "For civilization to exist, all people must abide by the rules."

I felt people watching me. Thoughts of Chalice and how the inspectors had escorted her out of the auditorium returned with full force.

Did any of the students overhear what we had said? I had been careful to make sure none of them had been standing by us in the yard, but I was still afraid.

My hands trembled as I concentrated on taking steady breaths. Maybe no one would report that we were late. I couldn't let anyone see me shaking. Naomi had warned me plenty. I knew better than this—to let my curiosity win. To listen to Sol's memories, to stand so close to him, to think so much about him. To let him into my dreams. I had worked hard to get to the A Level. I had to get to the University, there was no other way.

When I was ten I asked Naomi why we were different. Wasn't it just easier to be like everyone else?

To be fully human is the best gift you can ever have. And not until we create a larger world can human freedoms be restored. Find a way to create more land and civilization will spread out, and the Legislature's control will diminish.

I wanted to trust Naomi—but what would stop civilization from corrupting itself again if there were no controls in place from the Legislature? I glanced around the room and wondered what the class would be like if everyone were like me and we didn't have to suppress our emotions.

Rebellion.

Revolt.

Destruction.

You have to trust me, Jezebel. You've been schooled to only believe one way. But there are other options.

I didn't fully understand trust—I just knew that Naomi had pleaded with me more than once to trust her. She had failed at being the Carrier, and now it was up to me.

I forced myself to focus on my screen and chanted inside my head: *Don't screw this up. Don't screw this up.* I'd watched kids transferred to B Level for failing one test. I couldn't afford to be transferred.

The lesson continued. "Universal laws must be understood by the youngest of citizens."

I repeated the words to myself, committing them to memory. Most kids tested into A Level at the age of five. It took me until I was twelve. I was too skittish to handle it any earlier. I was late coming to the game, so I had to make every hour count even more.

Suddenly the lights flickered in the room, and our screens flashed red. I froze, feeling absolutely sick. The only other time I'd seen the screens turn red was during a security breach at the school, when a group of B Level kids tried to break in. They were all Demoted to C Level.

The students looked around, the confusion on their faces mirroring my own.

"Jezebel James," the voice coming from my screen said. By the stillness in the classroom, I knew the voice had been piped to everyone else, too. My entire body trembled. I wanted to disappear. Had someone overheard my conversation with Sol?

"Report to your childhood residence immediately."

I hadn't been to my childhood residence in four years. I struggled to take even a shallow breath. Why was I being sent there? Did this have something to do with what Sol and I were talking about in the school yard? My neck prickled with hot sweat, and I stared at the blinking words that scrolled across the screen, barely processing what it said. *Resume Ethics Lesson 28.*

Someone touched my elbow. I looked up and saw Sol standing over me. I broke out of my stupor and took out my earbuds with numb fingers.

"I wish I could go with you," he said. "Be safe."

I stood, my legs shaky. "I will." Dozens of paranoid thoughts collided in my mind. Was Sol an informer? But everyone was staring at me, and I stepped away from him and threaded my way around the desks.

Naomi was Taken only a few weeks after I tested into the A Level and came to live at the school. I hadn't been in any contact with my male caretaker since then. It hadn't been necessary. So why now? I had entered a new life, and David had remained in his old one on the other side of the river, working in his job assignment.

With a backward glance, I left the classroom, wishing Sol *could* have come with me. But we had to face our own fates. The hiss of the metal door seemed final somehow as it closed behind me. My footsteps echoed against the polished floor as I walked to my locker, the sound reminding me of the first time I had stepped into a school. I had been five, and Naomi had held my hand until we reached the doors of the Children's Center.

When she let go of my hand, it was as if all of my obedience training had fled. On the steps of the school, I broke down and cried. Naomi was horrified. *Jezebel, you mustn't cry,* she pled with me. *B Level girls do not cry—not if they want to be allowed to stay with their caretakers.*

That stopped my crying, but I spent the rest of the day swallowing against the permanent lump in my throat.

That same lump had returned now. I pushed back the memory as I grabbed my raincoat and umbrella from my locker and hurried to the exit, pulling the coat on as I stepped outside. The never-ending drizzle had lessened, but would become heavier as the afternoon wore on.

I crossed the schoolyard to the gates and pressed my hand against the scanner. Once through the gates, I turned down the street to face an empty stretch of sloping concrete. Everyone stayed out of the rain during work hours, and small apartments nestled against each other as if in cahoots to stand against the ceaseless rain. My dread increased as I neared the tram depot. Why was I being sent to my childhood residence? What had happened that required my coming?

Tears burned my eyes as I thought the worst. *Stop it! Crying is unacceptable.* I'd worked so hard to achieve the A Level; I couldn't let emotions control me now. Besides, I was about to enter the depot and would soon be among people.

There had to be a reasonable explanation. My caretakers had always followed every rule perfectly . . . or at least appeared to. So why did I sense that something was wrong? I knew I had been a challenge for Naomi—at least that's what she told me. *Jezebel, you mustn't laugh so loud. Jezebel, stop fidgeting. Don't hug me in public. Don't ask that question.*

I walked quickly through the driving rain, thinking of the things Naomi had taught me. What was the use of talking to David now? Naomi was gone. When I was admitted into A Level, the last thing I remember was the pride in both David and Naomi's eyes as they said goodbye. I didn't know it would be the last time I saw Naomi, and I left them behind without a tear, having learned to master my emotions.

At the depot, a few people stood waiting for a tram. They wore dark clothing, brown and indigo, standard for B Level citizens. A couple of them glanced at my bright jacket. I placed my palm on the kiosk screen underneath the metal awning. The gate for platform G opened automatically and I stepped through. I'd almost forgotten which tram to take across the river. Even the kiosk knew more about what was happening than I did.

Once out of the school neighborhood, the tram sped past the rows of brown and gray apartment buildings and three-story factories. Seeing the buildings reminded me of Naomi, who used to work in a clothing factory where they operated the machines that stitched royal blue jackets like mine. As B Level citizens, my caretakers were educated in useful tasks, allowed to choose mates from within their level, and produce a child—one per couple. My throat tightened as I thought about seeing David again, and memories of his face flashed into my mind, narrow and dark, with unusual green eyes.

When I turned five, I moved into the Children's Center where my formal education began. From that time on, I saw my caretakers once a month for a free day. I only let myself cry when I was in bed at night, after all the other children were asleep. It was then that I knew I was different. I knew later, too, when in the dead of night Naomi told me why my Harmony implant didn't control my emotions. I was breathless when she told me about the second implant—the key that made me the new Carrier.

Tram G came to a stop, and I stepped out of the sleek vehicle. A few gazes from the other riders followed me, and I wished I'd zipped up my raincoat to hide my jacket color. I stood on the empty neighborhood street for a moment, watching the tram turn a corner, until I was left alone in the stillness. Everyone who occupied the apartments on the street was working. I started toward my former building, then came to an abrupt stop when I saw who was waiting outside.

A man wearing a white jacket stood at the front entrance. In the gray atmosphere, the white of his coat almost glowed like a lamp. I knew immediately who he was.

30

Ruth's been Taken, Naomi had whispered one evening as she peered out the window. I stood next to her, on tiptoes, to look out the high windows of the apartment complex across the concrete expanse. A man with a white jacket was slowly walking around our neighbor's building, as if looking for something. "Who is he?" I asked.

"The Examiner."

And now, a man in a white jacket waited for me. I took a slow step forward, then another. I was in no rush to hear the news. It was now obvious that David had been Taken.

I blinked rapidly, fighting with everything I had against the tears. In the memory of my caretakers, I at least owed them the control that Naomi had taught me. The gravel crunched under my feet, and as I forced myself to walk, small pebbles scattered. The man in the white jacket watched me, not giving anything away in his expression. My stomach felt as if I'd eaten a large stone. I couldn't even swallow; my throat was too tight. Although I had been on my own for many years, it wasn't until this moment that I truly felt alone.

I forced myself to make eye contact as I neared the Examiner. His eyes were a watery blue, his face pale with a faint pink hue. He wasn't much taller than me, and his shoulders sagged away from his neck. When he held out his hand, I hesitated, then extended my own. He gripped mine briefly. His hand was dry and rough and cold as I imagined paper to be—the kind displayed in the City Center Museum.

"Jezebel James, offspring of David and Naomi James," the man said in a nasal voice. It was then that I noticed a leather satchel next to his feet, and he picked it up and gave it to me. He opened his mouth, then closed it, as if changing his mind about something. Finally he said, "This is your inheritance."

Forbidden tears stung my eyes, as I fought against them. Receiving my inheritance meant it was over—truly over. David was gone, my childhood past.

I clutched the bag, its weight heavier than I expected. Maybe there was more than one memento from the apartment. I wondered what David had chosen but I didn't want to peek with the Examiner still standing there like a statue, his gaze hard on mine.

With a glance at the door, I knew I couldn't attempt to go inside; it was prohibited. The rooms would be sterilized and a new couple assigned. I wondered if they'd have a child—someone to sleep in my room, in my bed.

I carried the satchel and made my way back to the tram depot with measured steps. The man's eyes stayed on me, and I gripped the handle tight to prevent my hands from shaking. I didn't want him to see.

CHAPTER 5

When I entered my dorm room, I turned on the lamp and stopped cold.

Chalice was in bed, sleeping, her back turned toward me.

Relief washed over me, and I turned the lamp off and listened to her steady breathing. She seemed peaceful in the glow of the streetlamp coming through the window, as if she hadn't been hauled off to Detention at all.

I curled on my bed and pulled a blanket around me, letting the tears escape. Chalice was back, but both my caretakers were gone, forever. It felt final somehow, more than when Naomi had been Taken. The emotions rocked through me, making me feel sad and angry at the same time. Why did I have to feel so much?

I could almost hear Naomi admonishing me, *Don't give them any excuse to send you back to B Level.*

I exhaled in disbelief, letting the tears run down my face

in the darkness. Perhaps there was an accident at David's factory. Perhaps he'd broken a rule. My chest ached as I worried it had been more; worried that it was something I had done.

The only things I had left now were memories and whatever was in that satchel. With Chalice asleep, this was my chance to see what David had left me. I reached under my bed for the satchel, then turned toward the light coming in from the lamppost outside.

The scent hit me first. Musty. Dry. A touch of old bark. I reached inside and pulled out a square object. It was Naomi's jewelry box. I knew the jewelry box would contain no gems, just as it never had when I was a child. The Examiner would have scanned it to ensure that it didn't. All gems and minerals were reserved for advancing technology. But I had seen images of jewelry on the WorldNet.

I tried to lift the lid but found it locked. Strange. I didn't remember it ever being locked. When I shook the box, something knocked against the sides. Trying to keep completely silent, I searched in the latrine for anything thin and sharp, and finally settled on a small pair of scissors.

Back on the bed, I pried open the lock and lifted the lid. My mouth dropped open.

It was a book.

I had never held a real book. Most of them had been destroyed in the Burning in the first year of the rains, but I'd seen one in the museum behind a protective case. How had the Examiner missed the book? His scanner must not pick up old paper or bindings.

My hands trembled as I opened the book, unsure of what I'd find. It made a rustling sound, and I paused, glancing over at Chalice. Her breathing remained even and undisturbed, so I carefully turned the front cover and read: *2061*.

As I lifted the first page, a delicate-looking piece of paper came loose. I picked it up, handling it carefully. There was strange writing on it—it looked like writing I'd seen on display in the museum—actual letters written by hand with curves and loops. It took me a moment to decipher the words, but once I figured out the first few, it became easier.

A hard lump formed in my throat. The paper was addressed to me and signed by Naomi, dated five years ago.

Jezebel,

Soon I will meet my fate. I don't know if I'll get to say goodbye one last time, and I don't know how long David will be around. We have always loved you, even though we were never able to speak it often. I'm giving you my caretaker's story—she is your 'grandmother.' Her name was Rose. You are very much like her. You know what she refused to reveal and that she gave her life after passing on the Carrier key. I hope Rose's story will help you be strong in your resolve.

Burn the book and this letter to ash after reading.

Your mother,

Naomi

My eyes pricked with tears. I exhaled and reread her letter. Were they the last words she ever wrote? What had happened to her? And David? No one returned from being Taken when the cycle of life was concluded. I squeezed my eyes shut, blocking out the thoughts that said I'd never see David again.

After a few moments, my breathing evened and I was able to look past the paper from Naomi and read the first line of the book. It was also handwritten, the ink faded. *January 8, 2061* was at the top, then the words: *Dear Journal.*

It was hard to believe that I was holding an actual record written in the Before by Naomi's caretaker, Rose. I couldn't quite think of her as "grandmother," although I knew that's what she would have been considered in the Before.

I tilted the book toward the light to get a sharper image and read the first sentence—words written nearly forty years ago.

Today I fell in love.

My face burned, and my hands went cold. Dread started in my stomach and crept throughout my whole body. I knew then that the story couldn't end well, and that explained why I had never even known Rose's name.

After the Burning, one of the first rules passed by the Legislature was Statute 3:1: *Romantic interludes are forbidden.*

Falling in love was the third way to get Banished.

CHAPTER 6

I woke with a start—Chalice was staring at me, her face inches from mine.

"Are you all right?" I asked, sitting up.

"Fine." But her voice sounded distant, and her eyes looked puffy and red. "Where were you?"

Had she seen the satchel? "My caretaker, David . . . he was Taken." My gaze wavered, and I hoped that she wouldn't see the sorrow that inflated inside me.

But Chalice didn't seem to notice. She moved back and peered out the window. Then she said in a voice not much louder than a whisper, "Why? He wasn't very old."

"The Examiner didn't tell me why," I said. "He only gave me the inheritance." I clamped my mouth shut before my voice could betray my emotion. I had only read a couple of pages last night, stopping when the fear in my stomach pinched into nausea.

Chalice turned from the window, and it was then I saw the deep red mark on her left arm.

"What happened?" I asked.

She brought a finger to her lips and shook her head.

I crossed to her and reached for her arm, but she pulled away. "They might be listening," she whispered.

"Listening?"

She clamped a hand over my mouth. With her other hand, she pointed up. I looked at the ceiling, but didn't see anything.

I stepped away. "No one can hear us," I said, hoping it was true.

"In Detention, they told me . . ." Her voice faltered, and I couldn't help staring. Something in Detention had changed her. She shook her head again and pointed at the ceiling.

"Are there listening devices up there?"

She nodded. I examined the ceiling from all angles, but still didn't see anything out of the ordinary. Maybe they just wanted to scare Chalice.

"Sorry about David," she said.

I exhaled, believing that she truly was sorry. Chalice was like that. She expressed her private thoughts without the blubber of emotion that always seemed to cloud mine. I nodded, unable to speak for a moment. She pressed something into my hands and I looked down to see the silver ring—a boxy emblem stood out from the simple band. "They let you keep it?" I whispered, more for Chalice's peace of mind than mine, because I actually thought someone was listening.

"Not exactly," she replied, her voice barely there. "This is a new one. It will bring you comfort."

Comfort? "It won't be comforting when I'm in

Detention." Why did she insist on so visibly breaking a rule? My gaze strayed to her right shoulder where a semisquare scar was obvious beneath the cutoff sleeve of her thin night shirt. The Harmony implant was secure.

I looked up at the ceiling again, but saw no sign of a listening device. I didn't understand the risk she was taking by wearing another ring. I handed it back. She took the ring with a shrug and slipped it beneath her pillow—like that was any type of hiding place.

"What was it like in Detention?" I asked, keeping my voice low.

She looked out the window. "Quiet."

"And your arm?" I whispered.

She blinked rapidly, but didn't answer. I watched her closely, looking for signs of emotion. Even if the Harmony implant wasn't compromised, would a very intense experience cause emotion to surface anyway?

"They didn't read the rules to you or question you?" I asked.

"They did some of that." Her eyes shifted their gaze to me, but I couldn't see anything beyond their steady blue.

"And . . . ?"

She tugged on the short hair curling around her ears, her fingers trembling slightly. "They asked me how I made the rings, how I learned about the symbols, and if you had helped me."

My breath stalled.

"Don't worry." Her eyebrow lifted slightly. "I told them you were upset that I was wearing the ring and had threatened to turn me in."

"That's not exactly true," I whispered, my heart thudding.

She reached for the ring again under her pillow. "If you change your mind and want to wear it, just let me know."

I shook my head—an automatic response.

Disappointment brushed her face for just an instant. Or had I imagined it? She slipped the ring on her finger and examined it. "I don't know why the Legislature is so worried about archaic religious emblems," she continued. "If they make us feel better, what's the harm?"

I stared at her. *What's the harm? She sounds like Rose,* I thought, remembering the pages I'd read from her book last night. Chalice met my gaze, and there was something hard in hers. Defiance?

"How can you say that?" I asked. "Religion used to incite wars. People *killed* each other over those myths. We've been taught that in class."

Chalice's eyes darkened to indigo, and her trembling hands clamped together. "Why would someone kill another person over a *myth*? How could a myth start a war?" She shook her head. "Maybe religious beliefs *aren't* myths."

"You shouldn't say that." My head started to pound. This was a dangerous conversation. "People are Banished for joining a religious cult." I imagined Chalice's thin form standing in the middle of a barge as it floated on the ocean farther and farther away from our city, until she was too small to see. Where would she end up? One of those barbarous Lake Towns?

"I'm not joining anything." Her voice was dead calm. "I just have a lot of questions about the prophets in the Before and the different Deities people used to believe in." She ran her fingers along the red marks on her arm.

I have a lot of questions, too, I wanted to say, *like what really happened to you in Detention.* Yet I didn't speak the words. My throat felt thick, and for a moment I wanted to hug her and tell her that I understood. But Naomi had told me not to hug people and not to be curious, so I just stood there.

While I focused on getting ready for the day, I wondered if the Examiner had any idea what had been inside the locked jewelry box. Would he have given it to me if he had? Maybe I should have asked him why David was Taken so early. I turned on my tablet to check the daily news report. It listed the names of those who were born, those who moved levels, those who were charged with crimes, and those who were Taken.

I found his name immediately: *David James. Taken.* My eyes stayed dry this time, but something squeezed my heart. The news report made it official, just another societal record, but it was personal to me.

When Chalice was in the latrine, I hid the satchel under my mattress, knowing it was a weak hiding place, but my options were limited. Although reading the first couple of pages had made me sick with apprehension, I knew I needed to finish it. I couldn't risk any notice by the government—something about the Examiner made me uneasy—but I did need answers. I knew that Rose refused to reveal where she kept the Carrier key, and that's why she died, and how I got it. But who gave her the key in the first place? Where had it all started? As soon as I finished reading the book and got my answers, I promised myself that I'd get rid of it as Naomi had instructed—and the sooner the better.

CHAPTER 7

Sol was waiting for me when I stepped out of the dorm building. He tipped his umbrella up with one hand as if inviting me to join him, while the other hand stayed buried in his pocket. His eyes studied me, questioning. The sight of him nearly made me turn around and claim a sick day. How could I face him after reading my grandmother's confession about falling in love? It was my absolute worst fear to have those feelings about him, and being around him wasn't helping.

"How are you?" he said, his question simple, yet perfect.

I couldn't sleep. I can't think. And I only want to be with you today. "Tired," I said, the finality in my voice putting a stop to further questions.

One of his eyebrows lifted, but he didn't press for more information.

We only had a few more days left together. At one point I had dreaded the Separation, but now I welcomed it. It would be freeing not to have to battle against myself during every moment. *Stop it,* I chastised myself. This was exactly what Naomi warned me about when she risked passing on an illegal book. I had to relax and stay calm. Stick to the rules. Sol's gaze was intent on me as I walked down the steps, and I ignored the warmth spreading throughout my body as I joined him at the bottom of the stairs. I plainly saw the concern, the questions, in his eyes, and it was killing me.

He glanced at me several times and stayed close while we walked the short distance to the school hall. I wanted to throw my arms around him and cling to him like a girl drowning in a fast river. Did he notice that my entire body trembled? That I was having trouble separating the emotions rolling over me—fear, grief, infatuation, fear again. Inside my pockets, I clenched my hands together, trying not to fall victim to his nearness. I stole glances at his profile, his shoulder. I looked at his hand and thought of how casually it had touched me the day before, sending my heart racing. Was that what Rose had felt?

By the time we reached the classroom, I had to take shallow, measured breaths, and Sol scanned us through the door.

Several students looked up as we entered but the news of my caretaker must have spread, because everyone looked quickly away. Chalice already sat at her desk and seemed to look right through me as I took my seat. The other kids refocused on their screens, determined not to miss one word of any lesson so close to the Separation.

"Welcome to Ancient Religion Myths 14," the desktop chirped as soon as my earbuds were in place.

I glanced over at Sol. His eyes were on me, questioning again. I gave him a nod, letting him know that I appreciated it. "Outside," I mouthed. He nodded, understanding.

My body relaxed. I could talk to him in the yard and tell him about David, and Rose's handwritten book and how she'd fallen in love. Maybe telling him about Rose's mistake would somehow save me from the same fate.

"What cannot be proven cannot be trusted," the monotone console voice said. "The idea of faith was invented by those who wished to take advantage of the innocent."

I looked at Chalice, hoping that she was listening carefully. She turned her head, biting her lip. She seemed smaller, shrunken against the seat. Her long sleeves covered the red marks I'd seen earlier, but they did nothing to hide the delicate dark beneath her eyes.

She shifted again, and I saw something on her hand. Was she wearing a ring again? I was stunned. Whatever they'd done to her in Detention hadn't been enough. Was it worth the risk to miss out on the University? To be Demoted or Banished?

"Faith is an idea created to control others," the lesson voice continued.

I'd barely had time to digest the words when the room flashed yellow. The metal doors automatically locked with an echo, and the desktop screen flickered into six words.

Inspection in progress. Please remain seated.

My heart flipped. Had they come for Chalice again? I wanted to scream at her for being so stupid. Hadn't they already done enough to her in Detention?

But no inspectors entered the classroom, and the panic continued to well within me. If they weren't inspecting the classroom, then maybe it was the dorm rooms. They would find my book.

Now *I* would be questioned. Sent to Detention to face whatever Chalice had, or perhaps Demoted. I'd fail as Naomi had failed. There would be no Carrier after all.

44

The blood drained from my face, and I gripped the edges of the desk to keep myself upright.

You are the last hope, Jezebel.

Why hadn't I stashed the book somewhere this morning?

After a few tense moments, the Ancient Myths lesson resumed, but the metal doors remained locked, which meant I was right. The inspection was taking place in our dorm rooms and I had to sit in the classroom while my whole life crumbled bit by bit. I tried to concentrate on the droning voice explaining why Buddha and Muhammad and Jesus Christ were false prophets of the world Before, and why all of their books of scripture were the first to be incinerated in the Burning.

"Because of these false teachings, society spun out of control," the lesson continued, forcing itself through the turmoil in my mind. "Freedom of religion turned humans into nothing better than wild dogs, ravishing each other, plundering their neighbors, cheating their own friends."

At that moment, I felt like a wild dog, too, wishing I could tear out of the classroom and erase all evidence of the book.

Jezebel, you must control yourself, Naomi said in my mind.

I am. I am. I am.

I imagined an inspector entering my dorm and searching through the room. He'd discover the book in an instant beneath my mattress. It would be taken to the High Inspector's office; Rose's words would be read, condemning her a second time. But now, I'd be the one facing sentencing.

It wasn't until Sol's hand reached across the space between our desks and gripped my fingers that I realized I was shaking. I wanted to tell him everything, how afraid I was, how I should have never even opened the book, but the room was full of students who were only too eager to get any competitor out of the way. And I didn't want to condemn Sol along with me.

To my horror, tears filled my eyes. I tried to blink them away, but they collected faster and faster. I pulled my hand from Sol's and wiped my cheeks before anyone could notice, but he'd seen them.

He leaned toward my desk, watching me carefully. He'd caught a glimpse of what I had tried so hard to suppress for so long, and now he would know I was weak and didn't belong in A Level society.

He glanced at the others, heads bent over their consoles. "What happened?" he whispered.

"David left me a book," I said as quietly as possible. "They'll find it during the inspection."

The silver in his eyes hardened to black, and I wanted to disappear. He must hate me. He had shared his memories, and now he certainly regretted it. He suddenly stood and crossed to the metal door. "Let me out! Let me out!" he shouted as he rammed his shoulder against the door.

Earbuds popped out as the entire class watched him in stunned silence. It looked as if the brilliant prodigy had gone insane.

But I knew he hadn't. Hot and cold twisted in my stomach.

The alarms blared, and within seconds the metal door slid open. Two inspectors waited on the other side and Sol ran into them. "I have to get out of here!" he yelled, appearing every bit like a madman.

The inspectors cuffed him and he didn't fight back— maybe not so crazy after all.

My tears started again as he was taken away and I knew he'd done it for me. Sol had just created the perfect distraction to help me hide my crime.

CHAPTER 8

We learned in Ancient Religion Myths 12 that hell is a place where wicked people burn in an eternal fire. But no one who claimed to come back from the dead ever admitted to actually seeing the place. They'd all seen bright lights, heard angels who sang in perfect tune, or had joyful reunions with deceased relatives. Did that mean only good people came back from the dead? Was it possible to be alive and exist in hell at the same time?

Whatever the ancients believed about it, when Sol disappeared down the corridor with the inspectors, hell became my reality. I couldn't breathe, I couldn't move. Every part of me was on fire while at the same time colder than ice.

The classroom door remained open while the students talked among themselves. I knew that in a few minutes order would be restored and things would be back to normal, but those few minutes might give me just enough time. My heart hammered, letting me know that I needed to move now or not at all.

I slipped out of the classroom, thinking up excuses in my mind if I was stopped by an inspector. The halls were empty as I hurried through them and out the door, flinching at every sound, expecting to be caught at any moment.

By the time I made it inside my dorm room, I was out of breath with fear. I rushed to the mattress and reached under it.

Nothing.

I lifted the mattress and scanned the empty space. "No," I whispered, as I searched under the bed, in the dresser drawers, in the latrine. "No no no." The book was completely and absolutely missing.

Standing in the middle of my dorm room, I was torn between the need to get back to class and an urgency to find the book. Finally, feeling like I was in a dream, I walked back to class. The door had shut, but the longer I waited, the more I'd have to explain. Lifting my palm, I scanned the door open.

Chalice and the other students looked up as I slipped into my seat. I avoided their collective gaze and stared at my console, trying to concentrate. Where had the book gone? How long until someone came for me?

But no one came for me, and somehow I managed to keep my turmoil hidden.

As Chalice and I walked back to our dorm after classes, she was painfully quiet, and I wondered again about the red marks on her arms. Whatever was happening to Sol right now, the worst part was that it had been in vain. When Chalice fell asleep for the night, I'd do another search, but I knew I'd already looked every place. The book was gone.

I followed Chalice inside, wondering if I'd be able to hold back tears until night fell. As soon as the door slid shut, Chalice turned to me and put a finger to her lips. Then she motioned for me to sit on her bed as I watched her pull the wardrobe silently a foot forward. On the wall behind, Chalice removed a square section of thick plaster by running her fingernails along a cut-out line.

I stared in amazement as she reached into the cavity of the wall and pulled out a small box. I rose from the bed and knelt beside her, my pulse throbbing furiously as Chalice opened the box to reveal the book inside.

I let out my breath, not realizing I'd even been holding it, my thoughts crashing around me. The book hadn't been discovered after all. And Chalice had hidden it for me. I looked over at her, trying to read her expression. She *had* to be different from the others—she had to care about me.

"Read it," Chalice whispered, looking around as if someone could see or hear us. "Hurry, then we have to destroy it."

But I was already shaking my head, and my pulse drummed with cold fear. "No," I whispered back. "We should destroy it now—it's already caused enough trouble." I couldn't shake the terror that had possessed me while I sat helpless in the classroom after Sol left. And I couldn't let Chalice get involved, too.

Before I could back away, Chalice pressed the book in my hands. "That's why you need to read it."

I pushed the book toward her. "There's nothing good in that book. I don't want to read about the rules some woman broke and how she failed society." I couldn't tell Chalice that I was desperate to read the book. But I was afraid too—to learn about Rose's falling in love. My breathing shortened. It was too much. Too hard. If I didn't read Rose's story, I could forget about how I was in the same danger.

"Jez." Chalice stood and held the book out to me. "If you don't read it, I will." She looked me straight in the eyes. She had a haunted look in hers. "Do you want me to get into trouble like Sol? Real trouble?"

"No," I whispered. Chalice had been through enough, and it stunned me to think of what Sol had done for me. What I wanted to know was *why*. Would I have done the same thing for him? Not if it gave away my state of immunity to the Harmony implant. Maybe this was a clue that Sol was more like me. Maybe he was immune, too?

Or maybe not. Maybe I couldn't see past my own heart.

"It's your inheritance," Chalice said. "And it's your caretaker's last wish."

"That doesn't mean it's right to read it," I blurted out. But even as I said it, I wanted to take the book from her. It was like I couldn't turn away. Naomi knew me more than anyone and somehow, David had saved this for me—hidden it for years. I couldn't dismiss that fact, and couldn't ignore that my caretakers wanted me to read it, despite the costs.

I stared at the book in Chalice's hands. As much as Rose's story repulsed and scared me, my curiosity was stronger than ever. "I'll read a few pages," I said, the words jarring in my throat.

Chalice moved to the door and sat next to it, listening for anyone who might come along the corridor. I sat on the floor as well and leaned against my bed, deciding to read only a few pages. But I kept on turning them, one after another.

There's no one I can talk to anymore. Neighbors spy on each other. Best friends turn each other in. Parents testify against their own children. I don't know if this journal will ever be read, or if it will be destroyed with everything else that seems to be attracting the zealots' attention.

I had heard of the zealots—the ones who were out of control. The government had to step in and save the people from them. I glanced at Chalice, my throat feeling thick. She nodded for me to continue, her back pressed against the door.

Tens of thousands have died—not from the incessant flooding as I might have thought, but from diseases, starvation, and destruction through mudslides.

Tens of thousands . . . later millions. I had never allowed myself to think of the deaths that must have occurred as the rain persisted and the earth underwent catastrophic changes. Sorrow came up from the hidden spaces in my soul, and my hands trembled as I turned the pages to read about the diseases. About the hunger and food rationing. But I needed to read this; needed to understand.

The light in our room had dimmed as the afternoon faded to night outside.

And then the first introduction to *him.*

The new edict was delivered by a man wearing an official-looking uniform—that of the new regime, or the Legislature, as they are calling it.

I discovered that I was holding my breath as I read.

When I opened the door and let in the officer, I was surprised to see he was no older than me. Probably about nineteen or twenty. He had the look of someone who had to grow up too fast and taken on heavy responsibilities too soon. Like me. I barely heard what he said as he spoke, but I did catch his name, although I won't write it here. I couldn't help staring up at him. His shoulders were broad, his arms long.

The overcoat he wore was a little short on his wrists, as if he'd had to dress in another man's uniform. Or maybe there weren't enough to go around, and they had to share when they went out on official business.

Stop, I wanted to tell Rose. *Stop and think.* But there were still more pages to read. My heart rate quickened as Rose described their first touches, their first kiss, what they said to each other.

We hid among the trees, eating apples. That's when he leaned over and wiped the juice from my lips and kissed me.

My face burned as I read. The emotions that Rose described were so close to the ones that I had worked to suppress. Emotions that I'd never let fully develop. But Rose hadn't suppressed hers. She'd embraced them.

Rose described how they met in secret, always hiding from others. Even though I blamed her for being so foolish for falling in love in the first place, I couldn't stop reading. Until the next words came.

I am pregnant.

I stared at the word: *pregnant.*

We'd been taught about the old ways of reproduction, when men and women produced children without regulation, without prefertilized eggs or controlling implantation. Children were conceived randomly, and there was no testing done after to gauge the best chances of survival and fitness. Infants who had disfigurements or other ailments weren't Taken, but allowed to grow up among society.

Reproduction and birthing were never discussed outside of class. We learned about it in twelfth year and left the rest of the details to the B Level. Women in the B Level were allowed to undergo in-vitro once they'd passed the caretaker exams and found a commitment partner.

Was Rose in the B Level society then? If this was the year 2061, then the population mandate had already been enacted. Everyone knew that was one of the first rules established by the Legislature so they could get the rampant diseases under control.

I can't tell him about the pregnancy. It would be too hard for him to hide such news. I'll have this child in secret, and my mother says she will pass it off as her own and take whatever punishment that might entail, since there has been a population mandate in effect for two years now.

I knew it. My pulse throbbed in my throat as I continued to read.

No one has any idea when the mandate will be lifted. So many children have died from malaria and other diseases from the damp. Even married couples must use contraceptives. It's very difficult to get a marriage license, and if you obtain one, children aren't allowed until the mandate is lifted.

I glanced over at Chalice. She was sitting on the ground with her back against the door. "She became pregnant," I said, my throat strangely tight.

Chalice nodded, but didn't say anything. She pulled her knees up and wrapped her thin arms around them.

I continued to read, my heart heavy as Rose wrote about her first weeks of nausea and how many times she feared being discovered, but she still refused to tell her boyfriend. Another blow came during that time, with the death of her "father," who'd been suffering from one of the damp diseases.

Then a new mandate:

Today, he came to our home, on business from the government. I could hardly keep my eyes from him, but forced myself to stare at the floor. A new system of fortification has been installed by the Legislature. A system where they can control us, at least that's the way I see it. Everyone is to report to the health clinic where each person will undergo a small surgical procedure and have a Harmony implant placed into their shoulder.

I do not trust the Harmony. They say it's perfectly innocuous, but I don't believe them. I won't get the Harmony implant, and they cannot force me.

The Harmony implant. Had she really refused to get it? I turned the next page.

They forced me. Used drugs to knock me out, and now I bear the Harmony scar like every citizen. But something curious happened and it didn't work like it was supposed to. I still have the same emotions. Even stronger, perhaps. I could pretend to be like everyone else, but then I am a fraud, and I refuse.

I read the words again. From what I could tell, she didn't have the second implant—the key—yet.

Something else happened. When I was coming out of the drugged state, I overheard a conversation between two doctors. It seems there is an underground building project that will be reserved for emergency purposes. If the rain never stops, there is a plan to create more land surface by building higher mountains. Something about generators. I'm determined to discover the plan.

My heart thumped as I read, not knowing if I really wanted to continue. This was the beginning, so many years ago, and whatever Rose had hoped for the future hadn't yet come to fruition.

I have joined up with the Carriers. I'm not sure how many of us there are, but we each carry a key that will activate the generators. A new hope for the future. It will be dangerous, but if things get too desperate, it will provide a new beginning. We will take back our humanity from the Legislature. Whoever can bring a stop to the rain will be the new leaders. If the Legislature gets control of the keys, then they will stop the rain, but they will continue in their absolute control, too afraid of the power of human emotion to disable the Harmony implants. We must destroy the Legislature, activate the generators, and give back dignity to the people. We must never let the Legislature know how much power we have.

It was all there. Rose and the other Carriers knew what they were up against. They'd started a plan to take over the Legislature, then to stop the rain. Even if it had been accomplished in Rose's lifetime, it would take generations for the earth to restore itself to even half of what it once was. The earlier generations would need to make all of the sacrifices for the benefit of the later generations.

I thought about what else Rose had said—there were more Carriers than just herself. Who had started the movement? And how many Carriers were left?

I was caught trying to cut out my Harmony implant. Carriers everywhere have been executed for one reason or another as they refuse to conform. If the Legislature knew these rebels were carriers, there would be an all-out war. I await my own trial now. And although I know there is no hope, I'll walk proudly to the judges' council. I may die because I believe in the power of love and the power of choice. No matter what they say, I still believe that people are good and can make right decisions. I believe the world can find redemption if given a chance. I refuse to tell them where I put the Carrier key. And I refuse to name the father of my baby— the Council will discover I'm pregnant soon enough when my belly grows in prison. My mother has promised to put in a petition to raise the child as her own in case I am not released. If I am sentenced to execution, I'll tell my mother where this journal is. I'll tell her about the key and where I've hidden it.

The writing ended, and I leafed through the remaining blank pages, wondering how long she lived after that. If Rose had only followed the rules, she would have had many more pages of her life to write about. But where would that leave me? Naomi wouldn't have been born, and I wouldn't be here, either. Maybe none of the keys would have been passed down, and I wouldn't be a Carrier.

My own grandmother had turned her back on the Legislature. She'd ignored the rules that were for her benefit. And my mother was a product of that. A shiver passed through me like a warning. *So am I.*

As if to match my mood, the rain came in thick torrents, slamming against our single window. The lamppost light cut through the darkness, but did nothing to dispel the feeling of gloom.

I looked up at Chalice. Her mouth was pulled into a tight line, and she gave me a single nod. "I saw you reading the book last night when you thought I was asleep. So I waited until you fell asleep and then I read it, too," she said in a low voice. "I'm sorry. It wasn't my business."

Surprisingly, I didn't feel mad, or betrayed—only worried. "You shouldn't have. Now we can both get into trouble."

Chalice lifted a shoulder. "Not more than I did wearing this." She held up her hand, displaying the metal ring.

"Why are you still wearing that?" Apparently Chalice hadn't learned her lesson in Detention. Or . . . I studied her. She was courageous. Fearless.

She was silent for a moment before she spoke. "It's not why you think. I'm not ready to go over the edge and get myself Demoted. This ring brings me comfort, that's all."

"It's just a piece of metal; how can that be comforting?" After reading about Rose's stubbornness, I couldn't bear to see Chalice act the same way, to take the same risks.

Chalice's expression was blank, impossible to read. How could she believe in any of the ancient religions when they had corrupted so many people?

As the silence filled with the driving rain outside, I closed my eyes, thinking of Rose's final words.

If I am sentenced to execution, I'll tell my mother where this journal is. I'll tell her about the key and where I've hidden it.

Rose didn't have to die so soon. Even now, thirty-seven years after her death, no Carrier had activated the generators. And the Harmony implants had protected the city from rebellions, saving many lives. Was that so wrong?

Naomi's voice popped into my mind. *You have been taught one way of thinking. But I will teach you another way.*

I put the book back in the satchel; I'd find a place as soon as possible to dump the thing. I didn't want to be caught with Rose's words. She had died because she followed her feelings, and that would be my fate too if I didn't learn to suppress mine.

I opened my eyes and exhaled. Chalice was looking at me. "Sorry about your grandmother," she said.

"She knew she was breaking the rules." I kept my voice hard, hoping to harden my heart as well, to push my emotions into a far corner. I couldn't let Chalice know that I was sympathetic, and scared.

"She was only following her beliefs," Chalice said.

"Sometimes a single person's beliefs contradict what's good for the whole."

Chalice released a sigh and climbed to her feet. "You sound like an ethics lesson."

Yes, I did. I shrugged for Chalice's benefit.

"What do you think happened to the man she loved?" Chalice asked, settling on her bed across from me. "Do you think he ever turned himself in?"

"I doubt it." I was suddenly tired. I didn't want to be in the same room with the book anymore. I didn't want anything to do with it. I didn't want Rose's sad words echoing around in my mind, and I didn't want to discuss it with Chalice, with anyone. We had been speaking quietly, but what if our room *was* being monitored? And what if Chalice decided to report me for keeping the book as long as I had?

I looked away from Chalice, toward the dark window, thinking of Rose's boyfriend. She hadn't mentioned his name, so it would be impossible for me to research, even if I wanted to. Which I didn't.

Rose had a chance to conform. Everyone knew the rules—right from the first classroom until our end cycle. They protected all of us from ugly lives of crime, dishonesty, immorality. From repeating the past.

My grandmother had deliberately broken the rules, and she wasn't afraid. Did I have the same courage? I didn't know.

Chalice was watching me, her face pale in the dim light and the circles beneath her eyes looking even darker. "I'll see if I can find something to burn the book with."

At least she agreed with me on that. As Chalice reached the door, I said, "Be careful." The image of Sol being carried away was still haunting me.

With Chalice gone, I stood before the window and stared out at the falling rain. I clutched the book in my hand, refusing to open it again. I didn't want to think of Rose's life of chaos and uncertainty, her world of constant death and the way she must have watched entire cities being destroyed.

Behind me, the door slid open. "Back already?" I said as I turned.

But it wasn't Chalice. Two inspectors entered my room, eyes trained on the book in my hands like they'd seen it right through the door. One of the inspectors held an agitator rod.

A flash of heat bolted through me, and it only took an instant to realize what had happened. It was as if I'd stepped outside my body and was looking down at my writhing limbs. My scream cut off when everything went dark.

CHAPTER 9

Cold and hard. The first sensations of feeling crept into my spine and brought me back to consciousness. Had I fallen off my bed? Tripped in the school yard? Then I remembered. The book. The agitator rod.

I dragged my eyes open. My mouth tasted acrid, and my body felt as if I'd run nonstop for hours, leaving me with no strength to move. The room I was in was smaller than my dorm and had no windows. It glowed faintly with a pale yellow, as if the sun filtered in from somewhere, yet there was no heat and no lighting system.

Like a prison. Had Rose felt like this? Alone, cold, in pain? I tried to block out her out, along with the unforgiveable rules she'd broken.

Someone whispered my name, "Jez."

I turned my head toward the wall next to me in the direction of the sound. There was a sliver of light coming beneath it. Was it a door? I pressed my hand against it. Solid rock.

"Jez, is that you?"

Sol.

I inhaled, wincing at the pain in my chest. The air passing through my lungs hurt—breathing hurt. "Yes." I squeezed my eyes shut for a moment, trying to get a handle on the pain. Why did my throat hurt so much? Why was Sol in the next room? Was this Detention?

"What's wrong, Jez?" the whisper came. "What did they do to you?"

"They . . . shocked me with an agitator rod," I said, having difficulty keeping the soreness out of my voice.

"Are you all right?" he asked.

"I . . . don't know." I rolled over, facing the wall. A shadow shifted in the space of light. Sol was on the other side. "Where are we?" I said.

"Detention."

I nearly laughed, but choked instead, and tears sprung to my eyes. I had done everything I could for years to stay out of Detention, and now, less than a week before Separation, here I was. The stone ground was cold beneath me and the rough walls were like nothing I'd ever seen.

"Can you remember anything?" Sol's voice again. It sounded as if he was whispering in my ear.

What did he mean? Of course I could remember.

"I'm sorry," I said, the cold floor causing me to shiver. "You shouldn't be here." I had to think of a way to exonerate Sol. It was my fault he was here.

His voice cut into my thoughts. "Jez, this is very important. Do you remember *why* you were shocked?"

I took a few more breaths, and my pain seemed to

stabilize as long as I didn't move. "My inheritance was an illegal book. I should have turned it in right away."

"This is the book you told me about in the classroom?"

"Yes," I asked. "I'm sorry I said anything to you. What . . . what did they do to you?"

But he didn't answer my question. "You remember talking to me in class?"

"Of course."

"You were shocked with an agitator, Jez. You aren't supposed to remember."

I let the information sink in. The Harmony implant didn't work, and now this. "The agitator was supposed to destroy my memory?"

"Just your memories over the last day or two," Sol whispered. "It's a method commonly used by the Legislature. Many times it's enough to deter the person from committing more criminal acts. They forget, and with the lost memory, their desire to rebel fades."

I didn't answer. I couldn't. Did they consider me a criminal now? Did they think I'd rebel? Would I be Demoted after all? And why didn't the agitator rod work on me? Was it because of the key?

"Jez, say something."

I heard the fear in his voice. The thought of someone like Sol being afraid of anything made me shiver all over. "I don't know what to say," I answered at last. "I remember everything. They caught me in my room, standing by the window, holding that book." I paused as I thought of Rose's words. "If the shocking had worked, I wouldn't remember what I read, either, right?"

"Right," he said.

I felt him waiting for me to continue. "That means . . . that means it didn't work and—"

"Jez," he broke in. "Don't let them know it didn't work. Don't let them know you remember what's in that book."

"All right," I said, or at least I think I said it. My words sounded so far away.

"Why didn't you destroy it in the first place?" His voice sounded calm again.

I hesitated. "It was my caretaker's last wish that I read it—it's the record of my 'grandmother.'" I didn't tell him that I'd also hoped it would help me expel thoughts I shouldn't be having. About him.

"Ah," he said.

My heart drummed with guilt at not reporting the book the moment I realized what it was. But even if I had to go back, even knowing that I'd be caught, I think I might have done the same thing. I might have still read the book.

"And you read it?" His voice again.

"Yes," I whispered.

"Let me guess." Sol's tone was slow, deliberate. "She talks about the Before."

I thought of everything I'd learned from Rose. "A little bit. But mostly she talked about the rains and how her life was changed when the Legislature formed."

There was only silence on the other side of the wall, and then the shadow shifted. I waited, holding my breath. I wondered if Sol was angry now, realizing what he got himself Detention for. What I cost him. This should have stayed between me and my caretakers.

"What was her name?" he asked.

His question surprised me, and it also worried me. I didn't want him punished anymore because of me. I regretted having told him anything in the first place.

"Jez." His fingers appeared in the opening at the bottom of the wall. "Tell me her name."

64

"What does it matter?"

He wriggled his fingers, and instinctively I closed my hand around them. There was no danger in it, I told myself. A thick wall separated us. Besides, who knew if I'd ever see him again? *Don't go there,* I thought, *or I'll stop breathing altogether.*

"Please," he said.

"Her name was Rose," I whispered.

"Like a flower." His fingers moved against mine, and his grasp tightened. I was glad he couldn't see me or the color spreading across my cheeks. The description of Rose kissing her boyfriend came to my mind. If Sol could make me feel this way just holding my hand, what would kissing him be like? I squeezed my eyes shut, forcing the thought away.

"She wouldn't turn in the name of the man whose child she carried," he was saying. "Even worse, she tried to cut out her Harmony implant. A serious crime of rebellion."

"How do you know all of that?" I asked.

His next words sent a chill through me. "She was executed December 3, 2061, a few weeks after her child was born. Her last request was to choose her method of death. Remember the case study?"

It sounded familiar now. I let the connection settle—my grandmother was the woman we'd learned about in class. In the case study, nothing more had been said of the child, only that it was relocated a few weeks after birth. The case study had been an impartial recollection of the events. But Rose's written words rushed through my mind—her worries, her fears, her love for the father of her child. She had been real. Not just a history lesson or a case study. She was my grandmother.

Then I remembered the conclusion of the case study.

"Death by fire," I whispered, horror sweeping over me as I thought about the barbaric methods of execution in the Before, and how some condemned criminals were allowed to choose the way they'd die. In Rose's case, her name hadn't been blotted out like the usual criminals. They had kept her name in the history lessons to be held up as an example.

Sol's fingers tightened around mine. "It *was* her, wasn't it?" he said.

I nodded, although he couldn't see me. I pictured his solemn gaze, his searching eyes, which seemed to understand me even when I didn't understand myself. I was grateful he couldn't see the tears that had started.

"Reading about her reminded me of you," Sol said. "Now I know why."

My heart thumped. He couldn't know, couldn't realize, that my caretaker had said the same thing in her letter. Did Sol know how I struggled to control my emotions? That I wasn't like the others? He had seen my tears. He must have guessed.

I waited a few heartbeats before asking, "How do I remind you of Rose?" I wanted to hear it from him.

"The case study had a description of her in it," he said. "Don't you remember?"

"Not really." I thought hard, but all I remembered was the sentencing and her listed crimes. I didn't recall any descriptive details.

"The study said she was uncommonly beautiful, and she was a danger to society because of it."

I froze. And that description reminded Sol of *me?* I was glad for the thick wall between us. I wanted to ask him more, but I was afraid the tremor in my voice would give too much away.

"She naturally attracted trouble," he continued, "caused men to fall in love with her. Made them lose their good sense and led more than one man to his downfall."

More than one man? The book I'd read only mentioned one boyfriend—perhaps he was the one she'd truly loved. I tried not to compare him to Sol.

Sol's voice continued rhythmically, like he was reading. With his brilliant mind, he probably *was* reading, straight from his memory. "Even if she'd turned in the man she loved, she still would have been imprisoned. The population was on a moratorium during that year. Not even married couples were allowed to reproduce." His tone was gentle. "The Legislature probably only kept her alive long enough to deliver the child. At least they were merciful on that issue. The child lived."

The child who had been Naomi. That's why I'd received the book as an inheritance. Naomi must have sensed something like this might happen and wanted to send me a strong warning. I couldn't let my feelings for Sol be discovered, or I would never succeed where Rose had failed.

Despite all of the education I'd received about how the Legislature was protecting us from our worst selves, it just didn't make sense that one of my grandmother's crimes had been her beauty. My consternation was threatening to become anger. I let my breath out slowly, trying to dissipate the unwelcome emotion. *Do not show anger, even if you feel it,* Naomi had told me more than once, her hands cradling my face as she looked sternly into my eyes. But this anger kept growing, despite my determination, becoming almost too big to hold in.

Sol pulled his hand away, and the shadow on the other side of the wall moved. It was closer now, darker. "Jez, listen to me."

His voice fell a notch, and I had to strain to hear. "Don't do anything stupid."

My breath caught at the irony. "Too late."

"No, it's not," he said, his tone urgent. "You've done nothing but accept your inheritance. Don't compound it. Do what they ask. Make them believe you don't remember the book."

"All right." Even from the other side of a thick wall, where I'd gotten him sent, Sol was trying to help me. "What about you?"

"I'll be fine."

A soft scrape came from Sol's side of the wall.

Then a whisper. At first it sounded like, "I'll miss you," but I wasn't sure. The shadow was gone. Sol was gone. Without a word of goodbye.

CHAPTER 10

The Council was made up of fourteen judges. Eight men and six women. They wore stiff-looking black robes, severely short hairstyles, and all appeared to be rail thin. No overindulgence in this group. I forced myself to stay in the present and not think of my grandmother standing before her own council.

I tried to stay calm. I had to get through this—I had to get to the University and become the scientist I was meant to be.

An inspector ushered me to my seat with no explanations of what to expect. At least a dozen other adults sat in the room, all staring at me. I glanced at them quickly, wondering what their crimes might be. It seemed we'd all be present to hear each other's cases—apparently there was no privacy. While we waited for the hearings to begin, I looked around the spacious room, taking in the marble pillars, the thick beamed ceiling, and the high, arched windows that framed the gray drizzle outside.

Finally, someone moved. The woman in the middle of the judges' bench clasped her hands together. She seemed to wear a permanent frown, which deepened as I met her gaze. I kept my expression neutral, although I was sure that she could see right through me.

Her long, skeletal fingers unclasped, and she said in a high, reedy voice, "Jezebel, offspring of Naomi and David, please step forward."

Already? I'd hoped to at least watch a few of the others go through their hearings so that I could prepare a little. I wanted to make sure I said the right things, followed the proper procedure and didn't mess anything up. I rose quickly, hoping the council would appreciate my eagerness to please, then followed the direction of an inspector who pointed to a sectioned-off area in front of the bench. The worn, crimson ropes formed a square, and as I approached, the inspector unhooked one of the ropes to let me inside.

I took my place and lifted my gaze to the judges. Most of them stared at me, but a few seemed to be looking right past me, as if they had little interest in the proceedings.

The inspector, who'd directed me to the ropes, read the charges from his electronic tablet. I kept my lips pursed as he began. "Citizen Jezebel James has been found out of compliance for the following: possessing an illegal item, in the description of a book. Citizen Jezebel James has also been found out of compliance for the following: reading said illegal book."

The inspector continued to drone through passage after passage of formalities. I didn't realize there was so much to say about such a simple crime. Finally his voice cut off, and my breath stalled. Would they hand down judgment immediately? Would I be excused and asked to return after they deliberated?

The room was eerily quiet as I waited.

The head judge spoke first. "Tell us why you read an illegal book."

I licked my lips, wishing I had Sol or Chalice's courage. They'd know what to say. Taking Sol's advice, I said, "I don't remember opening the book. I only remember picking up the satchel from the Examiner at my childhood home."

The judge's expression remained still, as if she hadn't heard me. She waited. I waited.

I spoke again. "If I'd known what was inside the satchel given to me, I wouldn't have accepted my inheritance. But since the Examiner gave it to me, I thought there might be important information inside the book."

Now the judge's expression changed. Her black eyes narrowed to slits. "Why didn't you turn it in when you opened the satchel?"

I looked down as I scrambled for an answer. What I said next could determine the rest of my life. "I thought perhaps the book had come into my hands for a reason." They certainly knew about my caretaker's letter. "My caretaker gave it to me for a purpose, perhaps as a warning—a warning that is meant for all of us . . ."

Several of the judges leaned forward, their expressions questioning. My heart sank. Had I said something wrong? Had I given something away? I plunged on, hoping that spending the last five years in their A Level classes had taught me enough to get through this.

"We must always follow the rules, even if we don't agree," I continued. "I thought the book was something I was supposed to read—even if I didn't know why yet.'"

That seemed to relax them, but it was hard to read their

placid expressions. The head judge nodded for me to continue.

Was this a good sign? I moved on, embracing the chance to defend myself. "I needed to experience the consequence of hiding something," I said, directing the focus away from the possibility that I had actually read the book and remembered what I'd read. "The consequence of being caught, and the consequence of standing before the judgment seat."

The head judge tilted her head, her eyes narrowing. What did that mean? She approved or she didn't approve?

She was still waiting for me to speak, so I said, "If I'd not had this experience, then I wouldn't understand the human condition fully as I move on to the University level." I let out the breath I was holding, hoping they'd believed my act and that it would be enough.

The judge's hands came together in a swift and decisive motion. "Three months arrest."

Arrest? I was being sent to prison? I opened my mouth to protest, to question, but stopped myself. Three months . . . how much would that set back my plan? Would I still be eligible for the University?

My eyesight blurred as I tried to appear steady and calm. Somehow I managed to nod to the judge's council while my mind raced. The inspector gripped my arm and led me from the room. I glanced at the other people waiting their turn. None of them met my gaze now. I was ushered into a side room where a metal cuff was secured around my ankle. It seemed to meld to my skin, flexible, but cool.

Then, we pushed through another door, this one leading to an outside platform in some sort of an alley.

"Where are we going?" I asked the inspector.

He didn't answer. Maybe I'd be sent to my dorm room

and just have to stay inside for three months. My hope grew just a little.

"Do people ever get released early?"

This time he did answer. "Never heard of it."

My heart sank. I thought I'd made a compelling argument, but it would be dependent on their belief that the agitator had worked on me. I had no way to ask. By the end of three months, how much of the life I'd created would be left?

I'd miss the final tests, the Separation ceremony, the first months of University. Would I still get into the University? Then I remembered . . . the Solstice. Surely I'd be allowed to enjoy the Solstice?

I was about to ask the inspector about Solstice when I heard the familiar sound of an approaching tram. It came around the bend and made an effortless stop. As the inspector guided me onto it, I noticed the dark windows. No one could see in or out. I took a seat on a narrow bench and the inspector sat across from me, his eyes locked on me.

The tram could have held two dozen people—or prisoners. Today it was empty except for us. Seconds later, the metal doors shut, and the dull lights came on. The tram lurched into motion, knocking my head against the shaded window.

After several moments, the tram slowed, and just as I anticipated it stopping, the car tilted downward and descended a hill of some sort. The hairs on the back of my neck bristled. Were we going to the lower levels of the city? The C Level? The docks? Maybe I'd be put on a work crew. But even that would be better than being Banished from the city, to where there was nothing but vast waters and uncivilized Lake Towns full of barbarians.

The air grew noticeably cooler, though that didn't bother me as much as the encroaching smell. I couldn't quite identify it. There were definitely chemical qualities to it, not strong enough to burn my eyes, but enough to create a bitter taste in my mouth. I looked at the inspector. He continued to watch me, seemingly unbothered by it.

The angle of the track steepened, and I clutched the bench as the speed increased until, suddenly, we came to an abrupt stop. If I hadn't already been holding onto the bench, I would have been flung to the floor.

The metal doors opened, and the inspector stood. I rose to my feet, my legs unsteady. The chemical smell was stronger now, invading every one of my senses. The inspector didn't seem to notice, but latched onto my arm and guided me out of the tram. As soon as we stepped onto the platform, the doors shut and the tram reversed direction.

It was pitch dark except for glowing beads of light to the side of the platform. The thin string of lights continued to the right, descending as if following a set of steps. Cold air penetrated my clothing, pressing against my skin and making me shiver. There was no doubt now that we were underground.

I folded my arms and inhaled carefully, trying to avoid breathing in the strange smell. The inspector kept ahold of my arm and led me along the strip of light. My vision adjusted slowly, and I began to make out the dimensions of a massive tunnel sloping gently downhill.

"Where are we?" I said, finally daring to ask another question.

His response was abrupt, and something about the tone of his voice made me shudder. "You'll see soon enough."

We continued to walk on the smooth surface that vibrated beneath our footsteps. It was certainly metal. Every few steps, I felt a gush of cold air touch my feet as if the floor were suspended somehow and air flowed beneath it.

When the inspector stopped and raised his hand, a door to the side of us that I hadn't even noticed slid open. He pushed me inside, let go of my arm, and stepped away. The door slid shut behind me, and I was left in complete darkness. Alone.

CHAPTER 11

I stood still for several moments, waiting for some other door to open up, for another inspector to take me to the next place. I waited for a voice to come through a speaker and give me instructions, to tell me what tasks I'd be sentenced to for the next ninety days.

But none of that happened. I was alone, with no sound or light, and no way to keep track of time.

The chemical scent was stronger in this room, but it didn't seem to affect me, so I stopped worrying that they were trying to drug me. Maybe I'd been sent to a facility that processed chemicals, and was going to be forced to work on an assembly line.

I reached my hands out in front of me, hoping to see a glimmer of my skin, but there was nothing in the blackness. I took a step forward, then another. Three steps later I touched a wall. It wasn't stone or metal, but a soft, pliable substance. I pushed my hand into the wall, making an indent. When I pulled away, it moved back into shape. I ran my hands along it, following until I was in a small circular room.

The ground seemed flexible. Crouching, I touched the floor. It was also malleable, like thick rubber.

I completed the circle and found the narrow door I'd been sent through. Nothing around the metal door indicated a way to open it, so I sat on the ground, pulled my knees up to my chest, and finally let the worries invade and the tears fall. There was nothing to do but wait.

My stomach hurt. My head hurt. My heart . . . ached. I had never been this far away from my dorm or school, and it was impossible to imagine that everything was continuing on as normal without me.

I wondered what Sol was doing at this exact moment. Was it day or night? Was he still in Detention? Or had he been released? Was he eating or studying? Was he thinking about me?

Just as I was about to drift to sleep, the room filled with light that seemed to be coming from everywhere at once.

I blinked against the brightness. The first thing I noticed was that I was still alone. The second, that the walls were a yellow-brown and the floor a pale blue. The metal door was the customary slate gray. I thought maybe I was dreaming, but my mouth was too dry and my stomach too empty for this to be a dream. I listened for the sound of a door opening, for footsteps, anything. Still nothing. But I sensed I was being watched.

I stood, stretching my stiff legs. Dizziness hit me in a wave, and I closed my eyes for an instant, trying to keep steady.

The door slid open.

The man who stood on the other side wore a pale blue

jumpsuit the same color as the floor. It was neatly creased along the sleeve and pant legs as if he hadn't sat all day. His eyes were the brightest blue I'd ever seen—almost piercing. He wore metal-framed glasses, which was unusual in our City since eye correction was done at a young age. And although he was completely bald, he looked only about five or six years older than me.

His eyes narrowed for an instant as he looked me up and down. "I'm Dr. Matthews." He looked at the tablet in his hand. "Miss J, follow me."

I wanted to ask who he was and what I was supposed to do here, but instead I kept quiet and stepped beside him, determined to do everything I was asked. What kind of doctor was he? He didn't stop, didn't wait, and I propelled myself forward. The light was dim in the corridor. The floor sloped, but he showed no sign of slowing down.

As I hurried to keep up with him, I tried to orient myself. The walls were made of the same yellow-brown padded material, and we were in some sort of tunnel. We were definitely underground, traveling deeper, but what was above? I looked for doors or other connecting hallways, but there were none, just the long winding snake of a corridor moving deeper and deeper into the earth.

My breath grew shallow as I walked. I hadn't eaten for a while, and my energy was fading fast. Time felt strangely off down here.

The doctor finally came to a stop and waved his hand against the wall. A brown metal door that matched the wall slid open and we stepped into a cavernous room, more brightly lit than the corridor.

The smell of food hit me immediately—cooked fish and something like sweet potatoes. I'd never smelled anything so good until this moment, and my stomach ached with anticipation. Eight tables were lined up in two rows in the room, and seated at them were about a dozen or so men and women, wearing the same light blue jumpsuit as my host.

The gazes that met mine were curious, but brief. The people turned back to their food and continued eating as if they were in a rush. One woman held my gaze an instant longer. I had just enough time to notice her very green eyes and long hair pulled back into a ponytail, before she, too, was eating again.

Dr. Matthews motioned for me to sit. As I took a seat, several feet away from the others, a young man came toward us from across the room, a plate in his hands. Instead of the blue jumper, he wore a nondescript beige. He was about the same height as Sol, but his hair was golden brown and cut short. His brown eyes were a shade darker than his tan skin. If I hadn't known better, I'd have thought he was someone who'd spent his days out in the sun.

I tried not to stare, but I couldn't help notice how his gaze flickered over me with mutual curiosity, lingering longer than the others' had. He set the plate in front of me and quickly turned.

I watched him walk away, then realized that Dr. Matthews was studying me very closely through those glasses of his, as if he were trying to analyze me on the spot. I felt like an insect under a microscope. His eyes didn't shift when I met his stare.

Eventually the smell of the sweet potatoes recaptured my attention and I, too, ate as if there were nothing more important in the world.

There was also the daily tube of vitamin infusion gel on the tray, meant to take the place of natural sunshine. I snapped the end of the tube and squeezed the bitter orange gel into my mouth. It always made me feel a bit nauseated for a moment. I knew many at my school mixed theirs with food, but I didn't like how it altered the taste of my meal.

When I finished, I set my fork down and looked up, surprised to see that the room was empty except for the young man in the beige jumpsuit and Dr. Matthews. The doctor was no longer staring, but seemed intent on reading something on his tablet. It was then I noticed a slight tremor in his hand. I heard something clink and looked over to see the young man move along the tables, picking up plates.

"It's time to report, Miss J," Dr. Matthews said.

I stood, wondering what my assignment would be. Perhaps the next three months wouldn't be so bad. Maybe they'd be so impressed with my behavior that I'd be released early and make it to the University after all.

I followed the doctor out of the cafeteria. The corridor was dim and it took me a moment to realize that the young man had fallen into step behind us.

The corridor turned gradually and sloped downward. A scuff sounded behind me, and when I dared a glance behind, the young man was gone.

Dr. Matthews stopped and triggered another nearly concealed door with his hand. "Here we are," he said. "We'll begin the report now."

I scanned the rounded room. There was nothing but a table and two chairs. Some cables protruded from the wall and rested on the table.

He motioned for me to take a chair and then sat down opposite me. "Let me see your ankle cuff."

I lifted my foot, and he pressed a narrow apparatus against it. The cuff expanded, and Dr. Matthews slid it off.

"The Legislature seems to think we need these to control our prisoners," he said.

I wondered what kind of prison this was.

"But our labyrinth of corridors is carefully monitored." He set the cuff on the table. "These get in the way of our testing more often than not."

He reached for the cables coming out of the wall. Each one had a circular pad at the end. "Hold still, Miss J." He pressed a pad on each of my palms. The tremor in his hands was back, and I wanted to ask him about it—did he have a disease? As soon as my palms were connected, the table's surface glowed and a screen appeared, much like the one in my desk at school.

"We're careful to make the appropriate assignments for the patrons in this facility," Matthews said. "A word will appear on the screen. Each word will have two images associated with it. Choose the one that is the most logical match, but do so quickly. We want to record your first instinct."

I pulled my gaze from his trembling fingers and stared at the screen, waiting for the words. My pulse thudded in my ears.

The word *apple* appeared. I'd seen images of the fruit and knew they came in different colors. Red, green, yellow. Unbidden, Rose's words came to mind. *We hid among the trees, eating apples. That's when he leaned over and wiped the juice from my lips and kissed me.*

I blinked and focused on the screen. When two images appeared, one of a burned tree and one of an old-fashioned ceramic bowl, I clicked on the burned tree. After all, apples grew on trees—it was a fact I'd memorized about the Before.

The next word was *tricycle.* I knew about this, too. It

was something that children used to ride, back when there were so many of them in the world. One image was of a smiling boy and the other of a knee, gashed open and bleeding. I studied the smile on the boy for several seconds until Matthews cleared his throat. I selected the smiling boy. I thought riding a tricycle sounded like fun.

The words continued to pop up, and I made my selections as quickly as possible. It felt like about an hour had passed when the screen darkened.

"Now for the second phase," Dr. Matthews said.

This time I was shown pictures and asked to choose the appropriate descriptor for images of plants that were harvested in the Agricultural Center. A few plants popped up that I'd never seen before. I studied them carefully, wondering if any of them were flowers, but they didn't have blossoms.

At the conclusion of the second phase, Dr. Matthews pulled the pads from my hands.

I glanced at him, wondering how I'd fared, but his expression was blank apart from a slight crease between his eyebrows. He escorted me from the room and led me along the corridor, eventually ushering me into a large room with a row of at least a dozen beds. It reminded me of a dorm room, but much larger. A door on the far side was marked with a latrine symbol, and above each bed was a square of metal attached to the wall.

"You'll sleep here," Matthews said.

I shivered at the austerity of the room. It was so bleak, so blank. The gray walls reminded me of the sky outside, and I wondered when I'd see the rain again.

"What will my duties be?" I asked.

I thought I saw a flicker of annoyance. "Your orders will

be given in the morning, Miss J." And with that, Dr. Matthews left the room.

I turned and scanned the beds. The mattresses were thin and the blankets on top were made of a heavy white material, just like the ones in my school dorm.

I crossed to the latrine and looked inside. Nothing unusual—a row of toilet stalls and two showers. Then I walked to one of the beds and examined the metal plate above it. I tried to wiggle it, but it remained sealed tight. I sat on the bed, having no idea what time it was.

Across the room, the door opened and two girls walked in, startling me with their sudden appearance. Both looked to be around eleven or twelve years old. One had reddish hair and a mass of freckles on her face; the other had dark skin, similar to the boy in the cafeteria. They glanced at me, then each climbed onto a bed.

"Hello," I said. One looked at me and nodded, the other merely closed her eyes. The lights in the room dimmed as if on a timer. Maybe we weren't supposed to talk to each other.

The door slid open again a moment later, and the young man from the cafeteria came in.

He quickly averted his eyes as he entered the latrine. Why was he in the girls' dorm room? Maybe he had to clean it? The two girls in bed looked like they were already asleep and hadn't noticed his entrance.

Maybe I could ask him about the prison—he obviously worked here in maintenance, so maybe he'd be willing to fill me in. I stationed myself a few paces outside the latrine, waiting.

When he stepped out, his brown eyes settled on me for an instant and I noticed they weren't just brown, but had some yellow in them, reminding me of sunshine. Or maybe it was just my wishful thinking about the Solstice that would happen in a few days.

He moved past me, but I reached out and grabbed his arm. He stopped and stared at my hand as if it were the oddest thing he'd ever seen. Then the sides of his mouth curled up into a smile.

He was *smiling* at me—actually smiling. Was that allowed in this place?

"Can you tell me what kind of prison this is?" I asked.

He glanced at the sleeping girls, and I detected a hint of wariness as he said, "Phase Three."

I dropped my hand. "Phase Three?"

"You'll learn your assignment in the morning." He shook his head, as if he'd said too much already.

But I wasn't finished with my questions. "What kind of assignments are there?"

Another half smile. "Phase Three assignments."

I let out a breath, cooling my frustration. I couldn't let some maintenance guy, likely a C Level citizen, detect my annoyance. "Why won't anyone tell me anything?" I pressed.

The young man suddenly leaned in, startling me with his nearness. His mouth was just inches from my ear as he whispered, "They're listening."

My heart stuttered. *Where?* I looked around the room, scanning for listening devices, but I saw nothing recognizable. "Can you tell me anything at all?" I said more quietly.

He straightened away from me. "Perhaps."

I refrained from clenching my hands into fists and managed an even tone as I said, "Please, anything would help."

He waved his hand in a wide arc. "This is the sleeping room."

84

I shook my head at his idiocy. His mouth tugged at the corners, and I couldn't help but stare in fascination. I'd never seen someone smile so much.

"The metal squares above each bed are scanners—tonight they'll collect data from your dreams."

This, I couldn't fathom. I folded my arms. "Really? How?"

"The scanners are the latest in discovery science. Just relax and try to sleep. Like I said, you'll get your assignment tomorrow." He took a step back, putting some distance between us. Perhaps he had more latrines to clean.

I exhaled and nodded. At least I had a little more information.

He walked past me and climbed onto a bed next to the far wall.

He was sleeping here, too? I tried not to stare as he pulled a blanket over himself and arranged his pillow. "Morning comes early," he said quietly.

I chose a bed three away from him, the sleeping girls on my other side. The lights dimmed further, set on some automatic mode, and I wondered if anyone else would be coming in for the night. I turned to find him watching me.

"What's your name?" he asked.

I stared, but his warm brown skin nearly blended into the darkness. "Jezebel."

"I'm Rueben. Welcome to Phase Three, Jezebel." He blinked slowly, but didn't take his eyes off me.

And that's how I fell asleep, staring into the warm brown eyes of a stranger.

CHAPTER 12

That night I dreamed of Sol.

I'm chasing him through the dank underground corridors of my new prison. Each time I nearly catch up to him, he spins away, running even faster. I finally give up and sit down in the middle of the hallway. A hand reaches out to me and pulls me to my feet. Sol is now Rueben, and he's laughing. And that's when I realize I'm crying.

I awoke—the lights hadn't come on in the room, and the girls were still asleep. Rueben was gone. I sat up, shivering, and discovered that my cheeks were wet and my covers thrown to the floor. I picked up my blanket and wrapped it around my shoulders. Curling back onto the mattress, I wondered if my dream had been recorded and who would be analyzing it. My head ached, a dull throb, making the dream of Sol/Rueben fade quickly from memory.

I waited in the quiet, not moving, filled with anticipation about my "assignment." I realized that although

I had escaped examination by the recruiters, I had probably landed myself somewhere much worse.

The door slid open and Dr. Matthews entered with three other people. They looked familiar and I thought I might have seen them in the cafeteria, but I couldn't be sure. Dr. Matthews's forehead was creased as he stopped next to my bed and frowned. "What time did you wake up?"

I had no way to know the time, but with all the eyes staring at me, I attempted a guess. "An hour ago."

Matthews typed something on his tablet, his frown apparently a standard when he was around me. His hands weren't trembling now.

"The sleeping powder doesn't work, either," one of the others said. I looked up, but missed who had spoken.

There was no change in Matthews's expression. "Come with us," he said. The others watched as I climbed off the bed, no doubt an ungainly sight. I needed a shower and a change of clothing, but it seemed that wasn't on the agenda.

We traveled the winding corridors for a few minutes before entering a large room with a bank of screens lining one wall, all displaying diagrams of different parts of the brain.

Dr. Matthews was still frowning as he hooked me up, yet again, to more machines. Another series of words. Another series of images. Heat crept along the back of my neck as the others scrutinized me this time, studying me and tapping notes on their tablets. What were they expecting? What were they looking for?

Despite their scrutiny, I focused on the test, determined to score high and earn my way out of this place as quickly as possible.

Back in the cafeteria for dinner, I noticed how everyone dressed the same, how everyone seemed to have the same expressions. Reconciled to their fates. The only person who appeared to be alive and thinking was Rueben, and it was hard to ignore the warmth of his eyes as they briefly met mine. *He must be immune to the Harmony implant,* I thought. There was no other explanation for it. Or was he just pretending to have these emotions in order to get me to trust him? Was he an Informer?

I lingered over the meal of meat and carrot pie. I was starving, but I forced myself to eat slowly so that I could be the last one in the room and alone with Matthews and Rueben.

"When do I receive my assignment?" I asked Matthews when Rueben was within earshot. He slowed his motions in clearing the table.

"You need more testing tomorrow," Matthews said. "For now you'll return to the dormitory."

"What did my dreams tell you?" I pressed on. All I remembered was that they were about Sol, but little else.

His frown deepened, and he said nothing. After a few minutes of silence, I picked up my plate and stood, my face feeling hot.

"No," Matthews said, finally speaking. "Rueben clears the plates."

I handed my plate to Rueben, but felt awkward; I was perfectly capable of clearing my own place.

"Can you point me in the direction of the dormitory?" I asked Rueben.

He opened his mouth, but Matthews spoke first. "You will not attempt to clear your plate again."

"I apologize." *Do not clear your plate,* I repeated to

myself. I was going to have to learn the new rules quickly if I ever wanted to get out of here.

Matthews's face relaxed a little, and he gave Rueben a brief nod.

"Follow me." Rueben set the plate back on the table and crossed to the door.

We walked quickly along the hall. It seemed that everyone was in a hurry in Phase Three, and I was out of breath when we arrived back at the dormitory.

Inside, he turned to me as soon as the door slid shut. "You mustn't do anything to attract attention," he whispered.

"I'm not trying to." I kept my voice low as well. "It's not like I was given a list of rules or anything. *You* won't say much, and Dr. Matthews tells me even less." The anger rose sharp in my chest, but I refused to let it spill. I focused on breathing in and out slowly, just as my caretakers had taught me.

Rueben glanced at the ceiling, looking for something.

"Can they see us, too?" I whispered.

"Yes." He crossed to one of the beds and sat down, still speaking in a low voice, but not looking at me. "What did you do to get sent here?"

I hesitated. Should I be telling the maintenance boy my list of crimes? If I wanted his trust, I had to tell him something, but I didn't want to screw up, either. "Will I be breaking another rule to tell a worker?"

His brows pulled together. "A worker?" Then his face relaxed. "Ah. You think I *work* here . . . like Dr. Matthews?"

"Well," I waved my hand toward the door, "You work in the cafeteria—"

He started to laugh—actually laughing aloud.

I was so astonished that I let the smallest of smiles escape.

"I don't work here. I'm like you—serving a sentence."

"You're a prisoner, too?" It was hard to believe, but maybe the maintenance work was his assignment. "Why did *you* get sent here?"

His eye glinted with something I couldn't describe. "You first."

I took a studied breath, trying to decide if Rueben was really going to trade information. "I was caught with an illegal book."

No reaction. "Anything else?" he asked.

"Not that I know of." I wasn't about to tell him, or anyone for that matter, about the conversations about the Before with Sol. Or that I had been shocked by an agitator rod and should have forgotten the contents of the book. "It's your turn."

But he completely ignored me and stood, then crossed to the door. He typed in a sequence on the tablet on the wall. The lights dimmed. Without turning he said, "There's something wrong with you."

My body stiffened. "*What?*"

"The other girls will return soon. We can talk in the latrine." His voice was barely audible. He walked into the latrine without looking back.

I stared at the closed door and then, before I could weigh out the consequences, I followed him inside.

He was leaning against one of the sinks, his arms crossed as he watched me enter.

"What could have possibly been in that book to make them send you *here?*" His eyes were a lighter brown in here, the yellow more noticeable. "Even if you did some illegal research, there's not much information to be found in a single book. Unless you were in an undercover lab."

I'd never heard of an undercover lab, but filed the information away. "I don't even know what 'here' is, or what, exactly, I'm supposed to do *here*," I said. "Tell me that, and I'll answer your question."

One side of his mouth lifted into a smirk. "The reason you're here becomes a little more obvious every time you open your mouth."

I folded my arms, mimicking his stance. "What kind of prison is this, anyway?"

Rueben raised his eyebrows. "The Legislature might have called it a prison, but believe me, it's worse."

His tone made my mouth dry. I swallowed, but it didn't help. I wiped my hands on my pants, then refolded my arms. "What do you mean?"

"Only kids they suspect to be Clinicals are sent here."

"Clinicals?" The name sounded odd, but familiar at the same time.

Rueben seemed to read my thoughts. "I'd be surprised if you'd heard of them—*us*. It's not something the general population knows about."

"So, are *you* one of these . . . Clinicals?"

"Yes." He said, reluctantly. "The kids who come here have displayed signs of being different, either in thought or action, which are always connected. But it takes a lot more than reading a forbidden book to get sent here."

"I didn't say I read it."

"You didn't have to."

I stared at him, wanting to protest, but something deep down stirred. An explanation? Was this what my caretakers had meant by being different?

Sol had known I was curious, and he had seen me cry on that last day. Chalice told me that I was too paranoid about breaking rules. But wasn't everybody? "What makes you think I read the book?" I asked.

"I can read it in your eyes."

"I disagree," I said, then clamped my hand over my mouth, realizing I'd spoken aloud.

"Of course you do," Rueben said. "You probably disagree with a lot of things. That's why you're here."

I shook my head, then stopped. He was right. I did disagree with things, but I always talked myself out of arguing, deciding to follow rules even if I disagreed with them. I guess it was part of what made me different.

"Jezebel," Rueben said in a strangely caressing voice.

I snapped my head up. The way he said my name made me feel like he'd just touched me—not with his hands, but with his words. I folded my arms again, feeling hot and cold, uncomfortable.

"Ninety-nine percent of the population never even *considers* disagreeing with what they learn in school, or with any of the Legislature's rules. You do it without even realizing it."

That's because immune to the Harmony implant and I'm a Carrier, I wanted to say, but didn't dare. "I make a choice to agree," I said in a slow voice. "Don't most people?"

He laughed, and the sound warmed me from my toes up, but I tightened my folded arms, unaccustomed to such unabashed displays of emotion. "Why are you laughing?"

"I'm a Clinical." Rueben's eyes shone, his words absorbing me again. "I disagree all the time. That's why I'm here—so they can figure out why I do it and fix me, and prevent it from happening in others."

I opened my mouth. Then I shut it. I couldn't look at Rueben because I already knew what he was going to say.

"Jezebel, you're a Clinical. Just like me."

My heart pounded madly, like it was trying to escape a cage. "I've never broken rules, at least until I read that book," I whispered fiercely. I wasn't counting what Sol had told me about the Before, the flowers, or the seasons. Or that the agitator rod hadn't done its job. My doubts had crept in. I was immune to the Harmony implant . . . did this mean I was a Clinical?

Rueben stepped toward me, making the small latrine seem even smaller. He was at least a head taller than me—like Sol.

"How did school work out for you?" he asked.

I bristled; he spoke as if I wouldn't be going back. "Great. I tested into the A Level when I was twelve. I'm at the top of my class now."

His eyes narrowed as if he didn't believe me.

"What?"

"They allowed you into the program that late?" he said.

I straightened and lowered my arms, clenching them into fists. "I had . . . issues to overcome when I was younger." I took a quick glance into those warm eyes of his, then looked away again. "Why? What about you?"

He ignored my question. "Did you spend a lot of time in Detention?"

"No!" I shot out. "I memorized the rules the first week in school. I avoided breaking even the small ones."

"Were you tempted to break them—even small ones?"

"No," I lied, perhaps too quickly. Even if I had been tempted, wasn't it more important that I had resisted the urge? "What about *you*? Were you in Detention a lot?"

He raised a finger to his lips. We fell quiet and both listened. Low voices came from outside the door; someone else had entered the dormitory.

Rueben left the latrine, leaving me alone. A few minutes later, unable to wait any longer, I exited as well.

The two girls from the night before were back, sitting on their beds. They both looked over as I walked into the room. The girl with the copper skin gave me a slight nod. But the freckled one stared past me, and I noticed she was shaking. Her face looked pale as if she was about to be sick.

I glanced over at Rueben, who stood at the end of the room, near one of the far beds. He shook his head slightly, as if warning me not to do anything.

I ignored him and crossed to the freckle-faced girl. "Are you all right?" I asked, touching her shoulder. She flinched when I touched her, but didn't meet my gaze. Then she opened her mouth to speak.

Her voice was high pitched like a young child's, but I couldn't understand anything she was saying—it was all gibberish. I threw a glance in Rueben's direction; he'd started walking toward us.

"What's she saying?" I asked as he neared me. Something wasn't right. I felt sick to my stomach as the girl continued her babbling.

"Come on, we need to stay away from Grace," he said, motioning for me to move away from the girl.

I stayed where I was. Something was seriously wrong. "We should try to help her."

His hand grabbed mine. "Leave her," he insisted. "They'll be coming for her soon, and you don't want to interfere."

I wavered. I didn't want to be in trouble in this place. I'd had enough of that. I followed Rueben to the far side of the room. The copper-skinned girl had closed her eyes, ignoring Grace completely.

"What's going on?" I whispered.

Rueben hushed me just as the doors opened.

Three men walked in, a couple of whom I recognized from my testing. They approached Grace, their faces grim. One held a tan jacket with extra long sleeves. Grace didn't pay them any attention until they grabbed her. Then she screamed.

"Stop!" I shouted, but Rueben pulled me toward him and covered my mouth.

"Hold still," he growled in my ear. I barely caught his next whispered words. "Don't call attention to yourself, or you'll be in the jacket next."

I nodded, and Rueben released his grip. I stared in horror as the men easily overpowered the young girl and thrust her arms into the jacket. Except they put it on backward, with her arms crossed against her chest, stopping her from fighting against them. With her arms confined, she could barely move, and the men carried out the still-screaming but completely helpless girl from the room.

Every part of my body trembled as the screams faded down the corridor. "What are they doing to her?"

"They put her in a strait jacket for her protection."

I stared at Rueben, trying to understand.

"Strait jackets are simple restraints from the Before," Rueben said, "when they didn't have Harmony implants to track criminals or ankle cuffs to control dangerous people."

Track? Harmony implants don't track people. They only level out emotions. My stomach went tight, like it might reject my dinner. "She's just a kid," I said. "She's not . . .

violent." Just saying the word *violent* frightened me. It was on the List of Failures, something that we didn't have in our world of Order.

Rueben must have heard the rising panic in my voice, even though I was trying to whisper. He put both hands on my shoulders and leaned close. "She's in overload."

With Rueben so close I noticed his scent for the first time—he smelled like he'd just been outside, in the sun, which was impossible. His usually warm eyes looked worried instead, as if watching Grace had disturbed him as much as it did me.

"The scientists raised the control level in her implant," he continued. "They adjusted it based on dream-watching and thought they had it right, but . . ." He looked away. "Changing the control level doesn't always have a positive outcome. In fact," his eyes were back on me, "there's only a sixteen percent success rate once someone hits overload."

"Level of control? Success rate of *what?*" I hissed, my mind trying to wrap around what Rueben was saying. I looked over at the copper-skinned girl, who had curled up on her bed and closed her eyes. It was like she'd completely checked out.

"Success rate of living through overload and returning to normal brain function," Rueben said.

I bit my lip, staring into his brown eyes, now dark with anger. Or was it fear?

"I don't understand, Rueben." I swiped furiously at tears that wouldn't stop and my chest felt tight as though I couldn't inhale enough oxygen. Something Rose had said popped into my mind. "I thought the implants were meant to protect us from a rebellion brought on by unreasonable emotion."

Rueben's fingers brushed my cheek, absorbing the tears on my face. "Don't fall asleep tonight, and I'll tell you about it."

CHAPTER 13

Rueben motioned for me to come over to where he sat in the dark. My hands felt damp as I climbed off my bed and settled on the one next to his. The remaining girl, whom Rueben told me was named Estee, remained curled up, and seemed to be asleep.

He started whispering, and I leaned forward to catch his quiet words. I tried to ignore how he smelled like he'd just been outside, beneath the sun.

"Most people are born with peaceful dispositions," he said. "In fact, scientists believe all babies are born with the same personality. So it makes sense that if we're educated the same way and grow up in the same social structure, our personalities will be quite generic."

I nodded. I could understand the scientists' conclusions. There wasn't much difference between the kids I knew. Sol seemed to have higher intelligence than most and Chalice liked to push against the rules, but they were the only ones who seemed different.

"But when the scientific model fails, even after all precautions are taken, scientists want to know why," Rueben continued. "Harmony implants don't just suppress emotions. They track our emotion levels and send the results back to the science board. And they can be programmed to control our brains on a greater level, affecting how you react to certain events or ideas."

I stared at Rueben in the dim light as disbelief washed over me. Although I shouldn't be surprised. If Phase Three could monitor my dreams, the Legislature could track us through the Harmony implants. But I wondered how Rueben knew so much. "How do you know?"

Rueben hesitated, then said in a quiet voice, "I wasn't born in the city. I'm from the relocation program. It's common knowledge there."

I shifted away from him, my heart pounding. I'd never met anyone born outside of the city—we were told they were barbaric and diseased and were never allowed within the borders. I studied Rueben for a second. He looked intelligent. He looked healthy.

"You're from a . . . Lake Town?" I tried not to let my prejudice show.

A slow smile crossed his face. "I know what you're thinking. Why aren't I shackled to the floor shouting nonsense words?"

"Well? Why are you so normal?" I asked, ignoring his smile.

"Your history lessons have been greatly manipulated."

Naomi would probably agree, but I still had a hard time believing it. Maybe he was an exception. "Where are you really from?"

"I was born in the Lake Town of Prairie."

I watched his hands move as he talked. His nails were clean, and I didn't see any signs of sores. "Where is Prairie?"

"A few days by ship." When my eyebrows crinkled, he said, "A ship is a very large boat."

"I know what a boat is." They transported people and goods along the river. I'd heard about Lake Towns in other parts of the world that relied on boats to house people because they weren't advanced enough to find alternate survival solutions like we had.

Rueben watched me, amusement in his eyes. He held up an arm. "Do you want to touch me, see if I'm real?"

"I—I know you're real, it's just that—"

"You didn't expect someone from a Lake Town to actually walk upright and speak?"

My face burned. "Something like that."

"Look, Jezebel, I'm not sure why I'm telling you all of this. One of the rules that Lake Town recruits are given before we relocate is that we aren't supposed to talk about where we came from." He hesitated, watching me closely. "But I feel like we're in this together—and maybe the more information we can share with each other, the better."

"I don't have any information to share," I said, too quickly. I'd promised never to reveal the secret of the Carrier key. And I wasn't ready to tell anyone about my grandmother or why she'd been executed.

Rueben nodded slowly, and I could tell he didn't exactly believe me.

I looked around the silent room. "And even if I did have any information to tell you, wouldn't we get into more trouble?"

He scoffed. "We're already in prison."

I let out a sigh. We were indeed in prison, but there was still hope—there had to be. I had to make it back to the University and become a part of the Science Commission. But I also had so many questions about the Lake Town, why Rueben came to the city, and how he knew so much. But mostly I couldn't stop staring at him, waiting for the barbarian to come out. Finally I said, "So how were you recruited?"

His face flushed, and he glanced away from me, as if he were uncomfortable. I still wasn't used to his display of emotion.

"In this city," Rueben began in a slow voice, "more people are Taken, due to life cycle or crimes, than are born each year. The population is dwindling."

"Dwindling?" I hadn't expected that.

"Yeah, so a certain number of people are allowed to earn citizenship each year," he said. "At the age of eight, Lake people become eligible to join the recruitment program. Usually the head officer of the town selects a handful of youth to recommend. The year I was recommended, I was the only one accepted for citizenship from the whole town."

Before I tested into the A Level, there were kids who lived at the Children's Center who didn't have caretakers. We were always told that their caretakers had been Taken. Now I wondered if some of them were from the Lake Towns.

Out there, in the vast waters, were other pockets of civilization. Living and breathing totally different lives than ours here in the city. "What was it like living in a Lake Town?" I asked. It was hard to reconcile my preconceived notions with the living, breathing boy who now sat across from me.

One side of his mouth lifted. "That would take weeks to

tell you. But information is harder to get out there—we don't have the WorldNet. We rely on stories handed down from generation to generation, and life is much harder in a physical sense. My family spent most of their time scouting for wood and metal pieces to add onto our floating barge."

I tried to imagine Rueben fishing for scraps of wood, his long arms snagging pieces out of the water. I blinked the image away. "So you must have been grateful to become a citizen in the city."

The flush was back, and he shoved his hands in his pockets. "There were some big trade-offs."

I waited until he met my eyes again. "What kind of trade-offs?"

He exhaled, looking past me. "I haven't seen my family for eight years."

"You mean your caretakers?"

"Yes." His eyes flickered to me, then away again. "And my two sisters."

"Sis-ters?"

His gaze slid back to mine. His eyes were no longer warm, but dark and cold like wet earth. "Siblings—my mother and father had three children . . . offspring."

Three? The silence dripped between us. I wondered how a large family could be allowed, even in such a primitive place. There was something else in his eyes that was hard to identify. Then my heart clenched. *Pain.*

"You miss them," I whispered.

He didn't need to answer.

I knew a little of what it felt like to miss someone. David, Naomi, Sol, Chalice. I blinked rapidly and said, "Does the B level in your Lake Town allow that many children in one family?"

His eyes thawed a little, but his voice was subdued. "There are no 'levels' in the Lake Towns, Jezebel. Caretakers are called parents just like in the Before, and adults are allowed to marry if they want to."

I let the information settle over me. No levels. Parents instead of caretakers. More questions swarmed. "If there are no levels, then how does the town function? How does everyone know what to do?" The true meaning of barbarians hit me. That must be why their society was so backward, why they had to live on barges hooked together, constantly in motion.

His tone was clipped when he answered. "Society functions in the Lake Towns just as it has for thousands of years, just as it did in the Before."

I clamped my mouth shut. That meant they suffered with disease, civil unrest, and crime. My eyes narrowed as I peered at Rueben.

"Why are you in here?" I asked over my thudding heart.

"I've been living in the city since I was eight years old," he said with a sigh, as though he expected the question. "Believe me, I've been through all the training and all the education. But, like you, my Harmony implant doesn't suppress my stronger emotions. So, like you, I'm considered a Clinical."

I waited for him to mention why he was in the prison. "Did you . . . commit a crime?"

He grimaced slightly, but his eyes brightened. "Failure to comply."

That could mean anything. "But you're from a Lake Town. That makes you different to begin with."

Rueben's gaze was hard. "Not different in the ways that you think. Different, yes, because I have memories of a family, of people who are free to make their own choices, of a place where people can fall in love."

His words stabbed at my heart. Why did he have to talk about falling in love? "If the Lake Town was such a good place to live, then why are you here?"

"I was chosen to come," he said, the bitterness swift in his voice. "It wasn't a privilege, but a duty."

"And now that you're here—in Phase Three—have you failed that duty?" Would he finally tell me what he had done to get here?

"It depends on your point of view."

I looked away. I didn't know how to process all of this new information. My eyes wound up on the dream monitor on the wall. The city was a place where things were controlled, and that control kept our society surviving while the others failed and became extinct one by one.

Rueben settled onto his bed, lying down and clasping his hands behind his head, staring at the ceiling. I glanced over at him, and as much as I didn't want to admit it, I was fascinated by his background. And his knowledge. What would it be like to be taken away at the age of eight from everything you'd ever known?

After several moments, he started speaking again. "I don't want to argue about who has the best life—whether it's in the Lake Town or here in the city."

"I don't either."

We both fell quiet, until I said, "I just didn't know . . ."

"I know," he said, and gave me a weak smile.

My mind was still racing, but I wanted to know more. "How does the Harmony implant record information?" I hated to admit it, but it seemed that I knew much less than I had realized.

"It tracks levels of emotion, recording things like increased body temperature, faster breathing, and perspiration output—all indicators of the presence of emotion. If you compare the Harmony technology to other sciences, it's still relatively new." He sat up again and swung his legs over the edge of the bed, resting his elbows on his knees. "A very low level of control is exercised over the average person."

I exhaled. Had Naomi known about this term *Clinicals*? Or had she just called it *immune*? "So is everyone being controlled right now?"

"Just enough to keep them in compliance," Rueben said. "It's a low level compared to what it has the potential to do."

I didn't like the sound of that. The kids in my class were already so controlled, so passionless.

"Once in a while, a person exhibits stronger behavior patterns than what is socially acceptable," Rueben said. "Like me and you."

"And the scientists are able to increase control levels," he continued, "in order to eliminate the powerful urges of various emotions."

"Can people tell when their emotions are being controlled?"

"Most of the time it's not noticeable, unless there is a big change. Like I said, most people don't need additional control—the lowest level is enough. When is the last time you saw someone rebel against an inspector?"

I briefly thought of Sol banging on the metal door just before he was cuffed, but he had done that to help me. "Never," I said.

Rueben gave a quick nod. "When's the last time you heard someone argue?"

I searched my memory. I could think of plenty of times when students informed on each other, but I'd never heard a real argument.

"What about kissing?"

Kissing? I stared at him. "What do you mean?" I thought of Rose and her boyfriend and the apple. Why was Rueben bringing this up?

"You know," he said with a slight smile, his teeth white in the dimness, "when a girl has a crush on someone. Boyfriend, girlfriend . . . kissing?"

"But that's—"

"I know it's against the law to fall in love here—or should I say to have a 'romantic interlude.'" He lowered his voice. "But have you ever *wanted* to kiss someone?"

I tried to shake my head, to say no. But I froze. Was he testing me? Was he part of the test to see if I had really read the book? To find out if I was truly a Clinical? Finally I answered, "Wanting to do something isn't the same as doing it."

Rueben closed his eyes. Then he started laughing. He opened them, and laughed louder. I looked behind me, worried he'd wake someone. I didn't know what the penalty would be for not sleeping, but after seeing that poor girl in the strait jacket, I didn't want to find out.

"Why are you laughing?" I asked.

He came over and sat next to me. Very close. He leaned against me so that his breath puffed against my ear. "You're definitely at risk."

"For what?" My body felt prickly all over at his nearness. I wanted to shove him away, but at the same time, I didn't want him to move. I wanted to ask him why he smelled like sunshine on the day of Solstice—did all Lake

106

people smell like him? He'd probably laugh at me again.

Rueben took a single breath, then said, "You're at risk for falling in love."

His words sent a jolt of fear through me. How could he know? He couldn't. This was a test—I *knew* it. I didn't want to fall into his trap. I didn't know if I had passed the other tests, but I'd pass this one.

"I won't break the law, especially that one."

I felt, rather than saw, him smile. "You already have."

My face got hot. "The book was a mistake. It was my inheritance, and I only—"

"I'm not talking about the book," he said, too close now. The prickles on my body turned to perspiration. Did he know about Sol telling me about the Before? Did Rueben know that I'd been shocked and it hadn't erased my memory? I felt like I might suffocate.

"You've failed every test so far," he said.

I scooted away from him, the mattress creaking beneath me. "How do you know?"

"I can see a lot of information on the instructors' tablets when I'm clearing plates in the cafeteria."

Panic shot through me, and I pulled away from him. He was learning too much about me. Had I really failed the tests? "I don't see how I failed; I only answered the questions."

"Exactly," he said. "When they showed you a red peony, you selected the color of 'blood' as the best descriptor."

"It *was* the color of blood," I said, thinking hard. Sol had described a valley of blood red flowers. I had merely repeated his description. Did that mean I'd given something away? "I still don't understand how I failed the tests."

Rueben reached out and took my hands. I flinched. The

only other person who'd held my hand was Sol. But I knew Sol felt nothing in return. Rueben was unsettling, his words and actions unpredictable. Emotions practically burst from him, reaching out and touching me. I pulled away, but he wouldn't let go. "What do you feel when I hold your hands?"

My face felt hot again. "I don't know—"

"Don't try to analyze it. Just tell me the first thing that comes to your mind."

"Nervous." I dared a glance at his face. "Warm."

A smile tugged at his lips. "That's what I thought." He stood, still holding my hands, and drew me against him.

"What are you doing?" I whispered.

His arms slipped around me. I tried to wrench away, but he held me firm, and my attempt was only halfhearted. "Now what do you feel?" he said in my ear, the warmth of his breath spreading to my fingers.

I tried to breathe, tried to move, but his grip only tightened. I hadn't realized how strong he was. "Let me go," I said. Something like fear grew inside of me, and I felt a scream bubble in my throat.

His was breath hot against my skin. "Kiss me first."

My entire body shook with astonishment, with anger. I made one more effort and got a hand free. Then I slapped him as hard as I could.

Rueben jerked back

I looked around frantically for something to use to defend myself, but there was nothing.

I moved against the wall and braced myself, expecting him to yell, to strike back. I imagined him becoming violent. Stories of rape and pillaging in the Before ran through my mind. My hand throbbed, but I'd be ready if necessary, using my fists.

But he didn't move. "That, my dear Jezebel, is why you were sent here."

My breath left my chest, and I stared at him, my hands still clenched. "Are you finished?" I ground out between my teeth. I used everything I had to hold back the avalanche of anger. I wouldn't let him get me into trouble. Not here, in this place. I had to get out and make it to the University. I had more important things to do than let this boy get under my skin.

He took a step toward me, and when I shrank back, he stopped. "Every other girl would have begged me to stop breaking the rules. But you . . ." He chuckled. "You hit me."

"You had no right to touch me, to . . ." He had no right to laugh at me. The trembling in my body reached to my toes. Maybe this was a game in the Lake Towns, but in the city, it meant Demotion or Banishment.

"I know," Rueben said. He stepped forward again, his eyes intent on me, one side of his face red from my mark. "And it made you *angry*." His lips moved into a smile.

I blinked, adrenaline still pulsing through me, but I was starting to realize Rueben wasn't really going to kiss me. "I'm not angry," I muttered, still seething.

He gave me a look that plainly said he didn't believe me. "You saw an injustice and reacted." His sounded . . . proud.

I shook my head. "I don't need any more trouble."

"You stood up for yourself." He touched my clenched hand, and I forced myself to relax it, forced the emotions to retreat, to be calm. "The scientists would love to put a stop to these kinds of reactions before they wreak real havoc."

"I wasn't . . . I'm not . . ." The breath left me, and I moved around him and sat back on the bed. There was no hiding from him. He'd seen my emotions firsthand. I needed his help, even if he was a part of the test. "What now?"

There was something like regret in his eyes. "They'll experiment. Alter your implant."

My entire body went cold. I had worked so hard to suppress my emotions. How would it feel not to fight them anymore? To feel and act like everyone else?

Rueben sat across from me this time, watching me closely, and giving me the space he'd stolen from me earlier. "I'm sorry, Jezebel. You're too much of a risk."

"I've never broken a rule—at least not intentionally," I said.

A small smile returned to Rueben's mouth. *"Never* intentionally."

"It's true."

"I believe you." But his expression said otherwise.

"Are you part of my test?" I asked.

His brown eyes held mine. "I hope you can believe me on this—I'm in the same test that you are."

"Then why did you say all those things to me, and why did you try to . . ."

"Kiss you?"

I nodded, my face hot again.

"I wanted to see what you were made of," Rueben whispered. "I need an ally."

CHAPTER 14

"I thought the testing was over, and I'd have my assignment by now," I said to Dr. Matthews a few mornings later. His trembling was back—it seemed to come and go. The testing was taking place earlier in the day than usual so that everyone could go above ground for the Summer Solstice.

His permanent frown deepened. "Your dreams weren't tracked last night, just like the previous two nights."

I suppressed a yawn. I hadn't slept much over the past few days. After Rueben's kiss test, we'd stayed up whispering during the nights. And the times we weren't whispering, I was worrying about the freckled-faced girl, Grace. Had she recovered or was her brain permanently altered?

On one of those nights, Rueben told me he'd been integrated into C Level when he first arrived at the city, but by the age of eleven, there were signs that he wasn't fitting in. He tested into B Level every year, but every year elected to stay in C. "I guess it became obvious that I wasn't exactly 'normal,' and when I refused to move up a level after passing the last series of tests, I was assigned here," he'd said.

"Why didn't you want to move up a level?" I asked.

"I blame it on the Solstice," he said. "Whenever I felt the sun on me, it reminded me of my family in the Lake Town, because that was the last time I was happy. And I thought about all the people who'd lived in the Before. I liked the freedom living in C Level gave me; there weren't as many expectations."

I was the opposite. I wanted to get as much education as possible, to find a way to save this city. How could Rueben just want to spend his days doing nothing? We had to prepare for the future and think about the next generations.

But, I did admit that the approaching Solstice made me forget my responsibilities just a little, as my body craved the sun, its natural warmth and golden light. I wondered if the doctors would bring Grace to the surface. Maybe it would help her.

Dr. Matthews's voice brought me back to the present. "We'll conduct the dream test again tonight."

I folded my arms on the desk in front of me. It felt like I'd spent my entire life in this small round room, surrounded by blank walls, with electronic images flashing before me. "Can you tell me what happened to Grace?"

Matthews kept his gaze on his tablet, but that didn't hide the tremor in his hands.

"Is that what's in store for me?" Perhaps I was feeling bolder because the Solstice was only a few hours away. Rueben said that it was the one time we'd all be allowed to go to the surface, under strict supervision. Even Matthews's frown had seemed softer today—perhaps he was looking forward to the sunshine as well.

"Will she get to go above ground for the Solstice?" I asked when he stayed silent.

He raised his head. Finally. "She doesn't concern you." His hands tightened on the side of the tablet.

"Maybe it would help her—"

"The sun won't make a difference," he snapped.

"Would it hurt to try?"

He ignored me and continued typing into his tablet. My hands clenched and unclenched as I tried to stop the tingle of anger growing in my body. I'd been in this place less than a week, and I'd already lost control of my emotions several times.

I remembered Rueben's warning about what they might do to me. To him. To all of us. *Altering*. Weren't we supposed to be finding a way to preserve future generations? Not destroying the one we already had?

I breathed out. I couldn't stand it anymore. The silence. The frowns. The unanswered questions. "Am I going through all of this testing only for you to *erase me*?"

His eyes lifted, and it felt like it was first time he really looked at me. Really saw me. I was struck again by how young he was, maybe nineteen or twenty. "Is that what you think we're doing here?"

My face reddened, and I tried to swallow the words that forced their way out. But I knew I could no longer stay silent, no longer pretend I was all right with all that was going on in Phase Three. The seeds of anger that had been growing inside me, suddenly sprouted, and there was nothing I could to do control it. "I saw what happened to Grace. She didn't do anything wrong. She's only a kid."

I was afraid he wasn't going to answer at first. "You don't know what you are talking about, Miss J. I advise you to keep quiet." His voice had a hard edge to it.

I stood and moved toward the door, knowing I couldn't get out on my own, but wanting to be as far away from him as possible. "And if I don't keep quiet, you'll alter me as well?" I knew this was a mistake, but the emotions were a flood now. "Maybe you should just alter me right now—save me from all these idiotic tests."

Matthews moved to my side with lightning speed, his hand flashing toward my shoulder. A stab of pain shot through it, but it was too late to react. Matthews stepped away, his face grim, an injector in his hand.

"I see you've been talking to Rueben," he said with a ferocious snarl.

I opened my mouth to respond, but my body went numb. Off balance, I tilted back and collapsed against the door.

There was a time when all I wanted to see was the sun. But now, I'd take the thick gray clouds, the cold rain . . . anything but this.

Without moving and without opening my eyes, I knew I was in a blacked-out cell. The floor was as cold as the wall I leaned against.

My shoulder throbbed where I'd been injected, but my head hurt even worse. I pulled my knees to my chest and cradled my shoulder. How long had I been here? Minutes? Hours?

Holding my breath, I listened. For any sound.

But I only heard my heart thumping as my pulse throbbed in my ears. I exhaled, letting my own rush of warm breath ripple over my hands.

Tears threatened, and in the blackness I let them fall. Shame followed. I'd let my anger surface at the worst possible time, to the worst possible person. Dr. Matthews had no doubt reported it, and I had lost all chance of an early release from this prison. If I'd had a chance at all.

Sol and Chalice were a fading memory; even Rueben seemed remote.

I leaned forward, away from the cold wall. My head was spinning—whatever Matthews had injected me with was making me dizzy. I had to get out of this place. I had to apologize to Matthews. I had to pass the tests. I had to go to the University.

I had to see the sun.

How could you be so stupid? I wanted to scream it, but only let it rebound within my head.

It would be six months until the next Solstice. If I missed this one . . . *I can't miss it.*

I struggled to my feet, bracing myself against the wall as a jolt of dizziness engulfed me. I took a step, ignoring the pulsing against my temples. My hands glided along the smooth, malleable walls until I found the metal door.

"Dr. Matthews!" I shouted. Then I started to bang on the door. "Dr. Matthews! Please let me out!"

I don't know what I expected—maybe the door sliding open and a guard waiting to shock me, or a scientist with another injection. But I didn't expect silence.

"Dr. Matthews! Someone! Please!"

Nothing again. I slid to the floor in exhaustion.

I closed my eyes and thought of the last Solstice, when Sol and I spent the whole day in the school yard with the other kids. We had left our raincoats in heaps on the concrete ground, turning our faces upward and spreading our arms, welcoming the yellow rays.

Wrapping my arms around my knees, I pretended the warmth was from the sun's heat. *Right now,* I thought, *right now, the sun might be out.*

"Please!" I croaked, my voice not much more than a whisper. I had no strength to stand, none to call out or to pound on the door anymore.

I had no strength to cry.

I'd been forgotten.

CHAPTER 15

I didn't move when the door opened. A square of yellow light settled on my legs and I peered through my lashes at the two men who stood there. Guards or scientists, I wasn't sure.

They spoke in low voices, but their tones vibrated through my ears and made my head throb again. One of the men leaned over and took my wrist, pressing against my skin to feel my pulse. Then he lifted each of my eyelids, shining a small light in my eyes.

I remained motionless—not by choice. My limbs felt as if they had been shackled to the floor.

Apparently, the men standing over me realized the same thing and lifted me. I was carried unceremoniously through the corridors and dumped onto a bed in the dormitory. The light was dim and several silent forms occupied various beds. The day was over, and night had come.

I had missed the Solstice.

The sun wouldn't appear for another six months, and I would be underground for three of them.

One of the men draped a blanket over me, and after checking the flat monitor above my bed, they shuffled out.

A tear formed beneath my half-closed lids, but it was so small, it didn't even have the strength to move down my face. It, like me, was depleted.

I wondered how long the sun had shone today. Did the kids in our prison cast off their jackets and dance around in the gold and white rays? Did their fair skin turn pink? Did anyone wonder where I was? Had Rueben missed me?

With great effort, I turned my head, looking for Rueben. His usual bed was empty. I turned the other way, trying to identify the sleeping people in the beds. One was the copper-skinned girl, the other a girl I didn't recognize.

My fingers started to tingle, and I was able to move them. Then the tingling spread along my hands and up my arms and I realized the numbness from the injection was wearing off. The tingling created a strange warmth in my body, as if there were a ray of sunshine within me, trying to emerge. It moved to my torso, my legs, and my feet. After several minutes, when I trusted my strength, I sat up. Eventually I made my way to the latrine on shaky legs. I washed the best I could.

I stared at my image in the mirror. My hair usual thick brown hair was lank and wet on the sides, my face dripping with water, my dark brown eyes bloodshot. I looked pale and sickly, despite my normal olive skin coloring, and again I wondered what they had drugged me with.

My chest tightened with anger, with sorrow, with frustration, but tears refused to come this time. I touched the image in the mirror as if I could feel a human connection that way, but felt only the cold rejection of the mirror.

I lowered my hands and braced myself on the edge of the sink. I had to get out of this prison. Rueben had told me he'd been here for nearly three months. But where was he now? The look of disgust in Matthews's eyes when he mentioned Rueben had frightened me. Had Rueben been punished for my outburst?

Taking a deep breath, I dried my face and hands, then left the latrine. I came to a stop when I saw someone waiting outside. "Rueben."

He put his fingers to his lips. There was bruising on his face and a wild look in his eyes.

"What happened?" I whispered.

He crossed to me. "My time is up. They've altered me," he said in a shaky voice. "I don't know how much longer I'll be coherent."

Fear threaded its way through my limbs. Was the wildness in his eyes just the beginning?

I reached up and touched the side of his face that wasn't bruised. "They hurt you."

His hand covered mine, lowering it. "I didn't go down easy."

"Oh, Rueben." I felt heartsick, and before I could think better of it, I wrapped my arms around his neck and hugged him like I'd never been allowed to hug anyone before.

His arms went around me, too, holding me tight. "I'll be fine."

"No you won't." My voice caught in a sob. "You saw what happened to Grace."

But he didn't respond, only tightened his embrace.

If I had the power to stop time, I would have done it right then. The next minutes, the next hours, were too fearful to comprehend. I buried my face in his neck, memorizing his

119

scent, feeling the warmth of his skin against mine. This moment, this space in time, was ours alone.

"That's what I like about you, Jezebel," he whispered. "You're not afraid to show emotion. You're real."

Cold seeped through my body, and with it came sadness. The exact reason he liked me was why I was here in the first place. It was also the reason that I'd met him. I had been taken away from Sol, only to find another friendship in the most unlikely of places.

Releasing my grip on Rueben, I looked him over. "Did you miss Solstice, too?"

He nodded slightly, his hands still on my waist. I felt the depth of sorrow in his eyes. "I'm sorry." As sorry as I was for myself, I was sorrier for him.

"You could kiss me and make it better."

My breath left for an instant until I realized he was teasing me. I pushed him away, and a grin splashed across his face. I bit my lip to keep it from trembling. I wanted to return his smile, but I knew once I did, I'd be crying.

He dragged the beds together so that he could hold my hand as we supposedly slept and I entered into the dream testing. Rueben wasn't being tested. He'd failed everything they'd put before him, just like I had so far, and altering was the next step in the research process.

I stared at him for a long time, even after he fell asleep. I memorized every angle and curve of his face, the way his chest rose and fell with his even breathing, the cut above his eye, and the way that, even in his sleep, he didn't relax his grip on my hand.

When I finally closed my eyes and slept, I dreamed bright vivid dreams of a woman named Rose with long, yellow-gold hair, skin freckled by the sun, and a smile that tortured my heart.

I woke to Rueben sitting up on his bed, staring at me.

I looked around the room. All of the others were sleeping.

"How are you feeling?" I said, turning back to Rueben. Would he be able to communicate if he'd already resorted to gibberish?

"I'm fine," he whispered in a hoarse voice. He reached for my hand.

"Are you sure?" I turned his hand over. "No shaking?"

"No."

"That's good, right?" I asked.

He blinked and looked away.

"Rueben?"

Releasing me, he scrubbed his hand through his hair, still avoiding me.

"Do you think it will still take effect?" I asked, sitting up. "Or maybe the altering doesn't work on you?"

Rueben stood and walked a few paces away from me. I didn't understand why he seemed so worried. This was *good*—he wasn't in overload.

I climbed off my bed and moved in front of him so he had to face me. "What's wrong?"

He met my gaze. The wildness of the night before was gone, and I only saw the Rueben I knew—the one who had all the answers in this prison.

"I don't know anyone who's made it through altering without going into overload," he said.

"But I thought you said there was a sixteen percent success rate."

"I know." Trepidation crept into his eyes. "That's what I

was told. But since I've been here, *no one* has escaped overload."

I clenched my hands together; it was like he knew more than he was letting on. "What are you saying?"

His hands rested on my shoulders, his fingers digging in as if he wanted to anchor me to the floor—prepare me for something. "I don't believe them, Jez." My heart tugged at the way he called me Jez. The last person who'd called me that had been Sol.

He exhaled. "What if . . . what if I'm the first one? And what if they increase the altering to the next level of control, until I do hit overload?"

I shuddered. I didn't know what the next level would do, but the fear in Rueben's eyes pierced me to the core.

My breathing slowed. "What do we do?"

"*You* will stay here. Don't do anything stupid. Do what they ask."

I closed my eyes for a second. Those were the last words Sol had said to me. And now here I was again, losing a friend to the unknown, being told to follow the rules again. I folded my arms to stop the trembling. "I don't want to be here without you."

"I'll still be here, just in another section. I'll find my own way out." He touched my arm, briefly. "Try to pass their tests. I don't want anything to happen to you."

"I don't care about *me*," I said, realizing how deeply I meant it. "I don't want anything to happen to *you.*"

Rueben's expression softened for a moment, then went firm again. His voice fell to a whisper when he said, "I'll find you again when we're both out of this place."

"How?" I whispered.

"I'll pretend the altering was successful," he said. "I'll figure out a way from there."

We stared at each other for a few seconds, the only sound in the room that of our beating hearts. I hugged him again, and this time I didn't try to stop the tears.

CHAPTER 16

I pretended to sleep while Rueben pretended to react to his altering. He started to mumble and thrash around on his bed. It wasn't long before the scientists came in and put him in a strait jacket. I sneaked a peek as they carried him out. Our eyes met for a brief instant, then he was gone.

The black hole in my chest expanded to every part of my body, dragging me into the darkest abyss of fear, the unknown. My ally was gone, and by the time we saw each other again—if ever—nothing would be the same. I looked over at the others on their beds, oblivious to Rueben's demise. Estee, the copper-skinned girl, was staring at the ceiling. The rest looked asleep.

Which one of us would be next? I closed my eyes, thinking of the parting words first from Sol, and now from Rueben. *Don't do anything stupid.* Did that mean I should try to pass the tests? Even if I had to lie about my first instincts?

My hope had all but vanished. Solstice was over, and Rueben was gone.

At the morning meal, I watched the scientists carefully, observing everything I could about them, from their short haircuts to the badges each wore on their shirt. Most of them carried an electronic tablet in their shirt pocket.

Matthews looked over at me more than once. His trembling wasn't noticeable today. I quickly returned to my pickled beet and carrot salad and kept my eyes on my food until it was time to go to the testing room again.

I stayed duly demure, trying to forget the image of Rueben being carried out of the dormitory. In the testing lab I answered questions without emotion, which really meant my answers came more slowly and weren't based on my first instinct. I wondered if it was enough to convince Matthews.

On the way to bed that night, I saw Estee walking slowly ahead of me, one hand rubbing her temple. I hurried to catch up with her. We hadn't spoken before, but I felt I had to reach out to her now.

"Are you all right?"

She turned and looked at me, and the panic in her eyes made me shudder. I took a step back. "Did they—?"

Estee let out a scream, cutting me off, and sank to her knees.

I wanted to run and hide, but I knelt and put an arm around her.

She jerked away from me and lashed out, clawing my arm. I stared in shock at the stripes of blood rising to my skin.

Estee twisted away and curled on the floor, cradling her head and screaming.

I staggered to my feet, pressing the bottom of my shirt against the slashes on my arm. As sickened as I was at the sight of her pain, I was relieved when the scientists hurried down the corridor, injected her with something, and carried her away.

Then, before I could remind myself not to do anything stupid, I followed. The drug they'd injected into Estee was taking rapid effect and she no longer thrashed, but her lungs were still going strong, her screams echoing through the hallway.

I stayed as close to the walls as possible and kept enough distance between us to give myself a chance to hide should they slow or turn around. The corridor sloped deeper into the earth. As the air grew colder, the hairs on my arms prickled.

They stopped at a door. When it swooshed open, I crept closer. I caught a glimpse of the interior of the room beyond. My stomach felt hollow as I stared into the room until the metal door closed and blocked my view. But I had seen enough. And it made me sick.

Fear pounding through me, I turned and ran the way I'd come. I needed to make it back to the dormitory before anyone spotted me. I was filled with adrenaline and a newfound resolve to pass every test put before me in the coming months. I knew for sure now that the last thing I wanted to be was altered.

I was afraid to close my eyes, knowing that images of the room would be lurking beneath my lids. But I hadn't had slept much the night before and, involuntarily, my eyes slipped shut. My dreams swirled with images of the room and the cage-like cells that lined the wall. There must have been two dozen cells made of thick metal bars. Inside the square prisons were people, my age or younger. A few had been standing and staring through the bars, their mouths open in silent screams, their hand clawing at the bars. But the rest . . . the rest weren't moving at all.

My body shuddered with a sob, waking me up. Holding a pillow against my chest, I wiped my cheeks. My breath stalled as I thought about my dream—now the scientists would know what I had seen as well. Had Rueben been in one of those cells, reduced to a science experiment? I tried to remember, but it had only been a few seconds, and I wasn't sure.

My head hurt with confusion. From the age of five, everything we'd been taught was aimed at preserving and saving our civilization—not torturing, testing, and altering it.

I had to make a plan. I didn't know where I'd start, but I had to find a way to get those people out of there.

Looking around in the near dark at the row of beds, the sleeping forms, the monitors on the wall, made me realize my prison was only temporary. I was comfortable, and I still knew my mind, but how long would that last? And what about Rueben? Or Grace and Estee? Were they the ones collapsed on their cell floors or had something even worse happened?

It was still the middle of the night, but sleep was impossible now. How could I just lay in bed, doing nothing, while they suffered? But what was the alternative? I'd be locked back into the dark cell if I broke any rules. My eyes burned with tears as a deep sense of helplessness settled over me. Just the fact that I was awake, and not feeding dreams into the monitor, might get me in trouble.

⁂

The lights flickered on, signaling another day underground, and Dr. Matthews walked into the room. I was dressed and ready. As I followed him through the halls, I counted the doors we passed and tried to memorize all of the turns and passages.

It was with mixed feelings that I entered the cafeteria. I noticed immediately that another boy was clearing the trays and dishes. They'd already replaced Rueben.

I may have only known him a week, but he'd made me feel safe and hopeful, and my throat burned from holding back my emotions as I imagined him in a cage, powerless.

Out of the corner of my eye, I took note of where each scientist sat—it was the same for every meal. Their tablets were either next to their trays or stowed in their various pockets. If only I could get ahold of one of their tablets, they might have the answers I needed to find a way out of this place.

But then what? Part of my brain argued. Outside, I wouldn't be hidden. If what Rueben said was true, they had a way to track me through my Harmony implant. There must be something—some way. I had to keep thinking.

I turned to Matthews. "What's the testing today?"

His hand stopped midmotion to his mouth. Then he proceeded to eat the bit of potato on his fork. I waited.

After chewing and swallowing, he said, "Today is the fear test."

Something told me to shut up, but I continued. "What does that mean?"

Matthews took another bite of his food—he seemed to enjoy making me wait. "We're going to find out what you're afraid of."

I didn't ask any questions after that. I thought it might

be better not to know. The food on my plate didn't look so good anymore, and I set my fork down, signaling for the new boy to come and pick up my tray. I wondered what he did to get himself here.

When Dr. Matthews finished, I followed him out of the room. Two other scientists came with us, flanking me on each side, Matthews leading the way. I wondered why there had to be three of them.

We turned and walked the opposite direction from the dormitory and the other testing rooms I'd been in. I tried to pay attention to where we were going, how many doors we passed. We took a sharp right, then walked up the sloping hall. For once we weren't going deeper.

I felt the change in the air before we reached the room. The pervasive cold had softened into warmth and moisture. Were we near the surface? My heart thrummed—maybe the test would take place outside. I may have missed the Solstice, but I'd welcome the rain with open arms.

Matthews stopped and waved his hand over the censor. The door slid open, and I peered into the shining cavern. Everything was bright white. The walls and the ceiling seemed to glow, and the floor was . . . water.

I gazed at the rippling turquoise water. It was beautiful—such rich colors of blue. Above ground, the puddles and the ponds were all as gray as the sky, and the ocean was dark and churning.

Squinting against the brightness, I stepped after Matthews onto a platform that circled the water around the perimeter of the room. Gently churning waves lapped against the sides. It was nothing like the raging swells of the ocean.

Matthews led us several steps in, and the door shut

behind us. A strange sensation crept over me—a feeling of being trapped. I'd been living underground for a week, and had been locked alone in a cell twice, but this was something different.

I peered down, trying to guess how deep it was. There were obviously lights beneath the surface, yellow mixing with azure, but I couldn't quite make out the bottom.

"Do you swim?" Matthews asked.

"No." I didn't know anyone who could swim—there was no place to learn. The ocean was too dangerous, and land area wasn't wasted with the creation of swimming spaces. "Is this a swimming pool?"

"Not exactly." Matthews said. We'd learned about swimming pools and the competitions that went as high as the world Olympics. But competition for physical excellence was no longer necessary. Our livelihoods weren't determined by our physical prowess, but by our intellect and ability to follow the rules. Things like winning awards and boastful pride had no place in our society.

Matthews stepped behind me, and two other scientists joined us.

I was prepared for more questions, but instead, Matthews shoved me forward.

I plunged face first into the water, plummeting down until I was completely immersed. I opened my mouth to scream, but water rushed in, choking me. I closed my mouth, gagging on the water. My body turned and tumbled, sinking lower as I tried to right myself toward the surface. I opened my eyes but everything blurred around me.

It felt as if my arms had been weighted down, slowing my reflexes. The water closed in on any oxygen I might have stored in the seconds before falling. Every part of my body cried out to take a breath, but knew instinctively to keep the water out of my lungs.

I focused on the surface and started kicking and clawing my way upward. Why weren't they pulling me out? Or was this the end? Matthews knew I couldn't swim. My head and chest felt like they were about to burst. The silent water seemed to work against my movements, keeping everything in slow motion.

My arms moved in wider circles, as if by their own will, and I shot up faster than I anticipated. I broke the surface, gagging and gasping for air, then started to sink again. Just as my head dipped below the water, I kicked my feet and thrashed my arms. I couldn't go down again.

The three men stood on the deck quietly watching me.

"Help me!" I screamed. None of them moved.

I sank beneath the water again despite my best efforts. If I'd been scared before, I was terrified now. There was only so long I could keep this up—the cold water was making my muscles numb. I clawed to the surface again, spitting and crying. This time I pushed against the surface of the water, shoving great scoops behind me, moving gradually to the closest side of the room, to the feet of the three stoic scientists.

Beneath the water again. The sounds of my own screams were cut off, and the vision of the men was blurry. I fought my way to the surface, only to inhale more air, and only to sink again and swallow more water. Under, above, under, above.

It seemed like an entire lifetime passed before I touched the deck, gripping it with my cold and trembling fingers. I screamed, and then my vision faded to red and black. I felt my grip loosen and knew I didn't have the energy to stay above the surface. Just as my last finger slipped, a strong hand clamped around my wrist.

CHAPTER 17

"You tried to drown me!" I yelled, my throat burning with bile.

I knew I was out of my mind with rage, but there was no stopping it now. I wanted them to alter me, here and now. Make me forget.

I stood shaking before the scientists, dripping wet and freezing. My clothing clung to my body and my hair hung in my eyes.

"How can you do this to people?" I tried to shout, but it turned into coughing and then gagging. I fell to my knees and retched.

The scientists simply moved back.

I took several deep breaths, waiting for my stomach to stop clenching. They continued to study me, typing into their tablets. Their tests no longer mattered to me. Had I passed the test by not drowning? Or was it like the ancient

Salem witch trials where the women were proved innocent only if they did drown?

The door was still shut, but I crawled to it and collapsed against the metal, staring at the gray blankness. I wanted to disappear. I had just fought for my life while three men stood by and watched, doing nothing. Had their Harmony implants replaced their hearts?

Hatred and shock collided somewhere within my body, leaving me breathless. I had never felt so much indescribable disgust at once. Maybe my grandmother's choice made sense after all. Being burned, being drowned, being lethally injected . . . they seemed like better options than living in this prison.

I sensed Matthews behind me, and the only reason I didn't hit or push him into the water was because my arms felt frozen. I could hardly feel any part of my body, but when the metal door slid open, somehow I stood and started to walk.

Numbly, I followed Matthews to the dormitory. I climbed onto the bed, still wearing my soaking wet clothes, and closed my eyes, ignoring the doctor, who was still in the room.

"No one has ever made it to the side before," he said quietly.

I didn't care whether that was good or bad. I didn't care what the test proved or didn't prove. I ignored him, and eventually he left.

What had happened to the other kids who didn't make it to the side? Did they drown?

I stayed on the bed, wet, cold, and uncaring. The meal hour came and went and still I didn't move. I had no desire for food, no desire for anything.

I must have fallen asleep, because when I was conscious of the room again, it was dark. The dimmed night lights glowed over the sleeping forms in the adjacent beds. I made it to the latrine and back to the bed, but then my strength was spent again.

I hardly even had the energy to dream. I vaguely remembered Matthews nudging me, trying to wake me to escort me to another test. But even if I'd wanted to, my limbs wouldn't respond.

I don't know how much time passed, a day or two, maybe three, but when I awoke in another haze I was in a different location. I peered around. My head felt fuzzy, like I was looking through some sort of curtain. A thin tube protruded out of my hand as a cool liquid was being pumped into my veins.

I blinked. The room was a sterile white, like the room with the water, and I panicked, struggling to raise my head and look at the floor, making sure it was solid. It was, and I fell back, drowsiness overtaking me again.

Someone was whispering. Someone was touching my shoulder.

I opened my eyes to a dark room. The lights had been dimmed—it was another night. Then I flinched as a face appeared inches from mine.

"Rueben?" I croaked. I tried to sit up, but he kept his hand on my shoulder.

"Don't move," he whispered.

I looked him over in the dim light. He was skinnier, but his eyes were the warm brown I remembered, and his contagious smile sent a jolt of warmth through me. Like being touched by the sun.

"How did you get here?" I asked, my throat burning.

"I should ask you the same thing," he said, looking me over with concern. "I've come to say goodbye."

"What?" I lifted my head, only to be met with darts of pain. I collapsed back onto the pillow. "Have you been released?"

"Not exactly. I've found a way out, and I'm leaving."

I stared at him, not sure if I believed what he was saying. The silence stretched between us. I reached out and grasped his arm. It was so strong, so alive, so warm—the opposite of what I felt. "Where are you going?" I whispered. I wondered how long he could hide in another level of society.

"Outside the city."

"Your Lake Town?"

"I won't be welcomed back there—they'll see my return as a failure. I'll find another place."

I shuddered. "But how will you get out of the city? You'll have to find a boat, and I've heard all boats are controlled by the city officials. The ones that aren't are controlled by barbarians."

Rueben held my gaze for a moment. "There are many different kinds of barbarians."

I thought of Dr. Matthews and the others standing by, watching me drown, and knew that Rueben was right. Still, I couldn't imagine leaving the city, the largest piece of land remaining in the world.

"If you leave the city, you won't be allowed back in," I said, feeling panic build. "I won't see you again."

"It's for the best. You don't want to be corrupted by my Lake Town ways." His smile was gentle. "And you shouldn't be worrying about me anyway. I'm more worried about you."

The irony burned in my chest. Here he was, talking about leaving the safe confines of the city, taking his chances among a foreign Lake Town, and he was worried about me. "They just did who knows what to you in that awful cellar, and now you want to face even more danger?"

He stared at me for a long moment. "I survived, Jez. But what happened to you?"

I looked away. "They tried to drown me." I closed my eyes against the memory of cold water filling my nostrils and ears.

"The swimming test?"

"When I reached the deck, I wanted to drown *them.*"

"You reached the deck?" His voice sounded incredulous. "I didn't reach the deck."

I opened my eyes. "You did the same test?"

"Yes, but they had to rescue me. I didn't even make it halfway."

A great shudder passed through me. How many others had had to endure the same torture?

His hand touched mine. "I have to go now," he said. "I want you to be strong—get better—pass the tests. Get to the University."

Tears burned my eyes and rolled down my cheeks. I didn't have the strength to wipe them away. "I don't think I will . . . I don't think I can endure any more testing."

He leaned close to me and pressed his lips to my forehead.

I was so surprised that I couldn't speak or move.

His fingers threaded through mine. "You're a strong person, Jezebel. I know you can make it. You have to. You're meant for greater things." He paused, his voice deepening. "Take care of yourself."

Then he released my hand and straightened; it felt like someone had ripped a blanket off me.

"Rueben, wait." Desperation bubbled up in my voice. "I want to come with you."

He shook his head. "It's too dangerous. If I'm caught, I'll be Taken. No second chances."

Before the swimming test, I had resolved to do everything perfectly, but now I didn't want to spend one more day here. I had followed the rules, and where had it gotten me? I'd been sent to prison for claiming my inheritance, and I'd missed the Solstice for asking too many questions. Maybe Rueben was right; those in the city were the real barbarians. I would just have to find another way to locate the generators. "I don't care if it's dangerous." "You can't even walk."

I exhaled. "I can."

He knelt by my bed and grabbed both of my hands, his gaze intent on my face. "You don't want to take the risk. You're better than me, and I'll never be what you can. I'm going to find my place in a Lake Town. I'll live my life out there—just making it through like everyone else. But you . . ." He brushed my hair back from my forehead. "You're exceptional. You could really be somebody."

If he only knew about the key, about what I was supposed to do. "My differences will only keep getting me into trouble," I said.

"Trouble brought us together."

My heart hammered at his words. His eyes seemed to pierce right through me, touching parts of my soul that I'd buried long ago.

"You wouldn't be in here if they wanted to kill you." He looked down at our clasped hands. "You're in an infirmary, hooked up to healing machines, while the others are sent to cages for more experiments."

"That's what frightens me the most," I whispered. But maybe he was right. Maybe it was too much of a risk. If I blew this chance at the University, how else would I get access to the generators? Closing my eyes, I pretended that he wasn't leaving and that I wasn't confined to a bed. I pretended that I could hold his hand forever.

"Jez, we can still communicate through tablets," he said.

"Too risky. They can monitor the messages." I didn't even have a tablet, but they were standard issue at University and I hoped to get one after I was out of this prison. Still, I knew it would be dangerous to try to contact Rueben.

"When you send me a message, you just have to type in a sequence code beforehand," he said. "After ninety seconds, the code with encrypt the message, and it can't be read after that."

Somehow I wasn't surprised Rueben knew something like that. "What's the sequence?"

"The beginning ten numbers are always the same," he said, then rattled them off. "But that last four numbers will change their order frequently. If one code doesn't work, transpose them and try again."

I repeated the numbers over in my mind. "You can also use it to do research on the WorldNet," he said. "You have to be careful though, because not only will the code encrypt the material you're researching, but it will also permanently destroy the link."

"A secure way to do research?"

"Yes, but also a destructive way." He gently tugged his hand away. "I have to go."

"Wait." I wasn't ready for him to leave. I wasn't

prepared to feel so empty. "How will you get across the district levels to the ocean without getting tracked?"

He hesitated, then pulled something out of his pocket. It was a square of thin metal.

I stared at it, barely comprehending. He pulled up his sleeve to reveal a deep gash with crisscrossed stitches holding it together. Blood stained his shoulder.

"You cut it out?"

His eyes were grave. "Now I'm untraceable."

CHAPTER 18

I stared at Rueben, waiting for him to tell me he was joking, but the wound on his shoulder made it plain. He'd cut out his implant. I turned over the metal piece in my hand, trying to imagine how painful it would be to do the same.

Rueben took the device. "I'll leave it somewhere outside to throw them off my trail." He squeezed my shoulder. "You'll be fine, Jez. Keep doing what you're told, and they'll release you. Soon you'll be on your way to the University."

He stepped back, his eyes on me, his gaze full of goodbyes.

It was like all the warmth was being sucked from my body at once, but my mind felt clear for the first time since I got down here. I couldn't stay behind, not without him. With a grunt, I pushed myself up, and before the dizziness could claim me, I pulled the intravenous tube out of my hand. Blood bubbled up, and I pressed the blanket against it to stop the bleeding.

My vision clouded over, but I forced myself to remain upright. "Take me with you. Cut out my implant." The Carrier key was in there, too. If that came out, I'd have a lot of explaining to do.

His voice sounded anguished. "You can't ask me that. You can't mean it."

"Rueben." I knew I was begging, but I didn't care. Finally my eyes were dry enough to look up at him convincingly. "Please."

"No, Jez," he whispered. "If something happened to you—"

"I'll be fine." I couldn't imagine him walking out the door and never seeing him again. *Sorry Naomi. I'll still find a way.* I pulled up my sleeve. "We have to hurry."

"No." His tone was firm now. "If we're captured together, our punishment will be worse."

"Worse than being in this place?" I nearly shouted, although I knew he was right.

He kept his gaze stern; he wasn't changing his mind. I reached out and grabbed the implant from his hand, catching him off guard.

I brought the metal square to my shoulder over the pale scar where I'd had been implanted when I was just a few days old. I took a deep breath and pressed down. Before I could pierce the skin, Rueben was at my side, trying to pry the metal piece from my hands.

"Damn it!" he shouted.

"Let go!" I shot back. I jerked away and brought the metal against my shoulder again, this time in the wrong spot.

"Jez, let me do it." His expression was grim, his tone resigned. "Look away and bite on the blanket."

"There are two implants in there, Rueben. Only take out

the Harmony." I felt his eyes burning through me. "I'll explain later," I whispered. I pulled up the blanket and clenched it in my teeth. I stared at a spot on the far wall, but ended up squeezing my eyes shut.

Rueben gripped my left shoulder with one hand.

I gasped as the fiery pain shot through my shoulder. I clenched my teeth harder, crushing and twisting the fibers of the blanket.

"Okay," Rueben said. "I got it out. I didn't see another implant."

I didn't have time to wonder about the Carrier key. I scrambled off the bed and retched on the floor.

Rueben's hand was on my back. "We need to wrap your shoulder. There's no time to stitch it here."

I nodded just as my stomach heaved again.

"Jez, maybe you should stay here."

"No," I gasped. I wiped my mouth and took a deep breath. "I'll be fine."

With Rueben's help, I stood, hoping that he didn't notice how badly I was shaking. "Let's go," I said with false confidence.

"You haven't told me everything," he said, his gaze fierce.

"There's no time now. We have to go."

He frowned but took my hand.

My body wanted to climb back on the bed and curl up until the pain passed. But I ignored my body. I took another deep breath and followed Rueben to the door.

He ran his hand over the console and it slid open.

"How did you do that?" I whispered, my stomach still roiling at the pain in my shoulder.

"I created a new employee," he said. "One that will be

discovered soon. We probably have less than an hour before they're alerted."

We stepped out into the deserted corridor.

Rueben and I ran, well, sort of ran, as fast as I could go. The pain in my shoulder seemed to have woken me up completely, infusing me with renewed energy. Thirty minutes ago I wouldn't have thought any of this possible.

I was breathless almost from the beginning, but I refused to slow down. Soon, Rueben had his arm around me, half supporting, half pulling me. We were ascending, which meant we were nearing the surface.

My heart raced, not only from the running, but from the anticipation of being outside again. It had been weeks. Weeks since I'd breathed open air or saw the clouds. I never thought I'd miss the rain.

I thought my heart would explode when Rueben opened the final door. I could barely hear his whispered commands because my ears were pounding so loud. He peered outside, then pulled me through, tossing our metal implants into the corridor before the door shut. We stepped onto the platform where I'd first arrived.

The tram tunnel seemed to extend a mile in either direction. "We'll have to walk the rails and hopefully get to the surface before another tram comes," Rueben said.

I swallowed against my dry throat. "Okay." The darkness made me hesitate, but soon our eyes adjusted well enough. Rueben jumped down onto the tracks below, then held out his hand. I nearly fell into his arms. He steadied me, then grasped my hand and led me to the tunnel wall.

We walked as fast as we could in the darkness, Rueben in front. I kept one hand on his waist and one on the wall.

After several minutes, the darkness faded.

"I think we're getting close." Rueben's voice came from in front of me, but echoed off the tunnel from all angles.

The wall started to vibrate, and I felt a rush of air against my legs. I grabbed his arm. "I think a tram is coming!"

We ran like mad. I hoped the tram would stop at the platform and buy us more time, but the walls vibrated harder, and the swirl of wind increased.

The track curved, and neither of us slowed. The light got brighter in front of us, but the noise grew louder behind us. It was nearly deafening.

"Rueben!" I screamed. There was nothing he could do, but I wanted him to know that I was there, with him, in our last seconds of life.

Suddenly he stopped and pulled me to the left.

"What are you doing?" I shouted as he tugged me across the tracks to the other side. Rueben pushed me against the wall, and held me there, pressing his body against mine. I clung to him, trying to forget that there was not enough room inside the tunnel for the tram to pass us without touching us.

"Don't move," Rueben said, his voice gruff in my ear.

I wanted to scream, to clap my hands over my ears and curl up in a ball, but I stayed against the wall—Rueben between me and the horror that was about to end our lives.

CHAPTER 19

M y body shook as the tram sped past. We clung to
each other, my hands around Rueben's neck, his
hands circling my waist, holding me against him.

The wind and the sound faded.

We weren't dead.

I let out a breath, and then I started crying. Rueben just
held me, not saying anything. He was shaking, too.

When I could finally talk again, I said, "How did you
know to cross the track?"

"I figured the tram would tilt as it went around the
curve," he said in a thick voice. "I just hoped that it would
lean enough to give us room."

I sagged against him.

"We have to hurry," he said. "There may be another
one. You go first."

It didn't take anything else to get me going again. My
ears were ringing, my heart hammering, and my body ready

to collapse. But I refused to take any more chances.

We continued toward the lighter, the growing grayness a welcome sight. When we turned another bend, the opening came into view and I increased my pace, Rueben easily keeping up. The final steps out of the tunnel were like coming out of the pool of water: I was gasping, but I was alive.

The fresh air hit me like a gentle caress. It was still night and the heavy gray clouds had never looked so beautiful.

"We need to find a place to hide," Rueben said quietly.

I looked around. It was a couple of hours from dawn, but some city lights were on. A light was on above the tunnel, marking its entrance, but it looked like we were behind some sort of a factory. I couldn't see any doors or windows, just cement bricks.

"Come on." Rueben grabbed my hand again, and as we walked along the back of the building. "How are you feeling?"

"I don't know," I said, truthfully. If I thought about it too much, I might collapse.

Rueben squeezed my hand, which was better than any medicine I could have received.

We rounded the corner of the building and stepped into a narrow alley that separated it from the next building. Several paces into the alley, we both stopped and stared at a metal door in the second building's side.

"How do we get inside?" I asked.

Rueben lifted his hand and ran it over the console. Nothing happened. "Let's keep moving."

We reached the end of the alley where it opened onto a street. We were definitely in the factory district, a place similar to where my caretakers had spent most of their lives.

I shuddered, realizing that it would be filled with busy workers in a few hours. How would we ever hide from so many people?

Rueben seemed to have the same hesitation. He stepped again into the alley and started walking back along it. Then he stopped, looking up. "Do you think you could break a window?"

I came to a stop next to him, following his gaze upward. "It's too high."

"Not if you get on my shoulders," he said.

Before I could protest, he pulled off his shirt. Deep bruises covered his chest and stomach, in various stages of discoloring and swelling.

I couldn't help but stare. "What did they do to you?"

He reluctantly met my eyes. "I'm fine." He lifted my arm and tied the shirt around my hand. "You'll have to punch it hard. Make sure you cover your eyes with your other hand in case any glass flies."

"Won't someone see the broken window?"

"Hopefully not until we're gone." He looked behind us.

"Okay," I said, trying to look away from his bruising. "But what will we do after?"

Rueben took my hand in his. "We'll hide in the factory until it closes again, then we'll leave like we're employees. We'll have to find a way to cross the south river without getting caught."

"Neither of us can swim," I said.

"No one in the city is taught to swim—for a reason." Rueben tightened his grasp. "We'll find someone to take us across. Then we'll sneak onto a trading boat."

The thought of getting on a boat made me uneasy, but I knew it was the only way. I hoped the Lake Towns would welcome runaways.

148

Rueben's eyes bored into mine with his next words. "If we get separated, or if anything happens to me, I want you to pretend that I forced you to do this."

"Rueben, I—"

"Please. We don't have much time." He pulled me into a rough embrace. His cheek pressed against mine, and I inhaled his warm scent. Then he released me just as quickly. He knelt down and helped me climb on his shoulders. I braced my hands on the wall as he stood, and when I felt balanced enough I made a fist with my right hand. The window was just large enough for us to crawl through.

Teeth gritted, I punched at the glass. My fist bounced off, and I stifled a cry.

"Try your elbow," Rueben called up. His voice sounded strained.

I unwrapped the shirt from my hand and wound it around my elbow. Then Rueben turned so that I was turned sideways, too. "One, two . . ." I said to myself and thrust my elbow against the window.

The window broke, but the impact nearly threw me off balance. Rueben compensated so I didn't fall.

"Now clear the glass and climb inside," Rueben huffed at me from below.

I broke the rest of the glass, working as fast as possible, knowing he was getting worn down. Then I placed my hands on the sill and hoisted myself in with a shove from Rueben.

The room I entered had a sharp chemical smell to it. It was a wide open space with several large tables piled with objects I couldn't quite make out in the dim morning light. I leaned out the window.

"Look for a rope or anything I could climb up with," Rueben ordered.

I turned and stepped warily into the room. My heart was hammering, but I had to get Rueben inside quickly. I reached out and touched one of the piles on the table. It was soft and pliable—fabric. I picked up the top layer. The fabric had been cut into various shapes. I tied ends together, creating a rope of sorts, hoping it would hold Rueben's weight.

Minutes later, I threw the fabric rope out of the window and peered over the edge. Immediately a bright light shone in my face. "Rueben?" I whispered, gripping one end of the fabric.

"Hello, Miss J."

I froze. Dr. Matthews stepped into view while someone else kept the light trained on me. The light reflected off his glasses, making it hard to see his eyes.

I moved back, startled, still clutching the fabric. How did this happen? No one had been around. It had only been a few minutes since Rueben helped me into the window. I turned, looking desperately at the tables behind me in the workshop. There was no place to hide.

Where was Rueben? My heart thundered in my ears and my legs felt heavy.

"Miss J.," Matthews's voice sailed up to me. "Please stay where you are. We don't want this to be more difficult than it needs to be."

I took another step back and released the fabric. It would do me no good now. They had Rueben. I heard footsteps and spun around, fear pulsing through me. They were getting louder, closer, but I couldn't see anyone. The light from outside glared through the window, bouncing against the tables and thick walls.

Suddenly a head emerged from a staircase I hadn't

noticed. I opened my mouth to scream when a familiar voice said, "Jezebel?"

I stared, my mouth still open. "Sol?"

He stepped onto the landing and came toward me, his face achingly familiar.

That face I'd missed so much.

What are you doing here? I tried to say, but no words came out.

Sol continued walking toward me, his dark gray eyes dancing, his lips moving. Sol was talking to me, but I didn't understand. His hand touched my arm, and my senses came back. Light, darkness, the scent of chemicals, and the touch of Sol's strong and steady hand.

"Jezebel," he said in his beautiful voice as he leaned close. "Congratulations. You passed the test."

CHAPTER 20

The sound of the tram is deafening, roaring in my ears.
I am alone. "Rueben!" I shout. But I hear no response,
only the tram growing closer, louder.

"Jezebel."

I tried to open my eyes, but it was as if they were sealed
shut. My body was relaxed, practically melded onto a bed.
Shadows moved across my closed lids, and I heard my name
spoken again. *Rueben,* I thought. *What happened to you? Did
you get away? Did they take you back to the prison?*

A brush of air moved across my skin, and I tried again,
finally opening my eyes to brightness and a familiar face.

But it was the wrong face.

Sol was watching me. I tried to lift my head, but it felt
fuzzy. "Where am I?"

"The hospice. A surgeon fixed your shoulder."

My shoulder. Had they discovered the Carrier key? Hot
and cold flashed through me.

152

Sol leaned back a little, and I could see the surrounding room. The walls were pale blue, the ceiling yellow. Some sort of a machine blinked green lights next to my bed. I lifted my right hand and saw a thin tube attached. My shoulder ached as I moved.

And that's when I knew. The pain in my shoulder was intense again. "I have a new implant, don't I?"

He nodded. "It's for your protection."

"Of course." I swallowed against the lump forming in my throat. What did I expect? To run away with Rueben and live in a Lake Town? Surrounded by sophisticated medical equipment and the familiarity of Sol's eyes, I realized I wasn't like Rueben after all—I was afraid. I was a product of the city—a world of order—it always would be. And I had a job to do.

"Hey," Sol said quietly. He was leaning over me again, his eyes gray like the rain I missed so much. "Are you all right?"

I couldn't speak, couldn't move, for if I did, I'd sink back into the nothingness that had been my prison before Rueben rescued me.

Sol smoothed my hairline, his touch gentle. Memories of our friendship and the feelings that I'd suppressed started to trickle back in, and I allowed myself to become absorbed in his steady gaze. The time separated from Sol hadn't dulled my feelings for him after all. It was like we'd never been apart.

Stop touching me, I wanted to say. His fingers against my skin were making my heart race.

But I didn't tell him to stop. I closed my eyes and let him continue. Let him think I was tired. Prison might have separated us for a short time, but it was as if no time had passed now. I thought about how much I missed him. How could I have even considered leaving for a Lake Town? *Because,* I told myself, *I don't want to feel this way around Sol.*

I opened my eyes.

"That's better." Sol exhaled, and his breath brushed my face.

I wanted to hug him. Hold onto him like Rueben had allowed me to do. What would Sol think? That I'd turned crazy? Well, maybe I was. Clinical, anyway.

I had to shake away my thoughts, focus on something else.

"What happened to—?" I couldn't continue.

Sol could always read my thoughts. "Rueben will be found soon." He was watching me intently, studying my face, like he always did.

"He escaped, then?" I couldn't quite meet Sol's eyes, afraid of what my face might reveal.

"He must have sensed us tracking both of you," Sol said. "There was no one in the alley when we came through."

Sol hadn't even seen Rueben. That meant he'd already fled. I wondered if he'd intended to climb up into the factory at all. My head started to pound again. Had Rueben set me up and then abandoned me? Had he always planned on going to the Lake Towns on his own? Was he not the friend I thought he was? Or had he been trying to protect me?

My breath left my chest as I considered the possibility that Rueben's final words to me were really a planned goodbye. *If we get separated, or if anything happens to me, I want you to pretend that I forced you to do this.*

Was that Rueben's way of telling me he was leaving without me? That it was for my own good?

I blinked and looked at Sol. He was still watching me, and my cheeks warmed beneath his gaze. Could he see my emotions?

"What will happen to him when he's caught?" I asked.

"Hopefully he'll be sent back to prison. After what he did to you—"

"He didn't do anything."

Sol's eyes narrowed. "He cut out your implant, Jez."

He did what I asked him to, and now he knows I have a second implant. I stiffened, remembering that Rueben had told me to let them believe he forced me to escape. But Sol wasn't *them.* He was my friend. I had to at least try to explain. "It wasn't what you think—"

"Good morning," a voice interrupted. Dr. Matthews stepped into the room. "I've come to say good luck. I'm on my way back to the prison."

Sol stood and greeted the scientist. I didn't like the look on Dr. Matthews's face. I'd never seen him not frown. It was almost like he was happy. Almost.

Matthews settled on a chair next to the bed, looking at Sol expectantly.

"I'll be back in a few minutes," Sol said.

I wanted to tell him to stay—that Matthews could say anything in front of him, but something in the back of my mind told me not to. I didn't know what was true anymore. Had this all been a test from the beginning? Was Rueben involved? How much did Sol know that he wasn't telling me?

With Sol out of the room, Matthews's familiar frown returned.

"Was this a test from the very beginning?" I asked. "From when I got my inheritance?"

Matthews's eyes shifted to the door, then back to me. "I

155

don't know about anything before you came to the prison. We were alerted that you left and told to find you and Rueben."

"Why does the Legislature even care about me or Rueben? Why don't you just have us Taken if you think we're a threat?"

Matthews's expression paled. "We'd never do that."

I almost laughed, but covered it with a cough instead. "I saw the way you destroyed the other kids—maybe they're still alive, but they're not who they used to be."

Matthews dipped his head.

Did that mean he agreed with me?

"You don't understand, Miss J.," he said. "The children who are altered are *not* Taken. They simply exist in another state of mind."

Anger charged through me. "Did you ever consider there are worse things than being Taken?"

Matthews seemed to hesitate at that. "There is nothing after our life cycles."

"You don't know that. You can't justify using children in scientific experiments." It was cruel beyond comprehension. At least *my* comprehension. I doubted the level of Matthews' thinking. He was just another man following government rules, no better, no worse than any other scientist.

Matthews leaned forward. "Only a very small percentage have tested as highly as you, Miss J."

"I thought I was failing the tests."

His voice was a sharp staccato. "Failure is in perception."

I exhaled. Of course. They were lying to me from the beginning, so why not about the test results? "Is testing 'highly' good or bad?" I asked.

"It's neither," Matthews said. "It is what you are, who you are. Adjustments will only be made if necessary."

"Are you going to alter me after all?" My shoulder burned as if in response.

"I don't know." He shifted in his seat. "You have a great depth of emotional sensitivity, something that is rare in our civilization. Regardless of your education, conditioning, and training, you're still influenced by your emotions. An altering might erase all of that before we can determine the causes. We want to put you through training in order to fully explore the depth of your condition."

"So I'm still being tested?"

"Essentially."

My stomach clenched so tightly I had to take a deep breath to concentrate. Would the training allow me to learn more about the generators? "You either want me to be like everyone else, or not like everyone else. It can't be both ways."

"We realize that, Miss J." His shoulders relaxed slightly. "But we think you'll be more useful to us with your emotions intact. You're being screened to provide research to the highest reaches of the Legislature—those who make decisions that affect the entire population of the city. We need to know if you're willing to continue as a test subject." He held up his hand. "Not in the extreme conditions of Phase Three though. We need your promise that you'll be willing to dedicate yourself to the city's success. We also need to know if your emotions are controllable through other methods. Only after all of that will you be a useful addition."

I was quiet a moment, letting the words sink in. "You're offering me a job?"

Matthews tilted his head. "I'm not offering you anything. You've already moved to the next level."

I exhaled, my pulse jumping. "What's that?"

"University. We'd like you to study neuroscience. We feel the more you know about the operations of the brain, the more useful you'll be in helping the government research cases like yours."

It wasn't exactly the scientist I wanted to become, but it was better than being Demoted. "Do I have another choice?"

Matthews didn't answer directly. "The success of your education will be up to you." He paused. "You may even sit on judging councils one day, Miss J."

My heart thudded at the memory of the black-robed Council of Judges. *That's not for me; I have an important assignment already.*

"You can't let anyone else know about it." He paused, glancing at the door. "Not even Sol. He'll know you've been released to the University, but not about your continued testing."

How could I keep this from Sol? I took a deep breath. "Then why is Sol here now?"

Matthews assessed me, his frown deep again. "We know you're comfortable with him. Sol will be taking you to the University when you're well."

It made sense, yet it didn't. It was after the Separation. I wasn't supposed to be with Sol, or any of the male members of my class for that matter.

Something was wrong here. Very wrong. Was Sol a part of this "testing"? I hoped not. I wanted him to be my Sol. My friend. The one I cared about more than anything.

In prison, all I wanted to do was pass the tests and get to the University, but now I wasn't sure. Rueben had showed me that there were other things to live for, that there was another life out there. And what if I failed as a Carrier? What then?

"And if I decide not to continue with this . . . testing?"

Matthews cleared his throat. "You'll be altered. Depending on the outcome of the altering, you'll be assigned to the level of society to which you can best contribute."

Maybe the altering wouldn't affect me, like it hadn't Rueben, but what were the chances of that? I'd be living in another place, at another level, away from Sol. I had lost one friend already; I didn't want to lose another.

"All right," I said. "I'll continue with the testing."

Matthews nodded, as if he'd expected it. He stood. "The best of luck to you, then." Something flashed in his eyes— was it compassion? Concern? It was gone as fast as it appeared.

"Thank you," I said as he left the room.

Sol was back inside in a moment, his gaze questioning. I put on false calm and said, "I made it to the University."

159

CHAPTER 21

The rain pelted against the tram windows, streaking across the glass as if in a furious race. I felt like the out-of-control raindrops as the enormity of what I'd committed to settled in my chest. Even with Sol sitting next to me, our arms nearly touching, I felt alone. I couldn't tell him about the testing. It would be another thing I'd kept from him. Rueben, and now this. I hadn't realized until now how freeing it had been to talk to Rueben, to someone like me.

The tram lurched to a stop, letting people off, boarding new ones. Those who stepped onto the tram were indistinguishable—all nameless faces, coats of gray and brown, dull eyes. I watched them closely, with renewed interest. Had any of them been to prison, been tested, or been altered? Did any of them struggle with emotions like me? Had any of them ever tried to remove their implant?

Were any of them originally from a Lake Town? The world suddenly looked very different.

I closed my eyes briefly as the tram started moving again, gaining momentum until it matched the speed of the assailing raindrops. Exhaustion replaced any nervousness I might have felt as we neared the north perimeter of the city, where the University climbed up several acres of mountainside.

I wished time could slow and all the people on the tram disappear so that it could only be me and Sol again. We'd talk like we used to. He'd tell me stories about his caretaker's grandfather, and I would tell him my worries about testing into the University. But that was all gone now, and time only seemed to speed faster with the moving tram.

I had toured the women's portion of the University the year before with the fifteen-year-old class. Chalice had been with me, and we'd eagerly speculated which profession we'd be selected to study. For a moment, I wished I was that innocent and unassuming girl again, with the wide-eyed view of what the future might bring.

Now, my path was tailored and completely controlled. I had no allies, only more secrets.

I glanced over at Sol, grateful that they let us at least travel together to the University. Would he miss me, too? Once there, we'd hardly see each other. The Separation had taken place at school without me, after which the sixteen-year-old class moved on to various vocations or to University level for more training.

"Is Chalice already there?" I asked Sol, wanting to say something, anything.

His gray eyes leveled with mine. "Yes, I saw her at opening assembly."

I felt relief. She must have stopped wearing her rings to class then.

The tram slowed and more people climbed off as more boarded.

When the tram started up again, I asked, "Did you get your first request?"

Sol's eyes stayed on the window. "I did."

"So, you'll be a neuroscientist after all?" I asked, wondering why he was ignoring me. *Look at me!* Maybe he was thinking of having to say goodbye. Maybe that meant he'd miss me after all. I pushed those thoughts away.

Realizing I'd be taking many of the same courses as him, I said, "I'll be training in neurology as well."

That got his attention. Sol looked at me, his eyebrows lifted. "I thought you wanted to specialize in geology."

"I did." How could I explain without giving anything away? "Maybe after a few classes, I'll change my mind."

He seemed to believe me, and I tried to forget the speeding tram, hurtling through our last minutes together as if they were of no consequence.

"I'm glad we'll be at University together," he said, his tone calm, as usual.

"Me too." For a moment, I wanted him to break. To really look at me and tell me that he'd miss seeing me every day. That he'd miss our talks in the school yard.

But he was calm as ever, observing everything, saying nothing.

The tram stopped and nearly everyone got off. The next stop would be the University. My heart rate sped up in time with the tram. As if in response, Sol said, "Are you ready?"

I blew out a breath. So he was noticing me. "Yes."

He gazed at me, but I couldn't quite read his expression.

"Why did you really choose neurology as your specialty?" he asked.

My heart thumped. Had he seen through my lie or was he just curious? "It was being in that prison," I said, thinking quickly. "There were some experiences there . . . things I thought I could help with. Make a difference."

He just looked at me. Then he said in a low voice, "That's what I admire about you, Jez."

"What?" My breathing felt shallow.

"That drive that comes from deep within you," he said. "Not everyone has that. Not everyone cares."

You don't know the half of it. You don't know how much I care. I stared at him for a second until he looked out the window again. I'd seen enough of the dull-faced people getting on and off the tram today to know that many people didn't care. Or maybe it was that they had no hope. No hope of hoping. People were assigned their lot in life almost from birth—they went through the motions, then life was over.

What's wrong with me? I'm thinking like my grandmother. "I guess there must be something wrong with me."

Sol exhaled, keeping his gaze forward. "How am I going to get through the University without seeing you every day?"

Heat rose in my neck. He still wasn't looking at me, but something like sorrow was etched across his features, making the heat spread to my face. *Don't say anything else Sol—it will only make it worse.*

I wasn't sure how to respond without giving anything away. Finally, I said, "I guess you'll just have to become a brilliant scientist to make up for my absence."

He just stared out the window. I moved my hand so that it brushed against his. "Sol?"

His gaze flickered to me, and he pulled away, his face paling.

I felt the distance like a cold night.

"Jez, we have to be more careful now." His gaze remained averted as if he were afraid to look at me. "Taking this tram together is an exception—"

"I know," I whispered, and I did. The Separation had taken place; we were no longer considered kids. The rules of association between male and female were stricter now. I looked down at my hands and folded them determinedly in my lap.

Sol bumped my shoulder with his, the movement imperceptible to the others on the tram. "I hate the Separation."

"Me too," I said. "But it's for the best." It was the only way for me, at least, to be better than my grandmother.

We settled back into silence.

It wasn't until that moment that I realized how much I already missed him. Even as I sat right next to Sol, it was like he was already gone from me. We wouldn't be able to whisper together or speculate about the Before. We were going to the University and would be expected to follow all guidelines of the Separation, which included girls living and studying separate from the boys.

Sol leaned back on the bench, his expression nonchalant. I tried to do the same.

The tram slowed in front of the University stop. It was all happening too fast.

"Remember," Sol said, "Don't do anything to get into trouble."

"And why would I do that?"

He looked at me, his dark gray eyes steady. Eyes that I

164

had seen in my dreams in prison. How could I say goodbye?

"Jez . . ." he began.

"All right. I won't break any rules." It came out as a stilted whisper.

The doors opened, and Sol and I stood. Through the doors I saw the two separate entrances to the University. One for men and one for women. Groups of students in clusters of umbrellas stood on the platform waiting to board. Sol and I slipped off the tram just as the students moved forward to climb on. We were separated in the crowd for a few seconds, then he found me and pressed something into my hand. "See you sometime." And then he was gone, walking toward the men's entrance.

I clenched my hand around the small object as the crowd shuffled past. I crossed the street and stepped up to the guard post, then raised my hand to the scanner under the guard's watchful eye, and he waved me through. I continued toward the building on a broad sidewalk lined with trees and dripping bushes. Other girls hurried past me, carrying umbrellas in the driving rain. I didn't open my umbrella, letting the rain drops pelt my face and hair, relishing the feeling after the time spent underground.

I looked toward the men's side and caught a few glimpses through the iron fence of others walking. Without an umbrella, my hair quickly became soaked, but I continued my slow walk. The University building up ahead was pale yellow and two stories, although in the rain it looked almost gray, meshing with the sky so that it was difficult to tell where one ended and the other began.

When I was quite alone on the sidewalk, I opened my hand. Inside my palm was a small stone. The color was unusual, a light pink with darker lines running through it. I lifted my hand so that I could inspect it as the rain pattered against my palm. Why would Sol give me a rock?

Then I noticed the carvings.

It looked like a cluster of leaves encircling each other.

Sol had given me a rose.

CHAPTER 22

My dorm room was at the end of a long corridor. From what I'd seen in passing, the other rooms contained two girls each, but I had a room to myself, a narrow space with a bunk bed of sorts. Bed on top, desk on the bottom.

Registration had been automatic. One swipe of the hand at the registration console had confirmed my presence, and I was handed an electronic tablet. My heart fluttered as I held it. I'd be able to check the news reports now and find out if Rueben had been charged or punished for a crime. I could also try using the sequence code to send him a message, but I knew I wouldn't dare.

I sat down at my new desk and turned on the tablet. Hesitating, I finally opened the news report. I looked back over the records, skimming through the names of those who were born, Taken, or charged with crimes. My hand froze when I saw Rueben's name. *Rueben Paulo: Criminal—Security One.*

I exhaled. He wasn't listed as *Charged* or *Taken*, so that was a relief. But *Security One* meant his punishment would be severe if he was caught. It also meant that I couldn't send him a message. Even if the message itself was encrypted like Rueben had explained, I worried that the Legislature could detect where the message had come from.

I opened the file called "Schedule" and saw that there was an assembly in less than an hour. It was as if I'd gone from one classroom to another, without so much as a hiccup.

I wondered why I'd been given a room to myself, but deep down I knew exactly why. They wanted to isolate me. I blew out a breath and looked around the stark dorm. I had brought nothing but an umbrella with me.

All I had left was a scar on my shoulder to remember Rueben by. The only tangible thing I owned besides the clothes I wore was the rose-shaped stone. It seemed so long ago that Sol and I had stood in the courtyard, talking about flowers and seasons. I slipped the rock under the pillow on the bed.

Sol's words on the tram came back to me: *The drive that comes from deep within you. Not everyone has that. Not everyone cares.*

"No, not everyone," I whispered to myself. "But my grandmother did."

I dropped my head in my hands, thinking of my grandmother. When I first read her book, I had been so afraid. I had been angry, too. How could she be so foolish and break such serious rules? What was the point of that? In death, she was nothing. She had had to pass on the Carrier key to her daughter, who passed it to me. Neither of them had been able to succeed in their mission.

What if I couldn't, either? Would I be able to pass on the Carrier key? I didn't have a daughter. Or would each month draw the city closer to final extinction?

A chime sounded on my tablet; orientation was about to begin. I lifted my head and slowly stood, reluctant to integrate into a new education program and start whatever testing the Legislature still had in store for me.

The hallway buzzed with conversation. I searched among the faces for anyone I might know, but came up empty. Roommates seemed to already be friends, and I was alone in the crowd as we walked in a group to the auditorium.

I found an empty row near the back of the circular room. I was the only one sitting in it until right before the lights dimmed. A girl slipped in next to me. I glanced over. "Chalice?" I whispered.

She looked at me out of the corner of her eye, but didn't turn her head.

"I was hoping you'd be here," I said, keeping my voice low.

Still, she didn't answer, except for a slight nod.

What was wrong with her? Her hair looked shorter than usual and her body thinner than I remembered. Her skin was paler, too.

A voice belonging to the president of the University carried over the auditorium, putting an end to my questions. "Welcome to the University. Before you divide into groups according to your assigned specialty, we have a few announcements to make. Please turn on your tablets."

I looked around the auditorium. There were instructors stationed throughout the room, their watchful eyes on the students. All of the students I could see were diligently staring at their screens. Boys sat separately from girls, as if there were some invisible line dividing us. I didn't see Sol anywhere. I turned my tablet on and peeked over at Chalice. She sat rigid in her chair, her hands lightly holding the tablet, the screen dark.

I sat through the monotonous announcements while sneaking glances at Chalice. She didn't move, didn't look at me, and didn't turn on her tablet.

When the president finished speaking, I followed Chalice out into the foyer.

"Are you all right?" I asked. No response. Was she being monitored and not allowed to talk to anyone? I continued to walk with her until we arrived at her classroom.

I wasn't too surprised to find out that she'd chosen Mathematics as her specialty. I stopped at the door—my ID wouldn't register for the Mathematics orientation. From the doorway, I watched Chalice take a seat, without a backward glance at me.

Late for my own orientation, I hurried to the classroom. I was the last in my seat and the instructor—a thin, gray-haired man in his forties—gave me a brief stare-down. Thankfully, he didn't call any further attention to my tardiness.

I took copious notes, typing in almost word for word what the instructor said in order to maintain my focus. Then I made it a point to be the first one out the door after the orientation.

Chalice was just emerging from her classroom when I turned down the hallway to meet her. I hurried to catch up with her. Maybe she'd speak to me now. "Chalice?"

Her gaze traveled slowly to look at me, her eyes resting just below my own. But there was no spark—nothing from our former friendship. Did this have something to do with me? Or with the rings she'd made?

"Tell me what happened," I said, but she didn't respond.

She didn't prevent me from following her down to her dorm room on the ground-level floor, one below my own. Stepping into her room, I stopped just inside the door as it slid closed behind me. There were two beds and two desks. She obviously had a roommate.

I waited for a moment, wondering if she'd finally speak to me, or look me in the eye. But she simply sat at her desk and placed her tablet in front of her. She didn't turn it on.

"Chalice," I said as I sat on the bed across from her. "Did they forbid you to talk to me? Just nod if the answer is yes. I don't want to get you into more trouble."

Her only movement was her breathing, which was as eerily calm as her other movements had been. Then I noticed that one of her fingers was swollen and red—the finger that she used to wear the metal ring on.

I stood and moved to her, picking up her hand. The skin was chafed and peeling, as if it had been burned. Chalice offered no resistance and didn't even seem to notice that I was examining her hand. What had they done to her?

"What happened?" I asked in the silence. "Did they take your ring?"

I scanned the rest of her, looking for any other signs of injury, but there was nothing. "Chalice," I said again, hoping that she'd snap out of her stupor. "Did they punish you for wearing your ring again?"

Her eyes lifted to mine and her pupils expanded for a few seconds, then reduced. For an instant I thought I'd seen something in her eyes—fear, apprehension—I didn't know what.

All that I knew was that Chalice wasn't herself. Something had happened to her. Something awful.

Then horror vibrated through me as I realized what had happened.

Chalice had been altered.

I don't know how I made it past Chalice's roommate, who stepped in at that exact moment, without breaking down.

"There are no visitors to the dorm rooms," the red-haired girl stated, her arms folded across her narrow chest. She had the sort of hard gaze and beady eyes that Sol and I used to predict belonged to student informers. I had to get out of here.

Tears stung my eyes, but I successfully held them back, mumbling an excuse as I pushed past the roommate. The corridors were completely empty; everyone had been obedient and gone inside to review their schedules and orientation notes. I sprinted up the stairs to the next floor.

Inside my room, I let out the tears that I'd been holding in.

Chalice—my defiant, energetic friend—had been altered. They had taken her essence. She might still be alive, but she was no longer Chalice.

I started to shake as the anger and sorrow of the injustice blended into a fierce ache in the pit of my stomach. I paced the room until it was dark. When a message popped up on the tablet informing me that I'd missed dinner and it would be logged into my report, I turned it off.

By the time the last bit of gray in the sky turned to black, I had my plan in place. I just had to find Sol.

CHAPTER 23

The rain fell in sheets, drenching me from the knees down as I walked across campus. I'd brought an umbrella, thinking it would look less like I was sneaking around. I hoped if I was stopped, I could use Matthews' name to gain some credibility. Surely, there was a link to my name in the University database that labeled me as a special test subject.

My feet were wet and cold, and I was still shaking—but this time from the weather. The lamp posts that dotted the campus looked like fireflies, high up in the sky, and the rain blocked out almost all visibility.

I had to tell Sol—tell him everything. About the altering, about me asking Rueben to cut out my implant, about my failed escape. We had to get help for Chalice. Maybe something he knew about the Before could help. Maybe there was a way to appeal to the Legislature. If not, I'd have to figure out how to help her myself. I didn't know if I could totally trust Sol, but he was all I had.

I walked along the fencing that separated the buildings of the men and women's dorms. There were still plenty of lights on in the boys' windows. Apparently the curfew wasn't as strict as in the girls' dorms, where the lights had shut off promptly at ten thirty. It was close to midnight now. I'd sent a message to Sol through the tablet, making it vague enough to not give too much away, but hoping he'd understand and meet me at the fence.

I looked through the metal bars, hoping to see a figure hurrying toward me. I didn't dare touch the bars, in case they triggered an alarm. The fence stretched up about ten feet over my head, topped off by rows of sharp spikes. If it wasn't for the green foliage lining the fence, it would look very ominous.

I waited a few more minutes, then started walking again, this time toward the front of campus. A glimmer of light came from the guard station at the front gate. I stopped before getting too close, throwing another glance over my shoulder, searching for Sol.

A guard sat inside the station, his profile clear. He was watching a monitor, his eyes half-closed. I took several steps back, concealing myself in the thicker part of the trees. I didn't know what exactly was on the monitor, but I imagined it included images of the fence.

My heart echoed the rhythm of the rain, and I crept away, putting distance between myself and the guard. I looked up into the trees and along the top of the fence, realizing there must be cameras at every angle. It was only a matter of time before someone saw me on the monitor. And if they were tracking me through my new implant, I'd be found for sure.

I moved toward the dorm building again, keeping an eye through the fence. Then I stopped. Someone was walking on the other side. *Sol?* The man moved briskly, the hood of his raincoat pulled over his head.

I took a few steps back, concealing myself in the trees, watching the man to make sure it was Sol. But he didn't stop, didn't slow, or even look in my direction as he continued toward the gates of the University. *Not Sol.* Where was he? Had he received my message?

My heart sank. It was more than thirty minutes past the time I told him to meet me. He'd either ignored the message, or wasn't able to get out of his dorm.

At least the guard hadn't seen me, I thought with relief. I'd send another message to Sol in the morning if I hadn't heard from him by then. I turned around and bumped into something . . . someone.

"Come with me, miss," a woman's voice said. Her hand gripped my arm.

"I'm sorry, I—"

"Save your explanation until we're inside," she said.

I hadn't even been at the University one full day, and now this. I walked with the woman back to the dorm building, her hand still on my arm. When we stepped into the lighted foyer, I noticed she was much younger than I'd assumed. Her hair was pulled back into a severe knot, but she appeared to be only a few years older than me.

"Sit," she said, with no other preamble. She took her own seat at the front desk and I grabbed one from the perimeter of the room, "What's your name? And what were you doing?"

I told her my name then said, "I couldn't sleep."

"No one is allowed to leave the building after curfew."

I lowered my eyes. I should have prepared a ready answer.

"This will need to be reported," she said. "Also, the tracking on your implant will be more closely monitored for the foreseeable future."

My throat tightened at the thought of garnering more attention from a government office. What if altering Chalice was one of my tests—to see how I'd react?

The woman typed something on a tablet. "Oh," she said in a quiet voice.

I looked up at her.

Her face had pinked. "You're already being tracked." She met my gaze, her expression wary. "What's your specialty?"

"Neuroscience," I gulped out. How long had I been outside, walking along the fence? Over thirty minutes. And had I been tracked the whole time? "So, you weren't sent by anyone?"

The woman started to shake her head, then stopped. Her tone returned to business. "I'll file my report and let the board hand down their restrictions."

"Restrictions?"

Her mouth twisted. "Read the orientation guide," she said, glancing at her tablet, "Miss James." Her mouth closed firmly.

"Can I go now?"

She nodded and watched me walk past her. Not until I was on the second level did I feel the penetration of her gaze lift.

I was being tracked. Probably since my new implant. Entering my dark room, I looked around, wondering if there were cameras watching me, too. With the light still off, I picked up my tablet. No message from Sol. I moved to the window and stared out at the rain.

Why hadn't he replied? Even to say he couldn't meet me?

It was too risky, I thought. Sol knew that. Would he be upset at me for asking him to break the rules?

This was Sol, I reminded myself. He's the one who'd been to Detention several times. He's the one who told me about his grandfather's album. But we were at the University level now. Maybe he was being tracked, too.

Maybe we were both being tested.

I wrapped my arms around myself, shivering from the damp.

"What is happening to us, Sol?" I whispered. But he wasn't there to answer.

Sleep was impossible, so I read the orientation guide before the pale morning arrived. By then my head hurt and my stomach pinched with hunger from the meal that I'd missed. I plowed through the guide, wanting to know everything.

Apparently the dorm buildings weren't locked, but students were expected to abide by the honor system code. If the codes were violated, restrictions were enacted. It was just before 7:00 a.m. when a message popped onto my tablet: *Restriction Order for Jezebel James: All instructors must sign you in and out of each class period for thirty days. Your dorm room will be sealed during curfew hours.*

My heart sank as I read the words. I tried the door of my room, and it wouldn't open. The restriction had already begun.

I turned back to the orientation guide. Curfew hours were 11:00 p.m. to 7:00 a.m. I waited two more minutes until the time was exactly 7:00 a.m. then tried the door again. It opened.

My stomach growling, I was one of the first to arrive at the cafeteria. A few other girls sat at the tables. When I entered the room, each of them looked up, knowing expressions on their faces, then they quickly turned back to their tablets, as if they didn't want to be caught staring.

I felt uneasy. Had the restriction notice been sent to everyone?

Two kitchen workers watched me approach the food table.

I picked up a bowl of banana-flavored yogurt. We'd studied fruits of the world, but I'd never tasted a real banana. I sat across from one of the girls, who didn't look up as I took my place. After a few minutes, she moved away.

I finished my meal, returned the yogurt dish to the cafeteria workers to be cleaned, then walked out, still feeling hungry. But I didn't want to stay in the cafeteria with everyone so silent and watchful. I'd report early to class.

I entered the same building as the day before, where most of the science classes were on the ground level. My first class was geology—what I could specialize in. The room was plain with a high ceiling, pale blue walls, and about a dozen desk consoles. I was the first to arrive, and the instructor looked up when I entered. He had a narrow face, wide-set eyes, and a scruff of graying hair.

I crossed to him and handed over my tablet. "I'm Jezebel James," I said. "I need to be signed into class."

"I was expecting you." He took the tablet and pressed a finger on the electronic box. His frown reminded me of Dr. Matthews.

I sat at a desk as others slowly filed in, taking their seats.

No one looked at me directly, yet it felt as if everyone were staring at me. My restriction had obviously been broadcast. Each time I glanced up, eyes averted. No doubt they were all studying me in the hopes that it would help them avoid being in the same situation—after all, I'd somehow found a way to get into trouble before the first class had even started.

I looked straight ahead and breathed out slowly, wishing I could ignore all of the stares and silent speculation. Even with my new restrictions, my focus was on helping Chalice. But how?

I needed to find Sol, to see if he could help. There was no one else that I could trust.

The instructor walked to the front of the class at precisely 8:00 a.m. and began his lecture. Everyone typed on their tablets, taking rapid notes. I typed just as furiously, not always comprehending exactly what I wrote.

My thoughts moved from Sol, to Chalice, to Rueben. Where was he now? Had he been captured? Had he made it to a Lake Town? Would I ever see him again?

The instructor's voice cut through my thoughts, "The first Lake Town was formed in the year 2052."

My fingers hovered over my tablet as I listened carefully. We had studied very little about Lake Towns in A Level.

"The town of Erie was named after Lake Erie, which used to reside in a state called Minnesota," the instructor said. I'd heard the name Erie before, but I hadn't realized it was the first one. "This state, of course, no longer exists, and over the course of three years, Lake Erie combined with the other thousands of lakes in Minnesota and eventually consumed all land except for the high point, Eagle Mountain."

A map appeared on our desk consoles. The Lake Town of Erie was a great distance from our city.

I clicked on the question icon on the tablet and typed in, "What is the closest Lake Town to our city?"

If the instructor wanted to answer, or if he knew the answer, then he'd see the question on his tablet and could incorporate it into the lesson. I just had to wait.

Finally, toward the end of the lesson the instructor said, "The closest surviving Lake Town to our city is Skyhill."

I typed Skyhill into my notes. It might be where Rueben was now.

The day passed slowly as I tried to stay awake in my next classes despite my lack of sleep and the soothing drone of the rain against the windows. Chalice was in two of my classes, but she didn't acknowledge me in either. I kept thinking of Skyhill. I had wanted to ask my geology instructor more questions, but I was afraid of raising suspicion.

Meeting Rueben had changed my perception of Lake Town people. I had never understood anyone wanting to live such a barbaric lifestyle until I met Rueben. Until I went to prison and saw what true barbarism really was.

Back in my dorm room after classes, I sent another message to Sol. *How are classes?* Nothing more. I fell asleep staring at the tablet until the bell rang for the supper hour. I ate quickly, speaking to no one, and hurried to the study lab, where I could use the WorldNet.

I found a console away from anyone else and typed in *first Lake Town*. The information that the instructor had given us popped up. I read through it quickly, not finding anything new. In fact, it seemed like the instructor had read the text to us word for word. There were a few links at the bottom of the information scan. I clicked on the one that said *Eagle Mountain*. An article from an ancient newspaper popped up.

My heart hammered as I read the first sentences: "Thousands flock to Eagle Mountain in a desperate attempt to reach higher ground. Roads have been washed out and cars left abandoned in the mudslides. The people keep coming, bringing only what they can physically carry. Meteorologists predict that this year will see record-breaking rainfall."

The year of the article was 2054. My grandmother had still been alive.

I clicked on the second link, and read, "Hundreds of house boats, fishing boats, and sail boats surround Eagle Mountain Lake. Fights break out on an hourly basis, but the oil has run out, preventing the town authorities from suppressing the skirmishes. The sound of gunfire is a regular occurrence on the waters."

I shivered. That was the beginning. When towns and whole cities flooded. This description was far different from the lifeless one we'd heard in class. The flooding had affected real people—men, women, children. Real people like my grandmother.

Tears burned beneath my eyelids. I exited the article, trying to distance myself from the brimming emotion. Where was Rueben now? What was he facing?

I typed in several more searches, hoping to bury my real inquiries beneath school-related ones.

I searched for *journal*, hoping that it wasn't a restricted word. To my relief, several links came up. "A record of a person's personal history or thoughts," one read. A journal wasn't a person, but a record.

I looked over my shoulder to make sure no one was watching me. Then I typed in *grandmother.*

A link was titled, "Oldest living grandmother." I pressed it, knowing I might be taking a risk. Clicking on a link didn't guarantee that it was valid, and links could disappear at any time since opening them would put it on the search radar. An entire government department was responsible for deleting illegal links. But with hundreds of millions of them out there, finding an illegal link wasn't impossible. It was just a matter of how long it would be available.

"Grandmother lives until 103," the article read. "Family surrounds her as she says her final farewells."

I inhaled. The article was dated just a few years earlier than my grandmother's journal. I wanted to read the rest, but after thirty seconds, the link would be on my permanent record, so I exited.

I sat for a moment, staring at the console screen. I knew I should start my science research, but my curiosity was in full force.

I typed in *flowers.* Several definitions popped up. I clicked on link after link, but there wasn't very much information. The last link had a small image. I leaned forward and stared at the bright yellow petals in the image labeled *Sunflower.*

Sol was right. It was beautiful.

I gazed at it for several more seconds before exiting. Then I began typing in random searches from my science notes, burying the sunflower image deeper and deeper, all the while wondering what had happened to all the flowers.

I spent the next couple of hours completing science work, but it was hard to concentrate.

Back in my dorm room, I was almost asleep when I

heard my door automatically seal with a soft whooshing sound.

I turned my face to the wall, letting the hot tears escape. This was a new kind of prison.

CHAPTER 24

I almost missed the morning meal, I'd slept so long. I was surprised to have slept at all, but I supposed that my body had finally caved.

Walking slowly to class, I took careful notice of the high metal fence between the buildings that separated us from the boys. Through the trees and the bars I caught an occasional glimpse of someone walking on the other side. Nothing much differentiated the boys' clothing from ours—they wore the same browns and grays, the same loose pants and shirts with long raincoats.

The rain fell in a slight drizzle, so I lowered my raincoat hood and let my hair become peppered with the mist. The boy I'd noticed walking on the other side of the fence did the same thing.

I stopped and stared. His hair was short, messy, golden brown. From this distance I could tell he was tall and lanky . . . just like . . . Rueben? I couldn't believe it. But it had to be him. It had to be.

Tracked or not, I hurried toward the fence, weaving through the bushes and trees to get there. Without touching the bars, I stared at the spot where Rueben had been. It was empty.

I drew back, my heart pounding. Had it been him? Had I imagined it? Or maybe it was some other boy, and he wasn't watching me at all.

Just to be sure, I called out quietly, "Rueben?"

There was no answer. A group of boys came into view, walking from one building to another, as if in a hurry.

I left the spot reluctantly and barely made it to class before it began. It was impossible to focus on my lessons as I wondered if I'd just seen Rueben. And if I had, how did he get to the University?

After classes, I walked slowly to the dorm, hoping to catch another look through the fence. But this time, there was no one on the other side.

On the morning of the science competition orientation, I awoke long before my door unlocked itself. I stood by it, waiting for the whooshing sound. As soon as I heard it, at 7:00 a.m. precisely, I left my room.

Tablet in hand, I hurried to the cafeteria and ate a bowl of orange-flavored yogurt. I was the first in the auditorium except for a group of instructors. I wanted to get a seat where I could watch people coming in, watch for Sol. He'd never answered either of my messages. I also watched for Rueben, as silly as I knew that was.

Within about ten minutes, students started trickling in. Then I saw him; Sol entered through the auditorium doors, walking with a group of guys. I wasn't prepared for the way my heart started racing. I hated it. Despite my caretakers' warnings, my emotions were never very far from the surface.

I couldn't help but stare at him; his hair was shorter, though everything else seemed the same. I waited for his gray eyes to find me. But he didn't look my way at all as he walked toward the front of the room. He was on the opposite side from me, so I left my seat and threaded through the people, trying to get close enough to talk to him.

An instructor approached Sol, greeting him. I hung back, watching, and, to my surprise, Sol walked with the instructor up to the podium and took one of the seats reserved for the presenters.

Sol was presenting?

Maybe that's why he didn't answer my messages—he was cutting me off. He'd made a name for himself at the University already and was afraid I'd ruin it for him.

I stumbled into someone as I turned. "Excuse me," I muttered and hurried to a back row. When I took my seat, I looked toward the podium again. At that instant my eyes locked with Sol's. I couldn't read his expression from so far back, but I was certain he was looking at me.

An instructor stepped up to the podium, and Sol looked away.

Had he seen me follow him to the front of the auditorium? Was he relieved I didn't speak to him?

My head pounded as the instructor introduced a student who'd quickly risen above the rest and would now introduce the annual science competition—Sol. If I didn't know him, I wouldn't have suspected that he was nervous, but his hands were gripping each side of his chair. He was anxious. *I would be, too,* I thought.

"The annual science competition was created for students to harvest new ideas in order to further promote the success of our society," he began.

He looked straight at the audience, but sounded like he was reading from a prepared speech. I leaned forward, willing him to look at me again. He never did.

"This year, the University is doing something unprecedented," he said. "Instead of having the men and women science teams compete against each other, they're allowing men and women to work on teams together. This will facilitate the development of scientific ideas that have input from both genders."

I barely processed the words as I listened to Sol. I just wanted to soak up his voice. But the longer he talked, the more he sounded like an instructor. I sank back in my chair, a heaviness in my chest.

"The teams will be randomly generated, and there will be no requests taken," Sol said.

I looked around at the students who listened intently at Sol's explanations. Nothing seemed to be bothering any of them. I didn't know which was more painful, being ignored by Sol and never seeing him, or being ignored and seeing him from a distance.

Again, I studied him as he spoke at the podium. Every mannerism was so achingly familiar that I expected him to suddenly turn to me and ask how I was doing. Tell me he was sorry he didn't reply to my message, that he had a good excuse.

But none of that happened, and I sat in the auditorium full of students, listening to him from afar like everyone else.

"Thank you, Sol," said the instructor, who came to the podium next. "The winning team will receive the opportunity to present their idea to the government board of science and have their project considered for implementation. This is an important honor and may result in being eligible for a position in O Level."

Murmuring erupted throughout the auditorium. Even though we'd all made it to the University, there were few positions opened each year for O Level jobs. They were highly coveted—the competition would be fierce. My breathing sped up. Moving to O Level could accelerate my plans as a Carrier.

I looked at Sol again. His gaze was on the instructor, his expression composed.

When the general assembly was over, we were told to divide into our specialties and convene in our classrooms, men mixed with women. At the end of class our science groups would be announced. Since Sol and I had the same specialty, we'd certainly be in the same classroom for today. I scooted out of my row and stood by the wall as others moved past me. I wanted to wait for Sol, to see if he'd talk to me on the way to class.

As he walked up the aisle toward me, I looked down at my tablet, trying to appear busy. But when he neared me, I lifted my eyes. His gaze had been on me, but quickly shifted when I caught it.

"Sol," I said quietly, but loud enough for him to hear.

He kept his eyes forward, although I knew he'd heard me. He walked past me, without another glance in my direction, past my pleading eyes. I fell into step behind him, and when the crowd dispersed, I whispered, "What's wrong? It's not against the rules for us to talk."

He slowed his step. "We don't know each other anymore."

I opened my mouth to answer, then shut it. He sped up. Even if I tried, I probably couldn't catch up to him without making a scene.

Just as I rounded the hallway to our classroom, he disappeared inside. When I reached the doorway, he was sitting in the front row, right by the instructor, surrounded by other students. I had no choice but to sit in one of the back rows where my only view of him was the back of his head and his shoulders, hunching as he typed notes into his tablet.

My eyes stung. How could he completely cut me off like that? If there was some reason we could no longer talk, then there would be no combined training.

First Chalice, now Sol.

By the end of the class period, I felt ready to burst. I had to literally force myself to stay seated. I wanted to rush to my dorm room and sort out my feelings by myself. But instead, I had to sit in class and keep everything inside.

You react too strongly, Jezebel. You need to be calm. Naomi's advice certainly applied now. I knew I was a Clinical, like Rueben said, and that probably explained why Sol could just cut me off like he had. He wasn't like me. He was like everyone else. I shouldn't have expected him to truly care. Yet I couldn't deny the memories I had with him— whispering together, his eyes watering when he talked about his caretaker, his need to share his memories. All that must mean something. Even if his Harmony implant was controlling his strongest emotions, wasn't there any room left over for him to care about me?

I straightened. What was I doing? Wanting Sol to care

about me—to *show* that he cared, to *say* that he cared? Maybe he was doing that already. By ignoring me, maybe he thought he was protecting me. He knew I was on restriction, that I was being watched and tracked, and that anything I said to him could bring us both down.

The tightness in my chest only grew worse. On one hand, I could understand why he was doing this, but I still wanted to talk to him, to have a friend. I knew we could never be more, but that didn't mean I wanted nothing at all.

The instructor's words filtered back into my mind, "And now, please check your tablets for the division of the science teams."

All eyes went to their tablets, and I inhaled sharply as I read the names in my group. Sol was first on the list.

CHAPTER 25

A few hours ago, I would have been elated to be on Sol's team. But that was before he told me that we no longer knew each other.

The students rose from their desks and shuffled out of the room for a short break. After that, we'd meet in our new teams.

I waited at my desk long enough to see Sol stand and turn. I tried to catch his gaze, but he was deliberately avoiding me. I took several deep breaths as I went out into the corridor and made my way to the next classroom where our team was assigned to meet.

I had only recognized Sol's name on the list, so I didn't know anyone else in the room when I stepped in. A boy and girl were already at the table.

"I'm Daniel," the boy said, lifting a hand. His face was round, his blond hair buzzed short. His blue eyes seemed calm and intelligent.

I offered my name then and looked to the other girl.

Her hair was pulled back in the typical tight pony-tail. It was reddish-brown, the red emphasized by her red shirt. I wondered where she'd gotten it—it was uncommon to see red clothing in the city. "Serah," she said with a nod, her pale blue eyes watching me curiously. *Will you be a competitor or a friend?* I could almost hear her asking.

"And I'm Solomon," a voice said behind me.

I took my seat next to Serah without looking at Sol.

The three of them began to discuss various possibilities right away; it seemed everyone had an idea, except for me. I tried to interject now and again, and I also tried not to notice that Sol's eyes were more green today than gray.

Daniel's voice cut in. "If we can create a cement compound that resists cracking, the Legislature would find that useful."

But Sol was already shaking his head. Not that I was paying any attention to him. "We don't have the time it would take—cement settles over time, thus it cracks over time."

Daniel rested his rounded chin on his hands. "That's a good point."

"Besides," Serah said, "that experiment has been done many times. And it has always failed. We don't have the same resources as the established scientists."

"It'll have to be something that hasn't been done by any other student group," I said. "Something that only we could come up with."

Sol scoffed. "What do we know that other students don't?"

We know a lot. Did the other students know about the Before, about the Phase Three Lab, about altering?

"Food additives haven't been done recently," Serah said. "We could come up with a new way to flavor meat or preserve vegetables. Or we could come up with a carrot-flavored yogurt."

I hid my groan. Yogurt already came in too many flavors.

I couldn't believe that Sol actually looked interested in Serah's suggestions. "Well, we should at least start the research on a few of these. Next time we meet, let's all bring what we've found."

Daniel and Serah hurried out of the room, intent on fulfilling their assignments. It was plain that our group had plenty of motivation.

"Sol," I said before he could disappear, too. I didn't like the catch in my voice, but I needed to understand.

He turned slowly, finally looking at me—really looking at me. It was almost like the old Sol—the one who could see into my soul, the one who I used to think cared.

"Jez, I told you—"

"I heard what you said, but I want to know *why*." I focused on taking steady breaths. I hated that his eyes were so green today.

"We're at the University now. Our genders are separated for a reason." His eyes searched mine, and I looked away before I could get absorbed in them.

"What about this project?" I said. "Why are we on the same team then?"

He shrugged, but I had seen it—a flicker of know-ledge—he knew we'd be on this team together.

"Did you plan this?"

"Just leave it alone," he said quietly.

I crossed to him, expecting him to step back, keep his

distance, but he didn't. "I know things are different now," I said. "They've been different since I went to the laboratory."

"You mean the prison?"

"Yes—which was a laboratory."

His brow crinkled. For once I was telling him something he didn't know.

"They did experiments in there on kids, Sol. They called them *tests.*" I watched his expression change to disbelief. "Look up the word 'Clinical.'" I stepped closer to him, almost touching him. "Because that's what I am."

He blinked, looking down at me.

A couple of students entered the classroom and their conversation died down when they saw us standing so close together. I stepped away from Sol and walked past the students, then out the door.

I gripped my tablet to my chest, feeling anger, elation, and fear all grappling for one space. My breathing was shallow, but I had at least told someone *something* about what had happened to me. And if I was Taken, the information wouldn't be lost forever.

The corridor was empty now. Every eager student had rushed to the study labs to start their projects. Someone gripped my arm and tugged me to the side. I turned with a gasp.

"In here," Sol said. We stepped into an empty classroom and suddenly I was facing him, standing so close that I could smell his scent—as if he'd just walked in out of the rain.

His eyes burned into me. "What *tests* are you talking about?"

I shook my head, anger overpowering all of my other emotions. "So now you want to talk?"

"Jez," he whispered, his voice sounding almost angry,

"I'm trying to protect you. You've been to prison, and now you're on *restriction.*" He looked toward the door and the empty corridor, worry on his face. Genuine worry.

"I just exchanged one prison for another." I couldn't keep the bitterness out of my voice.

Sol looked taken aback by my tone. But I was tired of thinking about Sol, thinking about our failing friendship. I needed information. "Have you talked to Chalice since you've been here?"

"No."

"She's been altered," I said in a rush. "Her personality has changed, and she's not the same person. We need to help her."

"You're not making sense—"

"Just listen to me. In the prison—the laboratory—they experimented on kids. They altered the level of control in their implants to see how much they could endure without going insane or comatose." I folded my arms as the memory of the cages surfaced. "I got out just in time, but my test isn't over."

One of his eyebrows lifted. "You're saying that scientists are experimenting with *insanity*? Jez, you shouldn't be talking like that. There are rules against heresy."

"You don't understand. The rules aren't what we thought they were." When Sol shook his head in doubt, I said, "I know . . . I know that might be hard to believe coming from someone who was petrified to break even one rule." I let out a breath. "When I was called to get my inheritance, the Examiner handed me the satchel with Rose's book. It's hard for me to believe he didn't know what was inside."

Sol took a step back. "You think the Examiner was

testing you? That they *wanted* you to read the book, and they wanted you to be caught with it?"

I nodded. "They set me up to get caught," I said, pleading for him to believe me. "And then thought they could make me forget what I read with the agitator rod."

He was silent for a moment. "What about 'altering?'" Sol folded his arms across his chest, listening, but looking unconvinced.

I stumbled on. "I saw the altering for myself. When I got to prison, I found out why I was being tested."

Sol watched me intently, clearly not believing me, and it was all that I could do to stop myself from crying.

"Rueben told me I was a Clinical—like him," I said.

His eyes narrowed. "What does Clinical mean?"

Voices sounded from the corridor, and Sol moved toward the door. I backed up against the wall. When the voices faded, Sol looked over at me. "I'm sorry for all the tests you've been put through, but Rueben was misguided."

My throat tightened. How could I get Sol to believe me?

He looked as if he were about to say something else, but instead he stepped out the room, the door shutting behind him.

I waited a couple of more minutes until I was sure I wouldn't cry, then I made my own exit.

That night Sol sent me a message: *I spoke to Chalice.*

I immediately typed back: *What did she say?*

Tomorrow, he responded.

I stared at the words on the tablet. We'd find a way to talk tomorrow. What had Chalice said to him? Did he believe me now? I wanted to send another message, but I didn't dare. I was already being monitored enough.

It was late, and I was sealed in my room, so I had nowhere to go. I opened the news report and scanned for Rueben's name. He was still listed as an uncaught criminal. Had he made it to a Lake Town safely? Was he traveling on the waters? I scrolled over to the weather report, wondering why they even had one. It rained every day, and had done so my entire life. The only useful information was a small countdown box that listed 172 days until Winter Solstice.

I climbed onto my bed and closed my eyes. My body felt tired and weak, as if it badly needed the sunshine. In the dark, I couldn't see my arms, but I knew they were pale and thin. Even my normally thick hair was limp and dull brown.

My mind took a long time to shut off that night. Just as I felt myself drifting into the gentle nothingness of dreaming, the seal on my door opened.

CHAPTER 26

I shot up in bed, grabbing the sides of the mattress. I had nothing with me but a small rose-shaped rock under my pillow. I was too petrified to grab even that.

Someone walked into my room, and the door slid shut behind them. The person crossed to the window, and that's when I recognized her.

"Chalice?"

She didn't move, but stared out the window into the dark night, holding her tablet against her chest. I wondered how she'd entered my sealed room.

I climbed off my bed, my thoughts spiraling with questions. I was afraid, but not necessarily of her. "What are you doing?" I said, keeping my distance.

She didn't answer.

I saw the puffiness beneath her eyes and how thin she looked. I touched her arm lightly, and when she didn't react, I laid my hand on it. She swallowed audibly in the silence.

"What happened to you, Chalice?" I whispered.

She moved slightly as if she heard me. I had learned once that the last thing to shut down in a body at the end of the life cycle was hearing. If she wasn't the same person after altering, perhaps she could still hear and comprehend what I said to her. That struck a new fear inside me. I'd seen what happened to the children that the scientists altered in the prison—what if this was just a more mild form, or a slower form, and she would go crazy at any moment?

I moved away, keeping an eye on her, but my thoughts turned bleak. What if Rueben had been altered, but the side effects were delayed? What if he was in some place, stuck, because he couldn't communicate like Chalice?

But she *had* talked to someone—Sol. Had she responded?

"Can you talk . . . to me?" I asked, adding in the last part, wondering if there was some sort of barrier between us created by the altering.

There was nothing for a long moment, and just when I was about to say something else, she turned to look at me and said, "Who are you?"

I was stunned. Had the altering made her forget me? How could she be at the University if she'd lost her entire memory? Wouldn't that affect her class work?

"Jezebel," I said, feeling sick inside. "We were roommates in Level A."

She stared at me, her body silhouetted by the window. I met her gaze, hoping that she'd remember.

"Why can't I talk to you?" she said.

"I—I don't know," I said, thinking fast. "Who told you that?"

She closed her eyes for an instant. When she opened

them again, they seemed vacant, empty. "I can't see you. I can't speak to you. I can't visit you."

My breath stopped. Her words sounded like she'd memorized them and had repeated them over and over. "You're in my room, Chalice, visiting me, right now."

"Yes," she said in a flat voice. "But I don't know why."

My heart hurt. My brave friend was gone. I could no longer hope that she was only pretending.

"How did you get into my room?" I asked.

"There was a message on my tablet to come here."

A cold chill spread through me. Who told her to come here? And how did she have the security clearance to open my door?

"I didn't know whose room it was," Chalice continued, her eyes narrowing as she studied me.

For an instant, I thought I saw some recognition there, but it faded in the dark before I could decipher it. "Why are you here? Try to remember," I whispered, taking a step closer to the door, not that I could get outside. I was taller than Chalice, but she was definitely stronger.

Chalice continued to stare at me. The light from the streetlamp light behind her made a faint glow around her head. Something flickered in her eyes. "Were we friends?" She sounded mechanical, like when Sol spoke at the assembly.

"Yes."

She held out her tablet and read something on it. "I don't understand."

I wanted to see what had just popped up on her screen, but I didn't dare leave my place by the door. "Understand what?"

"Why I've been sent to replace you."

"Replace me?" My heart beat wildly as I considered the possibilities. Were we swapping rooms? Or had I been kicked out of the University? Had my WorldNet research about the Lake Towns or flowers been discovered? I could barely whisper, "What do you mean?"

Chalice didn't answer, the glow of the streetlamp changing her pretty features into harsh ones. She slipped the tablet into her pocket, then removed something from her jacket and pointed it at me. An agitator rod.

I dove toward her just as a thousand lights burst inside my vision.

CHAPTER 27

My body shook with cold and burned with heat at the same time. I wasn't sure if Chalice was still in the room. All I knew was that I couldn't move, and I never wanted to move again. In fact, I didn't want to open my eyes. Ever.

There must be a limit to how much a body could withstand. Had I reached it?

The barest noise reached my ears. Someone moaning. I opened my eyes, groaning against my own headache.

Chalice lay on the floor against the far wall, where she must have fallen when we collided. She was cradling her shoulder.

I realized the agitator had hit us both, and we had been out for some time if I was to gage by the softening gray of the room.

I looked around the room for the rod; I wanted to reach

it before Chalice did. My head pounded and bright spots swam in front of my eyes, but it was my only chance.

When I spotted the rod by the door, I started to scoot toward it. The pain in my head broke out into a fierce throbbing. I kept my eye on Chalice as I reached for the rod, then scooted into the far corner of the room, keeping as much distance between us as possible. But her gaze was passive.

"I'm sorry," she whispered, then winced and grasped her shoulder again.

Sorry? I stared at her. Why was she apologizing? Did she finally recognize me now?

"Who sent you?"

She moved into a sitting position with another groan. "What happened to me?" Her eyes closed against the pain.

"I—You were trying to shock me. I think you got some of it, too."

"That would explain the pain." Her voice sounded almost normal, less mechanical. She removed her hand, revealing her shoulder. There was a wide red circle on her skin. "My scar hurts. I think my implant was shocked." She lifted her hand up with a grimace and studied her damaged finger. "They took my ring."

My breath caught. It was as if she was just realizing that her finger had been burned. I gripped the agitator in my hand and inched forward, still wary, but with new possibilities floating in my mind.

"Do you—do you remember me?" I asked.

Chalice focused her eyes on me. Her face was pale, and she looked even thinner in her painful state. "Of course I remember you." She looked down at her hand again, and her brows pulled together as she repeated, "They took my ring."

A dozen emotions rolled through me. "Chalice, why are you in my room?"

She lifted her head and narrowed her eyes as if she were concentrating, trying to remember something. "There was a message . . ." She brought her hand to her mouth. "Oh." Her eyes widened and tears formed.

I was astounded to see a tear fall down her cheek.

She seemed equally surprised and wiped the tear with one finger, then held it up, staring at it. "What's happening to me?"

"You're crying," I said.

She blinked and another tear fell. She wiped at her face and sniffled. Then she placed her hands on each side of her cheeks. "I'm crying—I'm really crying. It's like . . . something inside is trying to get out—to escape." More tears coursed down her cheeks. "Why do I feel so . . . I don't know what I feel."

"Sad?"

"I think so. The agitator did something to me—I'm not supposed to be like this." She stood up slowly, bracing herself against the wall.

"Actually, Chalice," I said, keeping the agitator in front of me just in case, "you *are* supposed to be like this."

She stared at me, her cheeks still wet.

"I think I know what happened," I said. "The shock reversed the altering." *And maybe much more.*

She swiped at her cheeks, her expression confused, so I continued. "After I was sent to prison, what happened at school?"

She sniffled again, then looked toward the window. The rain was barely a drizzle now, more of a mist. After several minutes of silence, I said, "Do you remember anything?"

Another tear dripped down her face. "I'm starting to

204

remember." Then her watery eyes focused on me. "They asked me questions after you left, but then nothing happened until the Solstice."

She grasped her shoulder again as if she'd had another rush of pain. "The morning was beautiful. We stood in the school yard, waiting for the sun to break through the clouds. I felt the warmth growing stronger and stronger before the sun actually came out."

I swallowed against my dry throat, imagining the fiery yellow warmth. Every part of my body yearned to feel the heat of the sun.

"Some of the kids laid down on the wet cement," she continued, "just soaking up the sun with their whole bodies. The boys took off their shirts."

I nodded. I'd seen them do that on other Solstices.

"My skin was just starting to turn pink when the school yard speaker announced I was to report to the director's office." She let out a sigh. "I didn't want to go, of course. I stalled a few more minutes, hoping that whatever they wanted could wait until the clouds came back." Another tear slid down her face.

When she didn't continue, I said, "Is that when they took your ring?"

She looked down at her hand. "I'm not sure. I didn't make it to the office. Two inspectors were waiting in the corridor, and they cuffed me. I don't remember much after that." She snapped her head up and looked at me. "Something happened to me. I can't explain it . . ." Her voice trailed off, and she wiped at her tear-stained face again.

"You were altered," I said. "I learned about it at prison. I saw it happen to other kids around me. Most of them were worse off than you."

"What do you mean?"

I told her what I knew about altering, what Rueben had told me about controlling the brain. "It affects each person differently," I added.

"Is that why I forgot about you?" Chalice asked.

"Probably."

She studied me. The darkness outside had faded now, replaced by the dull gray of morning. We had both been unconscious for several hours. It was nearly seven and my door would soon open. "So the agitator rod . . . do you think it reversed the altering?"

"I think so," I said. I wasn't letting go of the rod, my only protection. I didn't know what to think about Chalice now, although the tears had seemed real.

"And what about the tears," she said in a shaky voice. "I can't be seen crying."

Tears would definitely draw attention and reveal that her altering had been . . . altered. I wished I had time to tell her that I was having the same emotions, and that I had learned to control them since childhood, but I'd have to give her the condensed version. "When you feel the tears start, you have to think of something else, something that doesn't make you feel sad."

Chalice nodded as if she understood, but her face was marked in confusion. "I feel so tired." She leaned her head against the wall.

The door seal released, making a swooshing sound. I looked at Chalice. "You have to act like you did before—like you don't remember me," I said. Her eyes reflected the same fear I felt. I could only imagine the new emotions swirling around inside her. I'd been dealing with them my entire life—she was feeling them for the first time.

"Why would I be told to 'replace' you? What does that

mean?" By the haunted look in her eyes, I realized she'd just remembered what she'd come to my room to do.

The cold chill returned. "I'm not sure," I said. If Chalice was sent to shock me, then what was she supposed to do next? Take me somewhere? Would there be someone waiting for me in the corridor?

"Were there other instructions on the tablet?"

"I don't think so. I only remember one message—to come to your room. When I got here, I just knew I was supposed to shock you."

"And then I messed it up." I turned over the rod in my hand. "You're free now."

"Free?"

"Free from their control, but you'll have to learn to control yourself now," I whispered.

"How do I do that?" Her eyes budded with tears again.

"Take a deep breath and fight the tears," I said.

She followed my direction and the tears stopped, though her eyes were still red. "Why you, Jez? Why does the Legislature want to control me, and why do they want you replaced?"

Because I'm a Clinical, I wanted to say, but I didn't want to burden Chalice with too much information right now. I could tell she was in turmoil—fighting against a slew of emotions. "It must have something to do with the time I spent in prison, or the fact that I tried to escape."

"You *escaped*? They didn't release you?"

"When they caught me, they told me I'd passed their test, and I was allowed to come here."

She looked nervously toward the door. "Do you think they're waiting in the corridor for us?"

No one else had tried to come in—to 'replace' me, whatever that meant. Yet. Then it hit me. "Maybe this is another test," I whispered. "Maybe they wanted to see if you'd come in here and shock me. Maybe they wanted to know what I would do."

"So now what?" she whispered, her voice full of fear.

"Wait for the next test."

She grimaced, and I knew the feeling. I handed over the agitator. "You should probably keep this."

Chalice looked at it with distaste. "I don't want to touch that thing."

"It makes more sense for you to have it," I said.

"So if this was just a test—to see if I'd obey, or whatever—what do you think they'll do if they find out my altering was reversed?" she asked.

A chill crept through me. "Chalice, you must act as if you're still altered."

"What about the instructions to *replace* you?"

I clenched my hands together and breathed out slowly. "It was probably—hopefully—a test, and no one else will pick up where you left off." A cold sweat broke out on my neck. "I don't have any choice but to go through my day like usual."

Chalice pursed her lips together, her eyes darkening. "How will I know you're okay?"

I hesitated, remembering what Rueben had told me about a way to communicate messages through a sequence code. But even if Chalice and I sent messages that way, the chance of us being able to open the messages right away and read them before they became encrypted was very slim. Still, it was better than nothing.

I grabbed my tablet from the desk. With shaking fingers I clicked on the message icon. I selected my own name to send a message to. "A friend showed me how to send a private message. It will encrypt itself in about ninety seconds."

"Show me." Chalice leaned over the tablet to get a better look.

I typed in the sequence of numbers that I had committed to memory with Rueben. I hoped it still worked. He had said that the sequence was updated frequently, so I'd have to change the order of the last numbers, hoping one of them would go through. I transposed the last four digits and sent the message.

Immediately, an alert bounced back. *Message undeliverable.*

I changed the order of the last four numbers again. *Message undeliverable.*

On the third time it went through.

Chalice and I stared as the message to myself popped up on the tablet. Ninety seconds later the words *This is a Test* were replaced by strange circular symbols.

"Incredible," Chalice breathed. "Who taught you this?"

"A friend from prison." I met her curious gaze, and I couldn't help but add, "He's originally from a Lake Town."

Her eyes widened. "I thought the Lake Town people were illiterate."

"Not even close." I shut my mouth, afraid I'd said too much.

Chalice seemed to sense that I was done talking about it. "Tell me the numbers again so I can memorize them."

I repeated the most recent sequence that I'd entered. "I don't know how long it will be active."

Sounds from the corridor filtered through the door. Other girls were moving through the hallways, on their way to the cafeteria. "You should leave before the hallways get too crowded."

Chalice shook her head. "I'll wait here until everyone is gone. You go first."

"All right," I said. "Remember to act like you're still altered . . . You don't know me, and you don't talk to anyone."

She nodded, her eyes moist.

"Keep the emotion hidden," I said.

"I'm trying to," she said, but I heard the shakiness in her voice. Suddenly, she leaned forward and embraced me tightly. I hugged her back. For a brief second, we were the same.

CHAPTER 28

My pulse raced as I stepped out of my room, leaving Chalice behind. We couldn't be seen together. Especially after her failed mission that might not be a failed mission at all, but a test. I was worried about how well she would fare battling her new emotions.

But I was even more afraid of what the next test might be—would it involve Chalice again? Sol? Someone else I knew?

In the corridor, noise buzzed around me. I couldn't help but stare at people as I passed them, wondering if they, too, had been altered. Or perhaps they were Clinicals like me and had just done a better job of suppressing their emotions than I had.

I skipped the cafeteria, wanting to get to class early and be the first one in a quiet room, giving myself time to think. Once in class, I checked the incoming message I'd sent to myself. It had disappeared. Not only had it encrypted, but it had destroyed itself. I breathed easier.

I clicked on the news icon and scrolled through the names that were listed as criminals. Rueben's name was still there. A message from Chalice appeared on my screen. I opened it quickly in case it was coded: *Don't speak to Sol.*

I quickly replied: *Why?* But it took extra time to type in the numbered code, and a couple of students came into the room while I was typing. I kept my head bent forward, staring at the tablet and trying to shield it from view at the same time.

Message sent. I kept the message application on for a few more minutes, but there was no reply.

Why couldn't I speak to Sol? What had Chalice found out? Was this another test?

Worry gnawed at my stomach. I had already told him a lot—about Chalice's altering, the testing in the laboratories, and about being Clinical. Had he been altered like Chalice? I had forgotten to ask Chalice what they had talked about.

The geology professor began the lesson, saying, "We'll be discussing population today and the impact it has on our city."

I was at full attention. I wondered if he'd mention anything about the Lake Town populations.

"We presently have just under two million people in our city," the professor said. "We're also the largest city on the earth."

I ached to ask about the population of the surrounding Lake Towns, but I didn't want to betray my keen interest in the outside communities.

"Let's look up the history of populations on your tablets," he said.

I eagerly scrolled through the menu until I found the population chart. It started with the year 2089 and went to the present, 2099. The population had decreased by about three hundred thousand in the past ten years.

Two million still sounded like a substantial number, but I had never considered how many people that was—a seemingly large amount—yet to think our city might be the last major civilization to exist, the population was frighteningly small. Rueben had been right. Our population was dwindling.

I wondered how many people were out in the Lake Towns—surely many times more than here in the city. *Hopefully* many times more.

The professor talked us through each year. Then he paused. "The question came in: Why does the population decrease if there are new births each year?"

I thought of all those who were Taken before their life cycles naturally expired. It was an easy answer, but not the one the professor gave. "Disease is the primary reason for the dwindling population."

I typed in a question as well. The only diseases I'd heard of were easily cured with a day or two in the hospice.

It was clear when my question popped up, as the professor suddenly looked nervous. "Another question came in: Can diseases stop a life cycle?" He looked up, taking his time to answer. "Yes. There are diseases that exist in the C Level population which can cut life cycles short. Some children born into B Level have these diseases as well, regardless of the precautions taken during in vitro."

The words sunk in, and I tried to imagine a child succumbing to a disease. All around me, the students were completely silent. This was new information for all of us.

Possibly hundreds or thousands of people, slowly dying of diseases. I typed in another question, as several others did the same on their tablets.

I wrote: "What happens to the children?"

The professor said nothing. The silence among the students grew heavier as he read through our questions. Finally, he said, "The question is: Are these diseases curable? They are most of the time, at least in adults. It depends on how well the person has taken care of himself. I cannot say more. That is information regulated to the government's medical councils."

I had a new topic to research. What were these diseases and how was the government stopping them? And what happened to the babies born with them?

As the professor continued to talk, I marveled that children were still born diseased. B Level women were carefully screened before they were allowed to have a child. In A Level class, we'd been taught that only the most promising eggs were fertilized and placed in the woman's womb. All of the children I'd grown up with only suffered very minor illnesses. Was that because the ones who were less healthy had been relocated? What would they do with seriously ill children? Maybe there were hospice centers for them, although I'd never heard of any.

I had trouble concentrating the rest of the period.

After class, I hurried from the room. The men's classrooms were in the next building, with the general auditorium connecting the two. I hoped to catch a glimpse of Sol coming out of the men's building. Maybe from a distance I could tell if there was something different about him— something that might explain Chalice's confusing message.

I moved through the hallway, dodging students as it

filled rapidly. Had class let out early? It seemed everyone was outside of class, and they were all headed in one direction. I saw a couple of girls glancing at their tablets, then hurrying on. I stopped as people moved around me like a parting river. Finally I pulled out my tablet, too. A message flashed on the screen: *Alert. All students to the auditorium.*

My heart sank.

I hurried along with the rest, arriving in the auditorium in time to secure a seat in one of the back rows of the girls' section. Everyone was silent, except for some shuffling, as they stared at the front of the stage.

Three students stood there, heads lowered, their hands bound in front of them with something similar to the ankle cuff I wore on the journey to prison. I glanced around to look for Chalice. She sat several rows in front of me. Sol was nowhere to be seen in the boys' section.

The walls were lined with dozens of officials, as well as professors, their eyes hard on the students. The auditorium doors shut, followed by the unmistakable sound of them sealing into locked position—a sound I knew all too well. The tension in the room seemed to double.

I looked over at Chalice, but she stared straight ahead like everyone else around her.

A man wearing a white blazer stood up in the front of the room and climbed the steps to the stage. An Examiner. I hadn't seen him when I came in. If possible, the auditorium grew even quieter.

"Students." The Examiner's voice was amplified, his voice booming even in the very back rows. "We have an unfortunate situation at the University this week. These students were caught performing a religious rite."

A few murmurs sounded about the room, but then everyone fell back into silence.

One of the boys on the stage shuffled his feet. What was going through the heads of the exposed students? Their Harmony implants must not have been functioning correctly, or they never would have become involved in a religious rituals—it could earn them Demotion.

"We've brought them before you so they can name their coconspirators," the Examiner continued. "We believe there are more than just these three who are part of the cult."

My head snapped up as everyone started looking around at each other.

The Examiner continued. "We will not leave until every last person is identified." His voice grew louder. "We cannot afford to disobey the rules the Legislature has so carefully selected. We are one society with one voice. When we break off and form any sort of group, religious or otherwise, we begin to separate in unity and purpose, and such separation will be our downfall as a society."

I huddled in my seat, feeling sick for the guilty, wherever they were in the audience. Did they feel sick, too? Would it break them down into admitting the truth?

"We are truly disappointed as a University," the Examiner said. "Coming here and studying to be a part of the O Level society is a privilege only extended to the brightest of graduates. A breech of this magnitude is serious, and those on this stage will be Demoted. No one will leave until every member of the cult is brought forward. If we discover someone has not come forward, the consequences will be severe."

Now I knew why the doors had locked behind us. I looked down at my tablet. It was blank. It seemed our communication had been cut off as well. Everyone sat in silence.

The normally cool room grew warmer. I felt prickles of sweat beading at my forehead, and I wasn't even part of the cult. Minutes passed. No one moved, no one spoke. I discreetly wiped my hairline.

All eyes were on the Examiner as he stepped forward and pointed an agitator rod toward one of the students on the stage. The boy's eyes visibly widened as he followed the Examiner's movement. But before the boy gave any other reaction, the Examiner shocked him. The boy crumpled to his knees with a cry. His hands shot out in front of him but did a poor job of stopping his fall since they were cuffed together.

Everyone in the auditorium flinched, then seemed to collectively shrink.

Another step, and the Examiner faced the next student.

The boy stepped back, defenseless. I looked away as he screamed and fell to the stage.

The Examiner's voice boomed out, "Does anyone want to step forward now, or do you enjoy watching your fellow cult members suffer?"

In the boys' section, a young man stood up, his reddish hair cut so short that I could see his pink scalp. "I'm a member," he said in a low voice that I could barely hear from my seat.

The closest official immediately grabbed him and marched him to the stage. He took his place with the others after having his wrists clamped together. He was visibly trembling.

The Examiner raised his agitator. "Anyone else ready to come forward? Last chance to choose Demotion."

No one moved. No one made a sound.

Then someone to my left stood, a few rows up.

No. I almost said out loud.

It was as if time had stopped moving as I watched Chalice's thin frame grabbed by the thick hands of an official. What was she doing? I thought about the ring she insisted on wearing. Could she really be part of this cult?

My body felt cold and stiff, despite the warmth of the room, as I watched Chalice walk to the stage. I didn't understand.

Neither, apparently, did the other students on the stage. They looked at her with confusion and surprise evident in their faces. Of course Chalice wasn't a part of their cult—how could she be? She had been altered until just this morning.

"Very good," the Examiner was saying, a triumphant look on his face. He back turned to face the audience.

"This is my final request." His wide eyes scanned the auditorium, seeming to pierce through each person individually and collectively at the same time. And then, for a split second, so briefly that I wondered if I had imagined it, he looked directly at me. And I knew, even from that distance, that he was the same Examiner who'd handed me the satchel with Rose's book.

The officials surrounded the students on the stage and escorted them through a concealed door. The two on the ground were carried off. I continued to stare at the Examiner, though he no longer looked in my direction. I gripped my hands on the arm rests, stopping myself from jumping up and calling out to Chalice.

There was a faint whooshing sound, and I realized that the auditorium doors had been unlocked and opened. We hadn't been excused yet, but at least we weren't locked in anymore and the warmth in the room started to dissipate.

My tablet buzzed to life. I looked down and saw a

message had come in from Chalice. I clicked on it and was able to read it just as the encryption changed the letters. The first word was already a line of symbols, but the next three words were:

Don't find me.

I leaned forward so the girl next to me couldn't read the message as it encrypted itself and faded from my tablet. I didn't know what the first word of the message had said, but "don't find me" was plain enough.

Chalice had claimed to be a member of the religious group on purpose. But why? What had her message about Sol really meant? What had she found out? Had she remembered something from when she was altered?

I was sweating again with fear, with worry, with confusion.

The Examiner started speaking, and I had to reign in my emotions to pay attention. "We'd like to recognize a very special student for uncovering the illegal cult. Please come forward, Solomon."

My body trembled as Sol walked up to the stage. His expression was passive, accepting.

After a few words of praise for Sol, the Examiner said, "We'll return to our regular activities now, with what I hope is a serious warning."

I couldn't take my eyes off Sol. He looked like he usually did, his dark hair unkempt, his eyes a moody gray. I couldn't believe he would turn anyone in. He'd broken his share of rules in A Level, after all.

Then my mouth went dry as a new possibility entered my mind. Had *Sol* been testing me? Was he being given instructions like Chalice had been?

Suddenly I felt like I didn't know my former friend at all.

The assembly was over. The officials pocketed their agitators and allowed people to exit through the auditorium doors. I stayed in my seat as everyone else filed out of the room. Those in my row were forced to maneuver around me.

I couldn't look away from Sol as he spoke with the Examiner. They seemed deep in conversation, as if they were hanging on each other's words. A shiver went through me. I had told Sol about Rose's book, and now Sol was speaking to the same Examiner who'd given it to me. What was to stop Sol from saying something to get me into trouble? After all, I'd tried to meet him after curfew.

Forcing myself to breathe in steady gulps of air, I told myself to relax. This was probably part of some test. But I couldn't relax. Chalice being counted among the cult members sounded dangerous no matter what angle I considered it from.

Sol and the Examiner left the stage, and Sol walked up the aisle toward the back doors. I stood and left my row, waiting for him to reach me. Other students brushed passed me, heading out of the auditorium.

But I kept my gaze on Sol. He wouldn't be able to avoid me this time.

CHAPTER 29

"Are you an informer?" I hissed when Sol tried to move past me.

I turned and kept pace with him. Officials glanced at me, then let their eyes follow Sol. He was a school hero, making their job very easy.

Don't talk to Sol, Chalice had told me. But she was gone now. I was more confused and lost than ever. Had she learned something that made Demotion more appealing than staying at the University?

Taking a deep breath to push past my fear, I grabbed Sol's hand.

That got his attention.

He tore his hand away and turned with an icy glare on his face.

My words stuck in my throat for an instant, but my desperation drove me to ask, "What happened to you, Sol?"

He blinked slowly, and the iciness melted to just plain cold. "Science group is at four."

"Is that all you're going to say? Did you see Chalice taken away with the cult—the one she has nothing to do with?" I heaved a breath, lowering my voice so the passing students wouldn't hear. "What happened to the boy who told me about the fields of red peonies?"

His face changed color. Pale.

And then I knew. He was hiding something, certainly from me, and definitely from the University. The only comforting thing about it was that it might mean he was no informer.

His eyes narrowed, and I swear there were bits of fire in them when he whispered, "Meet me at three thirty."

He turned and walked away before I could badger him any further. I stared after him, wondering if I'd just made a big mistake.

I spent the next hours in class, trying desperately to concentrate. I took notes and followed along with the lecture, but all I saw was Sol's face—his piercing glare and the fire in his eyes when he said to meet him. It was the most raw emotion I'd ever seen from him.

During the lunch hour I ate quickly, ignoring the occasional glances from the other girls. How many of them knew I was friends with the girl who'd just declared she was a cult member? After lunch I went into the WorldNet lab and began searching for *deadly diseases*. Link after link was broken.

Anytime anyone had so much as a runny nose or cough, they were put into the hospice for a full recovery. No one I knew had ever had a severe disease—one that could break a life cycle. I thought back to the children behind the bars in the prison lab. Not only had they been altered, but many of them looked as if they couldn't perform the most basic tasks. Chalice had been able to fully function after her altering. So what was the difference?

The bubonic plague came up with a link. The plague had swept through Europe in the fourteenth century and then again in the seventeenth. I needed something more recent, though, something that happened after the Burning. Staring at the console screen, I remembered something my grandmother had written in her book: *Father has the damp disease, the one that used to be called pneumonia and treated with antibiotics. With no antibiotics available, there is nothing much we can do for his condition.*

I typed in *pneumonia* and then *damp disease*, but there was still nothing. It did give me an idea, though. Perhaps the names of diseases had been changed. It seemed they'd been changed after the Burning, so maybe they'd been changed again by the Legislature. I buried the links I'd read by typing in new unrelated searches.

When it was almost three, I made my way to the classroom where our science group had planned to meet. The room was empty, and I sat at a desk, waiting for Sol.

I thought of the events over the past few days: of being locked in my room during curfew, of Chalice coming to "replace" me, of her cryptic message about Sol, of his role in informing on the cult, and finally of Chalice's decision to be Demoted.

I covered my face with my hands as confusion rolled over me, a river of questions. At the top of the list was what had happened to Rueben. Had I really seen him on the other side of the fence? Or was he still on the water somewhere? Had he reached a Lake Town?

You shouldn't care about people so much, I heard Naomi's voice in my head. *But my teacher never smiles,* I had worried at the age of seven. *What if she's sick? Will she be Taken?* Naomi let out a familiar sigh. *Teachers aren't supposed to smile.*

No matter how I tried to talk myself out of it, I cared about people. Sol. Chalice. Rueben. The boys on stage today. Those kids at the prison. My whole life I'd been led to believe that I must not feel sad, or happy, or worried, or nervous, or angry, or frustrated . . . I must not feel anything.

But what if . . . what if the professors were wrong? What if the Examiner was wrong? The *Legislature?*

My throat tightened. If they were all wrong, did that mean Rose had been right? But she had been a rule breaker, someone who was foolish enough to get herself executed. Had she thought that death was really better than following the rules? I knew some people believed there was a place to go after our life cycles. Heaven. Paradise. Nirvana. But nothing could be proved, which meant death was a void in which there was no life. It was the end. I blinked against my forming tears. I didn't know what was right and what was wrong anymore.

The door slid open, and I scrambled to stand, facing Sol as he came barreling. His hair was messy, his eyes wide and wild, and he was out of breath. Had he been running?

I braced myself against the desk, steeling myself for whatever he might say: *Jez, I'm a student informer for the government. My job is to watch you.* Or, *Jez, word just came in that Rueben has been Taken.*

Sol said none of these things.

In a few quick strides, he was standing right in front of me.

"You're an informer, aren't you?" I demanded.

His eyes bore into me. "No."

"Then why did you turn in the cult members?" I folded my arms, hating that I missed him, *missed us,* even as he stood in front of me, making me angry.

"I can't explain," he said, his tone defensive. "But it was for their own good. They would have been worse than Demoted if I hadn't turned them in."

"What could be worse than Demotion?"

His gaze softened a little, and his voice fell below quiet. "Banishment."

Now that I knew about Lake Towns, Banishment might not be such a horrible sentence after all. There were worse things—I'd seen kids in cages, not even able to take care of their own bodily functions.

I dropped my hands to my side in defeat. I wanted to believe that Sol wasn't an informer, and that he wasn't supposed to spy on me. I had to believe. If I didn't, then there was no *us* and never would be again. "What about Chalice?"

His eyes clouded. "I don't know why she went with the cult. Probably felt guilty for wearing all of those religious symbols in A Level."

"That doesn't even make sense."

"Look, Jez," he said, grasping my arms and leaning in.

I flinched at his touch. He didn't seem to notice what he was doing. "I don't know why she came up on stage—if there was a way to help her, I would have, but that's impossible. Maybe you didn't know her as well as you thought you did. We're all walking a fine line. If you thought A Level was strict, University is worse. Only half of us will even graduate to O Level."

"Which is why you're trying to get rid of the competition?"

"Some might see it like that," he said, his hands still on my arms.

I looked down, and he seemed to remember himself. He dropped his hands, but then he took a step closer. Which was not good for me. I pressed further against the desk, but there was nowhere for me to go. If Sol wasn't an informer for the government, then why had Chalice told me not to talk to him? I had to find out what they'd talked about.

"What did you say to Chalice the other day?"

"I asked her what she knew about Clinicals," Sol said. "She hadn't heard the term before."

"Did you research it?" I asked, wondering if he had any idea what his nearness was doing to me—how I felt like I'd just been pushed near a blazing fire.

His eyes searched mine. "I didn't find anything, Jez."

"I'm sure the information is well hidden." It was impossible to keep the sarcasm out of my voice.

"You have to stop," he whispered, his eyes a dark gray tempest.

"Stop what?"

"Following me."

I let out a bitter laugh, not caring what he thought about my emotions. "You put me on your science team. So am I now messing up your perfect plan to becoming the student of the year? You're already the Examiner's favorite." I slid back onto the desk and sat, putting at least a little more space between us. "Were you talking about me on the stage? Telling him all my secrets?"

"You have secrets?"

I felt my face heat up. I couldn't tell if he was serious or teasing. Exasperated, I said, "Doesn't everyone?"

He stared at me, as if he could read exactly what I was thinking. "You have to stop talking to me, stop sending messages—"

"Give me one good reason, Sol." My voice shook with anger, but I didn't attempt to conceal it. "Why can't I talk to my friend?"

He closed his eyes. Good. He was exasperated. At least someone knew how I felt, if only marginally.

Sol opened his eyes, and I wasn't sure how to read his expression. The only way to describe it was maybe confusion. He touched my face, his fingers tracing my cheek, then he slid his hand behind my neck. This was different than anything he'd ever done—very different.

My heart nearly jumped out of my chest as his fingers stroked the back of my neck. He put his mouth next to my ear, his cheek against my cheek. I tried to pull away but my body refused to move. What was wrong with him? I was starting to get nervous. Scared, even.

"I don't know what's happening to me, Jez," he whispered, his fingers threading through my hair.

Goose bumps rose where he touched me and spread to my arms and legs. I couldn't answer. Couldn't breathe.

"All I know is that whenever you're in the room, I'm never close enough to you," he said. "When I don't see you, I think of nothing else. When you walk up to me in the corridor and make demands, all I want to do is . . ." He exhaled. "Jez?"

"What?" My voice sounded very far away. I felt frozen, but that was impossible because every inch of my body was burning up.

"Please stay away from me," he said in a pained voice.

I wrapped my arms around his neck and he pulled me to a standing position, tugging me against him.

Then the door slid open.

I was sitting on the desk, and Sol was standing three feet away from me in an instant.

Daniel entered.

"We've been waiting for you," Sol said, his voice perfectly calm and smooth.

How does he do that?

As for myself, I could hardly look at Daniel. I gave him a short nod and moved off the desk to sit in my chair.

If Daniel had seen anything, he didn't say so. The only indication that Sol had just been holding me was the way he stared at me now.

I could read his eyes like he could read my soul. His gaze was locked on me, but then he blinked, and it was gone—all gone—as if we'd been chatting about the science project and nothing more.

My body still tingled where we had touched. I tried to breathe normally, tried not to think of what Sol had said. It was beyond anything I'd ever considered before. What he'd said . . . what he'd implied . . . He was right. I did need to stay away from him.

CHAPTER 30

I stared at my tablet while Daniel, and then Serah, reported on their ideas. It was almost impossible to concentrate when all I could think about was being in Sol's arms. What would have happened if Daniel hadn't walked in? My mind spun and my body trembled as Sol's words replayed in my mind. *When I don't see you, I think of nothing else.* How could Sol feel that way about me? How could he feel like I did?

He wasn't a Clinical. After meeting Rueben, I should be able to spot them easier. So what had happened to Sol? How could he think those thoughts—and then confess them to me?

Perspiration broke out on my body as the voices of my team hummed around me. What did I do now? If Sol knew what I felt for him, where would that lead us? My hug hadn't been exactly innocent. I pushed out a breath, wishing I could disappear into my dorm room. It was awkward to try to carry on a conversation about science.

Finally I looked up to see Daniel's mouth moving.

"I considered Serah's idea about creating vegetable-flavored foods and thought we might start with sweet potato flavoring," Daniel said.

I suppressed a shudder as Daniel continued to talk about various vegetables and how we could inflict their flavors onto other foods like meat and dairy products. I didn't dare look over at Sol.

Serah nodded enthusiastically as Daniel talked. Finally, I glanced at Sol. My heart nearly stopped. He was watching me. Our gazes flicked away from each other, then back again. But his look didn't say "I miss you" so much as "can I trust her to keep her mouth shut?"

Serah took over next. "I thought it might be interesting to see if we can create a preservative that makes fish last longer."

I wrinkled my nose. My attention was finally diverted. Who needed fish to last longer? That was one food supply that we never lacked. The three of them discussed how much research we'd have to do to get the project started.

"You've been quiet," Serah said, looking at me.

I swallowed, audibly. Both guys were watching me as well. I took a deep breath, pushing away all thoughts of Sol's arms. "Why do we need to preserve fish? We aren't going to be running out. And . . ." I met the gazes focused on me. "Sweet potato-flavored anything sounds disgusting."

Daniel's jaw tightened, and Serah pressed her lips together. The only one who didn't look like he wanted to throw me out of the group was Sol. His voice was mellow when he said, "What are your ideas, Jezebel?"

So formal. With all three staring at me, I said, "What if we do something that actually benefits society? Makes a difference?" *Something that allows us to go to the C Level and find Chalice?*

Serah folded her arms.

Daniel jumped in. "Our ideas do make a difference. Preserving meat might not sound like a big deal right now, but it could have plenty of uses and—"

"Wait," Sol said, holding up a hand. "Let her finish."

My face flushed at the attention. I didn't want to argue, but I wanted answers about Chalice, and our science project might be a way to get some of them. "What if we cured a disease?"

Serah's mouth dropped open, and Daniel started to shake his head. Sol said, "Explain what you mean."

"Did you know there are diseases in the city actually killing people?" I said. "Ones that the scientists haven't been able to cure?"

Sol nodded. Of course. He knew pretty much all there was to know—all that we were allowed to know.

"Is this from the geology class earlier this morning?" Serah said.

"It got me thinking about it, yes," I said.

Daniel's voice cut in, suspicious. "What makes you think we could do something a group of skilled scientists aren't doing?"

He had a point. I'd mostly been considering the research we'd be able to do—that we'd *hopefully* be allowed to do—and not whether it would actually work. Although that would be obviously be a huge bonus. We'd all be named students of the year and I'd advance to O Level and get the security clearances I needed to find the generators.

"Many diseases in the . . ." I dropped my voice, "the Before were cured entirely, but what if there are links between them and the new diseases? We could study the old ones and track the similarities. Maybe some of the same medications will cross over."

"Don't you think the scientists have already tried that?" Serah said.

"I have no idea what they've tried or haven't tried," I said in a quietly. "That information hasn't been available for us to research. But if we could find even one thing that might help the scientists cure diseases, don't you think that would be of more value than sweet potato yogurt?"

Everyone was quiet for a couple of minutes; Serah looked like she'd decided never to speak to me again. Daniel didn't appear convinced, but Sol looked interested.

"We could at least request permission to do research on the current diseases and see what we're up against," Sol finally said.

I wanted to hug Sol. Again. Our eyes met and I looked away, guilt seeping through me.

Sol continued to discuss the timelines and when we'd have to meet next. Serah was out the door quickly, without saying good-bye to anyone. Daniel left a couple of minutes later after talking to Sol about one of their shared classes.

Then it was just the two of us again. I thought my heart would pound out of my chest. I didn't know what to say. I was too afraid I'd confess every thought and feeling I had about him. And now that I knew he felt the same way, I was consumed by tangible fear. This was real. This could change our entire lives. This could end them as well. Maybe I could act as if it hadn't happened. Maybe he regretted that it did. I kept my eyes on my tablet when I said, "Thanks for agreeing to at least consider my idea."

He didn't answer. When I looked up, he was staring down at his desk.

"Sol?"

He didn't move. I stood and crossed to him, wanting to touch him, but not daring to. He looked up, his eyes haunted.

I didn't want to ask, but did anyway. "What's wrong?"

He shook his head, standing from his chair, putting plenty of distance between us. "It's a great project, Jez," he said. "I don't think anyone's attempted anything like it—at least at our level."

"But what?" I prompted, breathing a little easier.

"I know why you're doing this," he whispered.

I waited, wondering if he really did.

He kept his voice quiet. "You want to do field research—visit the C level people—find Chalice."

I flinched. "Maybe."

"It's too dangerous, Jez," he said.

"*Everything* is dangerous," I whispered, tears rushing to my eyes. My voice felt raw when I added, "Just the two of us in the room alone together is dangerous."

He stared at me for a moment. "More dangerous than you know." It was as if his words had physically touched me. The back of my neck was on fire, and the room was suddenly too hot. But he didn't come any closer.

"Do you think it's possible to cure a disease?" I asked, moving the topic away from us.

"If it wasn't possible, then the scientists wouldn't bother trying." He held my gaze. I wanted to look away, but I couldn't. I wanted to step into his arms and hear him tell me again how he felt about me.

"Okay, then," I said, slowly, to stop the building tremor in my voice. "I guess we'll see what we can research."

I walked toward the door, feeling as if I were wading through thick mud. I had to force one foot in front of the other.

"Jez?" Sol said.

I stopped, but didn't turn, not wanting to see that look in his eyes. The one where he looked tortured and confused at the same time.

"I'm sorry for what I said earlier. It's not fair to you." He paused, and I waited with my back to him. So he was taking it back. I waited for him to finish. "You know I'll always protect you. I won't be the cause of you getting into trouble."

That was it. He wouldn't let this go any further. It was one slipup, one confession, and now it was over. I took a deep breath, when all I wanted to do was scream, and slowly turned around. "I can take care of myself, Sol." Tears splashed onto my cheeks. "Remember, I'm the one who hugged you."

He rubbed the back of his neck, looking tired and defeated. "But if Daniel hadn't come in . . ."

I waited for him to continue. He closed his eyes for a second and let out a sigh. Finally he opened them, his expression determined. "It won't happen again. I promise you." His eyes searched mine. I didn't know what he wanted me to say.

I wanted to cry and shout at him for ruining our friendship. But mostly, I wanted to hold him and be held by him and tell him how I felt the same way. But I knew that would only make it harder. For me. Whatever Sol was battling against, and however this came upon him, I felt it even more deeply.

I left the room. Sol didn't follow, and the door slid shut between us.

CHAPTER 31

M aybe I should request to be altered. Maybe I should
leave the University.

The night crept by and still I didn't sleep. I
couldn't get Sol out of my mind. Was his Harmony implant
no longer working? Did he have . . . feelings? Or was this
some sort of cruel test?

I let out a sigh and turned over, resting my head on the
inside of my arm. In spite of all the times I'd dreamed about
it, I never thought that Sol would actually say those things to
me. I closed my eyes, remembering how he was in A Level.
Always friendly and seeming to understand me. Had he felt
the same way then, and assumed it would go away when we
were Separated? Did he feel as much for me as I felt for him?

But *I* was always the one who was adamant about
following the rules. He'd been to Detention a few times. Now
that I thought about it, though, the reasons for his
Detentions—things like, *I slept in and missed class*—had

sounded like reasonable excuses at the time but I didn't know for sure whether they were the truth.

Could he be a Clinical? I dismissed that idea immediately. If he'd been a Clinical, wouldn't he have been put through testing like me?

Or maybe he was much better at hiding it than I was. I thought of the risk he took telling me about the Before. I thought of how smart he was, how easily he learned, and how he seemed to never forget a detail. Was it possible for someone to be as gifted as him and not have the full scope of emotions to complement his intellect?

Maybe that's why he was trying so hard to impress the professors. He was trying to keep their attention on his knowledge and not his emotions.

Of all people, Sol would know the danger in having feelings for me. He'd be able to study each angle and reason out in his mind to arrive at exactly why he shouldn't even be speaking to me. That he had failed and let his feelings get in the way was uncharacteristic.

I blew out a breath and pulled my blanket over my shoulders. The way he had looked at me, and the things he'd said, caused me to shiver in a way that made me warm to my toes.

When I'd hugged him, he'd immediately responded, as if he'd been waiting a long time to hold me. Our bodies had fit together perfectly, and for an instant I felt safe, like I had nothing to worry about.

I clenched the top of the blanket to my chin, and my breathing came fast. I ached all over. Ached to see him. Ached to wrap my arms around his neck again.

For a moment, I didn't place any blame on my grandmother for breaking the rules. But she'd been executed for it. I clenched my hands together and suppressed a scream of frustration. My eyes burned with unshed tears as I tried to push everything Sol out of my mind.

Our project was approved by one of the science professors, Dr. Luke. My science group met together every few days to discuss additional bits of research. Sol and I kept a careful distance from each other, maybe overdoing it, but it seemed to work.

Yet each night I clutched my blanket around me as if it could somehow replace Sol's arms, and had to talk myself into sleeping. It was impossible that Sol was experiencing emotions like I was. But if he did experience even mild emotions, they would seem overwhelming to him. That was the answer. Somehow his implant had lost its potency. The emotions he felt were confusing, and since we were close in A Level, he automatically focused them on me.

I breathed easier when I arrived at that conclusion. Now I just had to worry about how I reacted to him. I had to find a way to suppress the desire I had to be around him and to hear him repeat every word he spoke.

The weeks passed slowly as I tried to put distance between myself and Sol.

My restriction was lifted, but I now had no cause to break curfew. Sol had kept his commitment and there was no communication between us except for in our science group. It was just as well, and with diligence, I hoped to forget that anything had happened between us at all.

Today, Sol watched me enter the class right before our science group. He looked tired, with dark circles under his eyes and his face unusually pale. My first instinct was to ask him what was wrong, to take care of him in some way, but I pushed those thoughts away. As I sat at my desk, his eyes were on me. My heart flipped, but I chastised myself and quickly looked away, focusing instead on Serah and Daniel.

Sol was probably fine, and I wasn't going to even think about him today. I didn't waste any time presenting the information I'd put together. "Dr. Luke authorized us to view an image of a skin disease that might be a good candidate for our research." I pulled up an image on my tablet.

Serah's eyes widened as she studied the raised dots that ran along a woman's leg. "What is it called?"

"It's similar to what used to be called eczema," I said. "A skin condition that is prevalent in the C Level workers who spend every day working with hot water."

"And how is this deadly?" Daniel asked.

"The rash itself is only an irritation," I said. "Dr. Luke said those who carry the rash are more likely to suffer from River Fever, and it's more common in women than men."

Sol looked down at the notes I had forwarded to everyone. "The River Fever kills about one percent of the C Level population each year."

"Those are the numbers from a few years ago," I said. "I've requested to get current numbers and should have those any day. But whether it's one percent or higher, it might be something we can prevent if we find a cure for the rash itself."

Sol appraised me, his tired eyes actually looking impressed.

I hoped he wasn't becoming ill, but I quickly dismissed my concern. I'd kept my part of the agreement, and we hadn't spent any time together outside of this science group. I always arrived just a few minutes late so that I wouldn't have to face Sol alone, and I made sure that I was the first one to leave.

During the three weeks since Sol had told me we had to stop talking, I felt the distance widen between us each day. I should have been relieved. It hadn't become easier for me, but I trusted that it was for him.

After we discussed our ideas for curing the rash that preceded River Fever, I made it a point to be the first one to leave the room, Serah right behind me. Over the past couple of weeks, she had softened toward me and was actually actively interested in the project now.

"Wait, Jez," Sol's voice called behind me.

I paused at the door as Daniel and Serah filed past.

The door slid shut, and I stayed by it.

"Can I talk to you outside?"

I hesitated. *Now* he wanted to talk to me? What did he have to say that he was worried about being overheard in the classroom? This was definitely going against our agreement. I slipped out the door, not looking behind to see if he was following. Exiting the building, I walked around the corner, and stood under an awning. It was dark outside; streetlamps lit the way back to the dorm buildings. I was in plain sight of anyone passing by, but the campus seemed quiet—most students were inside somewhere out of the rain.

Buttoning my jacket against the cool air, I waited for Sol. A few minutes later, he came around the corner.

"I just wanted to say thanks," Sol said as he approached.

I folded my arms and peered at him through the shadow cast by the awning. "So you had to tell me out here?"

"It's too risky inside. I don't want anyone to . . . walk in on us."

239

I didn't exactly believe his answer, but I decided to let him finish whatever he wanted to say.

"I want to apologize for being so brusque before, too," he said. "I don't want you to feel like this is your fault in any way, when it's mine. You're just being yourself, your friend self." His voice was low against the sound of rain tapping the awning overhead. He took a step forward, his eyes holding mine.

My heart hammered. *Don't come any closer.* I couldn't look away from the dark gray in his eyes.

"I don't want you to worry about me," Sol said. "I'm not going to say any more crazy things or break any rules."

"That's good to hear." I wished he wouldn't look so serious, so pained.

He shoved his hands in his jacket pockets and straightened. "I'm pulling myself off of this project."

"Why?" I was shocked. Sol was a key member of our group, and without him and his relationships with the instructors, I didn't know if we would succeed.

"Because it's not getting easier," he whispered. "It's getting worse."

The rhythm of my heart changed at the soulful look in his eyes. I was grateful for the darkness because I was sure my cheeks were turning red. "But I haven't been following you or sending messages; we barely speak."

"I know." He looked away. "It's for the best—for both of us."

He was right, but I didn't want him to be. "How do you know it's best?" I couldn't breathe right. "Maybe I can help you."

He looked at me, his brows drawn together. "Don't you understand? I can't be around you—it only makes it worse."

"Sol, I've had . . . emotions since I was born. My caretakers taught me how to suppress them. I didn't know until I went to prison that there was a name for it—"

"You told me. You're a Clinical. But I can't found any information about them." His voice sounded as frustrated as I felt inside. "How do you know that you were told the truth?"

"It makes more sense than anything else, at least for me," I said. "For you, I think the only other explanation is that your Harmony implant is no longer effective."

Sol tilted his head, watching me closely. "Do you think I'm a Clinical?"

"I don't think so," I said slowly. "You would have been struggling with emotions since childhood." I hesitated. "How long have you been . . . feeling like this?"

He didn't have to think about it. "Since I met you."

I looked away from his absorbing gaze, trying to let the information sink in. We'd been friends for over a year. This wasn't going to be as easy to explain as I thought. "Are you sure?" I said, not daring to meet his eyes.

"I thought I was going crazy at first. I watched you even when you weren't watching me, just to see if you felt the same way."

My chest felt like it might explode. He shouldn't be saying these things to me.

"You were always different, Jez," he continued while I remained silent. "And it's not because you're a Clinical, or whatever you call yourself. It's because you're *you.*"

If it was *me*, then maybe he was right, maybe it would be better if he left the project.

"I thought it might get easier," he said in a subdued voice. "After the Separation. But it hasn't." He took a step toward me. There was nowhere for me to back up. "No matter how you define it, or explain it away, I know what this really is."

"What?" I whispered, my heart beating so hard that I thought I might not hear his next words.

"I've fallen in love with you."

CHAPTER 32

stared in horror at Sol. "There must be a cure." But even as I said it, my heart was soaring. He said he loved me—it was what I'd hoped for, and never thought possible. But I couldn't let this happen, and I couldn't let him know what I felt in return. Our lives depended on it.

If anyone found out what he'd just admitted to me, he would be Taken. Not sent to Detention, or Demoted. Taken. His life cycle would end. Forever.

I wouldn't let that happen.

"I can only think of one cure," he said.

"You're wrong. You don't have to be Taken. There are ways to stop your emotions." I looked around to see if anyone was coming toward the building, but everything was quiet. I turned back to Sol, to find him watching me.

"Should I ask to be altered?" he asked.

"No," I said in a rush. "It's still an experimental science, and some people can't tolerate being altered." I had never told him how we reversed Chalice's altering. That was definitely not an exact science and I didn't know if it could be duplicated.

"I can't put you in danger," he said in a dull voice. "I'm willing to pay for myself, but what if you're incriminated as well?"

It was possible—highly possible. It wasn't as if I hadn't thought of it from all angles, especially after reading Rose's journal. I had never expected to deal with Sol's feelings, just mine, and this was worse—infinitely worse. "Just stop thinking about it, Sol," I said, pleading now. "Forget what you just said to me. You look like you haven't slept, and you'll get sick if you don't take care of yourself."

"Sleep is the last thing on my mind." He lifted his head to look at me and spread out his hands. "I thought if I left the project, it would help. But now . . . I think the only solution is for me to leave the University."

"No," I said, shaking my head. "I can't let you to do that. If anyone leaves, it should be me."

"Don't say that, Jez" he said. "You didn't ask for this. It's me, all me."

I bit my lip, gazing at him as my eyes burned. "Sol—" my voice broke.

We stared at each other. We stood a couple of feet apart, but it felt there were only inches between us.

"What if . . ." he whispered, "What if the rules could be changed?"

"That's impossible." I thought of the Council of Judges that I'd been sentenced by. The entire government was based on rules that were set up to protect the city from itself, and everyone had to follow rules or our society would fall apart. The rules were essential to our survival until more land mass was created. Otherwise the List of Failures would take over. I had read my grandmother's journal. There was no mercy.

"Serah and Daniel thought that curing a disease would be impossible," he said. "I wondered about it myself at first. But here we all are, trying something that we thought would never work." He paused, moved closer, and lowered his voice even more. "*You* believed in the impossible. You came up with the idea."

He was standing too close to me. I couldn't think straight. I wanted to touch his face and erase the tiredness from his eyes.

"That's the difference between you and me," he continued. "I might know every lesson ever taught to us, but you want to make things better for everyone. You care about others whereas I . . . I care only about you."

I stared at him as the sound of rain grew louder against the awning. I suddenly hated the rain. If it hadn't started raining, then our society wouldn't be slowly dying and none of us would be in this mess. I swallowed hard. "Sol, you have to learn to care about yourself." I took a small step to the side. One more step and I'd be standing in the rain. "You can learn to forget me. You can learn to control your emotions like I have."

His hand touched mine; I hadn't realized how close he was. I hadn't moved far enough away. His touch sent a shiver through me; I wanted to run through the rain back to the dorm while at the same time holding him close.

"Don't leave the University," I begged, selfish panic overtaking me. "You're the most promising student." I couldn't tell him my other reasons.

"If I stay I'll eventually become like them," he said. "Unfeeling, uncaring. Ruthless. I saw the way you looked at me when you found out I turned in the cult members. I don't want you seeing me like that." His voice softened. "But you . . . the Legislature needs someone like you. *You* should stay."

I shook my head. This wasn't happening. I couldn't believe we were having this conversation, couldn't believe what Sol wanted to give up. "The government needs your mind, Sol. You're smarter than half our professors. It would be a waste if you worked at a lower level." I took a deep breath and continued, "Besides, I can't be the only brilliant scientist."

"Jez, finish the science project," he said in an urgent voice. "Visit the C Level population. Help find a cure. Find Chalice. Bring her back to the University. They'll listen to you when you win the science competition. They'll grant your request—"

"You have to stay here, help me finish the project," I cut in, trying to keep my voice steady. I met his gaze, and his eyes seemed lighter, with pale blue-green mixed in with the gray. Like the sky right before the Solstice.

He shook his head, and I remembered how his eyes had moistened when he'd talked about his caretakers in the school yard. Sol might not be a true Clinical, but he felt emotion, somehow. "I don't know how you've suppressed your emotions for so long. I feel like I'm going to break in half if I don't do something about it."

I looked around quickly. Seeing no one, I grabbed his hand. "Sol, let me help you. This is manageable. Please don't leave the University." I grasped his other hand, and whispered, "Please don't leave me."

He closed his eyes as we stood hand in hand. I didn't dare move. Didn't dare wonder what might happen if I buried my face against his chest and wrapped my arms around him.

When his eyes opened, they were wet. "This is goodbye, Jez."

"No," I said, tightening my grip on his hands.

Instead of pulling back, he leaned forward. His lips pressed against my tear-stained cheek.

"Don't leave," I said, wrapping my arms around his neck, taking a risk in the shadows.

He held me for a few seconds, his face buried against my neck. It wasn't a fierce or possessive hug like the one in the classroom, but one of someone who'd already given up. All too soon, he released me. One of his hands smoothed my hair back. "I care about you too much to jeopardize anything."

I took a staggered breath. "Just give it some more time." I held back a sob. "Leave the science group, but stay at the University." He clenched his jaw, but I pressed on, "Please. If it doesn't work then you can leave the University."

After a long moment of avoiding my gaze, he said, "All right."

Relief poured through me. I wouldn't see Sol at the science group, but at least he wasn't throwing his intellect away on a lower society level. This also meant we probably wouldn't have a chance to talk for a long time after this, if ever again.

He was already turning away when I stopped him with a question. "Before you go, can you tell me if you ever saw a picture of when it first started to rain?"

"No images," Sol said, "But my caretaker's grandfather had some news reports on the origins of the Burning."

I held my breath, listening.

247

"It wasn't the people who started the Burning, Jez." Sol looked directly at me. "They're the ones who stopped it."

"But the people were the ones who cleansed the evil from the earth," I said. The rain had increased, and now it dripped from the awning, splashing near our feet.

"No," Sol said. "My caretaker's grandfather told me that when it didn't stop raining, the governments of the different nations turned to scientists for answers. Global warming was among the topics debated."

"My grandmother's book talked about the meteorologists holding international meetings," I said.

"That sounds about right. But no scientist or meteorologist could come up with a satisfactory explanation and it only continued to rain. Every day . . . Are you sure you want to hear this?"

I nodded, a pit in my stomach, but I wanted to know.

He looked nervous now as he glanced around. "The religious zealots were the ones to be executed by the governments."

My stomach lurched. "For not stopping the rain?"

"For not finding the cause." His eyes were on me again, gauging my reaction.

"My grandmother's book said that criminals were killed—it didn't say anything about religious zealots."

"She may have not known. News was getting harder and harder to come by with the devastating floods."

I nodded. He was probably right, but that didn't make it any easier to stomach.

"The zealots said that God was punishing the people—that the earth had been cursed."

"So their god made it rain?" I stared at Sol.

"Yes. According to the zealots, God was making it

flood." After several heartbeats of silence, he said, "They thought God would stop the rain if they could get rid of all evil and sin."

Just the fact I stood here, in rain that hadn't stopped in forty years, was proof enough that the zealots had been wrong. "But why attack the zealots? It wasn't their fault. It wasn't anyone's fault."

"Science and religion have always been at odds—but the world was big enough to contain both in the Before," he said.

"Until it started to flood," I said.

"Until the world started to shrink, and the scientists took over, eventually becoming the Legislature."

I let out a breath, trying to comprehend it all. My mind was spinning.

"When the Legislature formed, new rules were put into place to protect the diminishing population," he said. "There wasn't room for disobedience."

"And those who disobeyed were executed," I finished.

"Yes," he said, his voice quiet. "Like your grandmother." His hand brushed my cheek. "Jez . . . I'd better go."

My eyes stung with tears. "All right." I reached for his arm, but he moved back.

"Goodbye, Jezebel." He stepped into the rain, walking backward for a few steps, then he turned away.

He walked to the corner of the building, and then he was gone. I closed my eyes, seeing his gray eyes and feeling his final touch on my cheek long after he'd disappeared. It took everything I had not to follow him, not to run after him and beg him to stay.

I'd seen the pain in his eyes—the confusion, the hopelessness. He was truly afraid, and I knew what that was like.

Tears sprung up again, and I wiped at them furiously. Maybe he'd change his mind. Maybe he'd show up to our science group tomorrow after he had a chance to consider it.

I was shivering in the cold. The rain was now a full downpour, and my shoes were soaked, my feet numb. Still, I couldn't move. I wanted to stay in this spot—the place where I'd last touched Sol.

I probably would have stood there for hours if the message icon on my tablet hadn't lit up. It was from Sol. My finger hesitated over it, not sure if I could handle whatever he had to say.

Finally I opened the message and read: *Sorry*.

One single word. Nothing more.

CHAPTER 33

I n my dorm room, I stared at the final message from Sol until my eyes slid shut from exhaustion. I couldn't bring myself to delete it. It had been five days since I'd last seen him. He never showed up for the science group, and although I tried to catch glimpses of him coming in or out of the men's buildings, I didn't see him anywhere. I knew he was around, but he'd obviously been careful to avoid me completely.

I kept the rose stone Sol had given me in my pocket now. It was the only way that I could make him real. He might have found a way to avoid me, but all I had to do was touch the rose stone, and I felt him near.

Daniel and Serah were totally mystified about why Sol had been taken off the project. To avoid their speculation, I spent every spare moment in the chemistry lab, concocting various creams using plant leaves delivered from the Agricultural Center—anything that might treat River Fever.

251

The University had given us clearance to start a test group in two weeks. We would go to one of the C Level training centers, and ten women would be assigned to try our ointment.

So far the forerunner was the Lemon Balm plant. Its small jagged green leaves made a nice oily pulp that was surprisingly cool and moisturizing on the skin. But even with the science project moving forward, each minute and each hour thoughts of Sol battled inside me as I worried and wondered how he was doing.

I checked the news reports to see if any information came through. But there were only the standard reports on weather and the status of certain criminals. I had sent him a couple of short messages, but there had been no reply.

It was as if he'd disappeared.

The morning arrived that we'd be leaving for the C Level training center. I woke early and slipped out into the corridor. It was nice to be able to come and go as I pleased, but my freedom from restriction was only bittersweet. Everything inside of me ached. Everything wanted to see Sol, if only to know he was all right, that he was working on controlling his emotions.

I met Daniel and Serah at the University entrance where Dr. Luke joined us a few minutes later. We carried our vials of batch #12 cream, made primarily from lemon balm leaves and watercress, in a satchel, ready to be distributed and administered to our test subjects. Each woman would report in at the end of each day with her progress.

As the four of us climbed onto a tram that would take us

to the training center, my stomach was in knots. The last time I'd been on a tram, Sol was sitting next to me. How he'd managed to avoid me for so many weeks, I had no idea. A couple of times I thought I'd seen him from a distance, but it always turned out to be someone else.

Dr. Luke sat across from us, absorbed in whatever he was reading on his tablet. Serah and Daniel were quiet, staring out the windows as the tram sped through the streets.

It was just barely raining, a mist really, and the streets were bare. Everyone was at work, fulfilling one more day of assignments in order to make it to the next. At one stop, a couple of officials climbed on. They looked in our direction, but when they saw us traveling with a professor, their interest waned.

I had lived in the B Level district my whole childhood and had never been to the C Level areas. The factories and housing units sped by as we descended one hill after another. I hadn't realized how close the C Level streets were to the ocean.

Serah and Daniel both sat straight up. "Look at that," Daniel said, pointing out the window across from us.

Since the rain was so light today, it seemed the fog had lifted as well. From our seats we could see beyond the rivers and the massive docks, out to the ocean.

The ocean was a dark gray mass, churning angrily, with white caps cresting the waves. I stood and crossed to the window.

There were boats everywhere. Everything from rudimentary rafts to the sleek black vehicles belonging to officials. Large fishing vessels moved slowly through the water, the rails covered with seagulls that stood wing to wing.

"I've never seen the ocean this close up," Serah said.

"Neither have I." I exhaled in amazement. The clarity of the day showed just how big it really was.

The tram continued to move toward the ocean. I thought of Rueben arriving at the docks and trying to find a way across. Where had he gone? There weren't any Lake Towns within sight. It was like heading into a vast nothingness.

Serah touched my arm. "Look over there." I followed her direction. A cluster of officials stood together on a dock. A raft-type boat bobbed in the water a couple of dozen paces away, like it was coming into the dock. But the officials had formed a barricade, blocking it.

Dr. Luke turned to look. "Those must be Lake People." He shook his head. "They'll never be allowed to dock."

I stared through the window, trying to get a better glimpse of the people on the raft. There were four people, two of them quite young—children who were maybe five or six.

The tram turned a corner, and I lost sight of them for a moment. Through gaps in buildings, I could see that one of the Lake People, a tall man, was standing in the raft, his fist raised.

"What do they want?" Serah asked Dr. Luke.

He was reading something on his tablet again. Without looking up, he said, "Now that they are over the disappointment of not being allowed to enter the city, they're probably begging for food."

My heart ached. I thought of the desperate people who had come all that way. The tram slowed and came to a stop in front of a building that blocked the view of the ocean.

Dr. Luke looked up. "We're here. Gather your things."

We each picked up our satchels and followed the

professor off the tram. I hoped for another glance at what was happening out on the water. "Do the officials ever give in and offer some food?"

Dr. Luke shook his head. "They would be foolish to do so." He glanced at me, probably surprised by my questions.

I fell silent. I didn't want the professor to wonder about me too much.

We arrived at the training center and entered a narrow room with beige walls and beige floors. Metal chairs lined the walls, and there was nothing in the center but a single table. I wondered what type of training took place here. No one was in the room yet, and Dr. Luke told us to sit down and wait.

The professor disappeared through a door, and Serah and Daniel took a seat. I crossed to the windows to see the ocean again. The rain had picked up, making the view hazier than before. The officials had abandoned their barricade, and the raft of Lake People was nowhere to be seen.

Dr. Luke entered, followed by ten women. They all wore gray or blue shirts and pants. Their hair was cropped short to their scalps. They might have looked like men, but for their delicate features, and they were all quite thin. It was their smell that surprised me—like spoiled food.

One woman glanced at me, her eyes bright with curiosity. I nodded in a friendly way, and she quickly looked away.

They sat along the wall, their hands clasped and their expressions blank for the most part. They all seemed oblivious that we'd come to help. I wondered what their skills were and what sort of jobs they did.

Daniel launched into an explanation of the treatment we were giving them. The women seemed a bit more interested after that. Serah asked the women to pull up their sleeves. I winced as the women revealed arms covered in irritated red rashes. It looked much more painful in person than in the image I'd seen.

Serah handed the ointment samples out to the women and I followed behind, demonstrating how to apply it. I held my breath more than once, trying to grow accustomed to how the women smelled. No one met my eyes as I worked.

Daniel wrote down the names of each woman and a few details about them as Serah and I helped the women one by one. I asked the first woman what her job was. She glanced at me for an instant then lowered her head. Why wasn't she answering? I knew she'd heard me.

When I moved on to the second woman, I tried not to gasp. Her skin was worse than the first woman's, with red welts raised high above her skin. When I applied the ointment, she winced, but didn't pull away.

"Where do you work?" I asked her.

She seemed less reserved, or maybe more intelligent than the first woman. "We boil 'n preserve vegetables."

"Is it hard work?" I asked.

She gave me a strange look as if she didn't understand the question.

When I finished, I moved onto the next woman, the one who'd seemed curious when she first came into the room. "Do all of you work with food?" I asked.

She nodded. I was surprised to see how green her eyes were.

I lowered my voice and asked, "Do you know a woman named Chalice?"

The woman opened her mouth to answer, and I was appalled to see that she had several broken teeth in her mouth. Weren't the C Level people taught to care for their teeth?

"Who wants t' know?" the woman whispered back, seeming to understand I didn't want to be overheard.

"She used to be at the University with me. She was Demoted."

The woman's eyes glimmered. She actually looked excited. There was more emotion on her face then all the other women put together. "We don't 'ave any University people on my team. No one's new." She glanced over at the other women, but they didn't seem to be paying attention. "When someone's Demoted, it takes 'em a while to recover from punishment."

"Punishment?" Wasn't living under the conditions these women were in punishment enough? I looked down the row of women, seeing anew their damaged skin, limp hair, pale complexions, thin bodies, and expressionless eyes.

The woman laughed, actually laughed. No one seemed to notice—perhaps they were used to this woman's display of behavior. "Never 'eard about the punishments, eh?" Her voice remained low, so I had to stay close to hear, even though my nose wrinkled at her odor. "Maybe less of you'd break rules if you knew 'bout the punishments." She gave me a broken-toothed grin.

"What type of punishments?"

Her green eyes brightened. "Break you hard . . . s'you don't get any mighty ideas of moving up to no higher level."

I shivered. *Break you hard* . . . Serah was nearly finished with her five women. I had fallen behind. I wanted to question the woman further, but I settled for asking, "If you see my friend Chalice, can you let me know in your report?"

The woman gazed at me, distrust in her eyes.

"I'll bring you a gift next time—something from the University," I said.

The woman's eyes brightened, but still she looked like she was considering.

"My name is Jezebel," I said. "What's yours?"

She hesitated, then finally said, "Ruth."

"Thank you, Ruth." I touched her hand, and she raised her brows.

I moved onto the next woman and hurried to catch up with Serah. When I finished with the others, Serah and Daniel were waiting for me.

Daniel went through the reporting procedure until all the women seemed to understand. The official who'd accompanied them agreed to help them if there were any problems. We watched the women leave the room, their little packets of cream in their hands. Just before stepping through the door, Ruth looked back at me.

We followed the professor out the way we'd come, and I slowed when the ocean came into view. There seemed to be even more boats now, all heading in different directions, but no sign of the raft. Fog had crept in, clinging to the edges of the docks. Soon, the afternoon would fade to dark, and it would be impossible to see the ocean.

As pre-approved by the University board, we'd be allowed to visit our test subjects in two more weeks. They'd fill out their reports daily, and on the fourteenth day, we'd complete our observations and record the progress in person.

On the tram ride back to the University, I stared out the window at the gray, hardly processing the passing buildings. I couldn't get what Ruth had said about the Demoted out of my mind. What kind of punishments were they subjected to? Were they sent to an experimental lab like I had been? Were they altered?

My eyes stung. I missed Chalice, and knowing what might be happening to her made me want to find her all the more. Was it true what Sol said? That if this science project was successful, I might be able to make a special request?

But if Chalice was 'broken' and had no desire to return to a higher level, or was incapable of it . . . I shuddered. I'd seen her when she was altered—she hadn't remembered me then.

Would she remember anything now?

CHAPTER 34

We were nearing the University when the tram came to an abrupt stop. Daniel, Serah, and I jerked forward. Dr. Luke looked up from his tablet, bracing himself against his seat.

Two officials stepped onto the tram, carrying small transponders. The tram was nearly full with passengers by now. At each stop farther from the ocean, more and more people had boarded.

The serious look on the officials' faces told me not to ask any questions. They approached each person, holding the transponders to each shoulder and scanning their Harmony implants.

They were identifying us.

They were looking for someone.

My heart raced as the officials moved through the crowd, starting on the opposite side of the tram from where I sat, checking Harmony implants one by one. I heard Serah

260

inhale sharply next to me, and Daniel was gripping the sides of his seat, his hands turning blotchy red and white. If I didn't know any better, I'd think both of them were afraid. And then I started noticing other people's reactions. Most were dead calm, but a handful looked genuinely nervous.

Had Rueben been right? Were there Clinicals all over the city? Did some of these people, like me, have a secret they were worried about being uncovered?

As the officials moved to the middle of the tram, my mouth went dry. I looked out the window toward the University. Even from a block away, I could see that there was a crowd gathered in front of the gates.

Something big was happening. They must be looking for someone connected with the University. I looked at the people inside the tram.

One official stopped in front of our professor across the aisle and held up the transponder. For a split second, I thought I saw a trace of nervousness cross Dr. Luke's brow, but it was gone as quickly as it'd come.

"What's going on?" Serah whispered next to me. "Why are they blocking the University entrance?"

"I don't know," I whispered back, but dread had pooled in my stomach. The officials were getting closer. Then, on the outskirts of the crowd, I saw Sol. His tall form stood out clearly among the officials. He wore a black coat, matching his dark hair. It looked as if he'd been standing in the rain for a while with no umbrella or hood.

And he was staring right at the tram.

My throat tightened. Did he know which tram I was on? Was he with the officials on another manhunt like he'd been for the cult members?

Fear surged through me. Everyone on the tram had

noticed the crowd at the University by now and had started to murmur, their voices questioning.

I glanced over at the officials. They had moved on from our professor; who had returned to looking almost bored. Had I imagined his anxiety?

One of the officials reached Daniel. Soon it would be my turn. My hands felt slippery with perspiration.

Everything seemed to slow as I thought about what they could possibly arrest me for. I'd done some research, yes, but it was all explainable under the guise of science project. I had kept every curfew and every rule for weeks. Besides, anything else might be a test, right?

I had controlled my emotions, and if anyone knew what Sol had said to me, he wouldn't be out in that crowd. The transponder readout must have been satisfactory for Daniel because now the official was moving onto someone else.

Instinctively, I scooted away from Serah and sidestepped my way toward the door. Sol was still watching the tram, his eyes so focused that I imagined he could see right through the metal sides and into my heart.

No matter how I tried to talk myself out of it, I was sure this had something to do with me. Had I asked Ruth too many questions? Had they found Rueben, and he named me as an accomplice after all? Or had Sol confessed his secret to the University and they were waiting to arrest us together?

I slipped through the people as slowly as possible, trying to avoid attracting any attention. The doors to the tram now stood open, but there were several officials just outside, their eyes searching for something. Or someone.

I froze. It would be impossible to leave the tram. I looked up the street again. Sol was on the other side of it now, standing near a building. Our eyes met, and I knew for sure he'd seen me this time.

The tram started up suddenly, and the officials shouted for it to stop. We were thrown against each other as the tram jerked to a stop again. I used the jostling to move to the other side of the tram, hoping I could escape the transponder reading. One of the officials announced, "If you've been cleared you can leave. This tram is now out of service."

I moved with those leaving, my heart pounding so hard in my ears that I couldn't decipher the conversations around me. One glance behind told me that Serah had noticed my escape. She stared after me, her eyes hard and small.

I turned from her quickly, hoping to get off before she could alert anyone. Sol was watching me climb off the tram. I met his gaze and wished that I could ask him what was happening. He gave me a slight nod and then suddenly disappeared into the group of officials. Where had he gone? Was he going to turn me in now?

I exhaled and continued walking toward the University, relieved my implant hadn't been read, but knowing there was really no place to hide now. They could find me in my room or track me.

More people were leaving the tram, and we moved as a unit toward the University gates. It looked as if the officials had set up check points to evaluate each person before entering. I could see another tram beyond the University, facing the opposite direction. It had been detained as well. People were coming off that tram and being divided up, some of them ushered to the gates.

I glanced behind me. I couldn't see Daniel or Serah yet, or even Dr. Luke. I didn't know what I'd say to explain my actions to Serah. I was now about half a block from the University gates, and didn't know what to do. If I was who they were looking for, I'd surely be caught at the next check point.

Everything in my body screamed to run, but there was nowhere to go. I tried to keep my pace normal, acting as if I had no worries.

Then I saw Sol. He was coming straight toward me, threading his way against the crowd. I didn't know whether to get out of his way or to wait and face him. There was no expression in his eyes as he walked toward me, but he stared straight at me.

It was starting to grow dark and the twilight hour was a dirty gray as the rain drizzled from the endless clouds above.

Then Sol took a hard right, straight into an alley between two buildings.

I nearly stopped walking, but forced myself to move. He had been looking right at me before he turned. Did he want me to follow him?

My stomach gripped as I tried to decide what to do.

As the crowd moved past the alley, I turned and went into it, too. I didn't dare look behind me. Up ahead, Sol was nearing the end of the alley. Without looking back, he turned toward the right.

I hurried down the narrow street, wanting to run, but if I were caught I'd have to come up with some explanation and running wouldn't help my case.

When I reached the end of the alley, Sol was nearly half a block ahead of me down the small tree-lined street. It was the neighborhood where the professors lived and in between the apartment buildings were small parks filled with trees and unused benches. Some architect had been overly optimistic that anyone would actually use these areas in the drizzling rain. The ones in the B section had been renovated into more apartment buildings years ago.

Sol's dark jacket disappeared in the foliage up ahead. I

slowed my step even more and glanced around. The street was empty; it seemed all the excitement was reserved for the University.

I moved toward the spot where he'd disappeared. I kept glancing around as I approached the area, expecting officials to burst through the alley at any moment, or for a professor to come out of his apartment building and question me.

With a deep breath, I crossed the street and stepped into the trees. The street lamps hadn't come on yet, and in between the trees it was as dark as night.

Something grabbed my hand. I gasped. "Sol?"

His other hand was on my waist. I inhaled sharply as my heart stuttered. "What are you doing? What's going on?"

"I had to talk to you," he whispered, his mouth close to my ear.

I shivered, not from cold, but from his nearness. His hand moved to my back as he pulled me into a hug. I was so surprised that I held my breath, not knowing what to think.

"Are they looking for me?" I asked.

But he didn't release me; in fact, he held me tighter. This wasn't good. I thought the weeks of separation would have put more distance between us, would have helped him forget. Maybe he had. But there was something wrong now, and he seemed scared.

"Sol," I said, reluctantly pulling way. "What's going on?"

He let me move away, but still leaned close. "It's Chalice."

Chalice . . . not me. "Where is she?" My heart thumped in dread, but at the same time I was relieved that this wasn't about *me*. Had she escaped? Why were they searching for her at the University?

"She was Banished," Sol said.

My stomach twisted. I'd expected him to tell me that she was in a prison somewhere, being punished, or questioned, or that she'd escaped and they were looking for her. As horrible as it would be to learn that about Chalice, hearing about her being Banished was not what I expected. I grabbed at Sol's shirt, feeling as if I might blackout. "What do you mean?" The words themselves seemed self-explanatory, but I hoped with all my heart I hadn't understood.

"She was Banished from the city," Sol said.

"I thought she was Demoted." And then punished. But at least that sounded better than Banished.

"I found the listing on a professor's tablet," he said. "I read the full report."

"What did it say?" I wondered how he came to be on a professor's tablet.

Sol looked around at the darkness, then lowered his head to mine, and spoke quietly. "I don't have time to tell you everything, but she confessed while she was being held— something about how she'd reversed her altering."

I inhaled. They must have tortured the information out of her.

"Do you know anything about what she confessed?" Sol said.

I hesitated only for a second. "Yes." I felt Sol's gaze on me, but I couldn't meet his eyes. "We reversed the altering by . . . accident."

He groaned. "That explains it."

I was afraid to ask what he meant. I was afraid to think about it.

"You and Chalice have some very dangerous information. Chalice is gone now. About an hour ago, a notice went out to the University that you're under criminal investigation."

"So the tram stop and the officials at the gate . . . are for *me?*" My mind reeled—the officials, the transponders, the blocked gates—everyone was looking for me.

"Yes." Sol's voice was thick with concern.

I wanted to throw up. I would be Demoted, maybe Banished. "When was Chalice Banished?" I choked out.

"Yesterday." He watched me intently.

Tears burned in my eyes, but I forced myself to stay composed. "What else did the report say?" I took a step away from him, putting distance between us. I had to think; I needed as much information as possible before I had to face questioning.

"Jez, we only have a few minutes before they find us," Sol said.

I swallowed against the thick dread in my throat. Would they Banish me, too? "It isn't right they Banished Chalice. It was my fault that it happened. We agreed not to tell anyone." I looked up at Sol. "Even you."

And just like that, Chalice's final message to me was suddenly clear: *Don't talk to Sol.* Chalice knew that if Sol learned our secret, he could be implicated, too. And by standing here, with Sol, I was doing just that.

"Don't you see, Jez," he said quickly, "if we knew how to reverse the altering by ourselves, the people could become more powerful than the Legislature."

"So they'll do anything to stop this information." I exhaled. "And all the people they've altered could be reversed." Tears gathered in my eyes. I thought of Chalice and wondered what was happening to her. Was she floating on a raft in the vast waters, traveling aimlessly at the mercy of the great swells? Suddenly I understood why she went with the cult. She was trying to hide the reversal. She was trying to protect me.

"She . . ." my voice faltered, "was trying to protect me." Tears fell onto my cheeks now. "She thought if she got Demoted and put enough distance between us, there would be no connection between us, nothing to link me to the crime."

Sol's fingers touched my tears, absorbing them. I leaned into his warm hand. The temperature was dropping fast as the darkness settled in. I had missed Sol so much, missed seeing him, talking to him. With him so close I was experiencing the pain anew. My heart hurt for Sol, for Chalice. "Don't you see, Sol? She was Banished because of me."

"Don't say that."

"It's true . . ." Suddenly I wanted to tell Sol everything. "She went through punishment after she left." I took a deep breath. "A woman in the C Level told me today. We were there applying our test cream and I asked if anyone that had been Demoted was in their group. She told me about the punishments. She said they break you."

Sol was quiet for a moment. "They must have dragged the information out of Chalice."

"When she gave herself up as a cult member, it must have become obvious that she was no longer altered. And someone got her to admit how it happened." My chest hurt, and it was hard to breathe.

We probably only had minutes left before someone discovered us, but all I wanted to do with whatever time I had left was lean into Sol and wrap my arms around him. I wanted to feel safe, even if it was for only a moment. Even if it wasn't real.

What if this was our final moment together? I hadn't known when my last would be with Chalice or with Rueben.

And now, I was facing Sol. We could be caught in a matter of minutes—seconds. There was nowhere to hide.

Anger burned through my chest. We were all just waiting to be caught. We were all one infraction away from Demotion or Banishment. The image of the Lake People on the crude raft and the group of officials who'd refused to help them kept coming to my mind.

It was just a matter of time before someone broke a rule, even unknowingly, and they'd be replaced in a heartbeat.

Our lives meant nothing. We were only a number to them. We were an instrument to push the life cycle forward. Even my experiment with the C Level women had no meaning anymore. What did it matter if there were ten less women in the city? They had no choices—nothing to look forward to, nothing to celebrate. They worked themselves to the bone day after day, with nothing to show for it but a miserable disease. Their life cycles would come to an end, and no one would even remember who they were.

My breath was shallow, and I moved a fraction closer to Sol. I couldn't imagine not ever seeing him again. But that's what was about to happen. There was no way out.

"Are you all right?" he asked.

"No." I reached out slowly and touched his face. He inhaled but didn't move. Maybe he sensed that we were in our last moments together. "I'm sorry about all of this," I said, "about you risking this meeting to tell me what's going on."

He blinked. "I'll always protect you," he said, his voice sounding hoarse.

"I know," I whispered. "That's what makes this so hard."

He tilted his head, his expression confused.

"It's my turn to protect you," I said. I rested one hand on his shoulder, then moved my other hand behind his neck. I lifted up on my toes and hesitated, gauging his reaction. He didn't move, but continued to stare at me.

I lifted my chin and pressed my mouth against his.

CHAPTER 35

Sol didn't move for few seconds, and I thought he might be in shock.

I had just broken a rule that could get him Demoted. I didn't worry about myself; I was already a lost cause.

But he didn't pull away or run into the street calling for the authorities. Instead, his mouth moved against mine.

My entire body burned as we kissed, and I wondered if this was what it felt like to be burned at the stake. The final seconds of life when the pain was beyond feeling, and the soul leaves the body, becoming something else entirely. Our bodies pressed together, fitting perfectly, filling every curve and angle.

His lips were warm and his tongue hot against mine. I clung to him as one of his hands slid behind my back and the other through my hair, pulling me even closer.

It was as if everything in my life had culminated in that kiss. All of the emotions I'd suppressed in the last sixteen years, all the times I'd watched Sol or thought about him, all of the days I'd spent in prison afraid, all of the nights I'd spent reading his last message to me. I was finally able to release all of my emotions at once, into Sol.

I broke away to breathe, and then Sol's mouth was on mine again. Less urgent this time. We were communicating in a new way, a silent, yet complete way, where only our souls were speaking. Every touch, every kiss was an affirmation of the emotions we had finally allowed ourselves to share.

"Sol," I gasped, wondering if I might self-ignite. He murmured something but kept on kissing me. It was another long moment before I forced myself to break away.

Sol groaned and pulled me toward him again.

"Wait," I said. His lips went to my neck, to my ear, as his hands cradled me. "I have to tell you something."

He lifted his head and smoothed the hair from my face. For a moment, I was mute. I couldn't believe I was here, with Sol, kissing him. Every part of my body tingled; I was floating above the world. But my time was up.

It was now, or never. "I love you," I whispered.

Sol gazed at me and touched my cheek. His fingers slowly trailed along my jaw, then my neck. I shuddered at his touch and the new fire that came with it. He leaned into me again, and his breath brushed my mouth.

"I have to tell you something else," I said, the words sounding like part of a dream.

He didn't stop his pursuit and kissed me once more, then lifted his head, his eyes hazy.

"I'm going to turn myself in."

His eyes changed immediately, and his grip tightened, holding me fiercely against him. "No, Jez."

"Listen to me," I said. "If you take me back to the University, then they'll think you caught me when I left the tram group."

"I'm not turning you in" Sol said, his voice rough.

Voices came from somewhere down the street, accompanied by footsteps. It wasn't hard to guess that the officials were expanding their search. Someone had realized I'd escaped the check point.

"You don't have a choice," I whispered. "The officials are coming now."

"I've been doing some research . . . there's a place you can hide." His grasp tightened. "That's why I brought you here. You have to trust me on this."

"What are you talking about?"

He spoke in my ear, sending a shiver through my body. "Come with me."

There was no place to go—the street was on one side of the small park, apartments on the other. Sol pulled me through the tiny park and stopped at the wall of a building. He crouched down and pushed away the dirt and littered leaves. There was a metal grate or door of some sort.

"What's down there?" I asked.

"Your escape."

He lifted the door with a grunt.

I peered into the pitch black hole. Even in the darkness, I could see there was no semblance of light.

"There's a ladder that takes you to the bottom," he said.

Someone shouted in the street; it sounded very close. My heart raced as I looked down into the blackness. "What about my implant? They'll be able to track where I went."

"You should be deep enough in the ground that there will be too much interference for them to read your location properly."

I exhaled. Could I do this? Could I trust his research? "How deep does this go?"

"I'm not sure," Sol said. "But you'd better go now. I'll return as soon as I can. Then I'll explain everything."

I stared at him.

"Jez, you have to go down there." His gaze was fierce. "Now. These officials don't have trackers, but it won't be long before the government sends out authorities who do."

I was shaking with cold, and my heart was hammering. Sol grabbed my hand and helped me get my footing on the first rung of the ladder. He leaned down and kissed me, his mouth hard and demanding. The shouts of the officials faded into the background for a second. The kiss was over all too soon.

"Be careful," I said to him.

He brushed a hand against my cheek. "I'll return before morning," he said in a strained voice. He kept ahold of my hand as I descended the first few rungs, then released it with a squeeze. Without a word, he replaced the metal grate.

Darkness completely engulfed me. I felt it pressing against me, sliding over every part of my body. I clung to the cold metal rung and held on tightly as I listened to Sol's distant voice. "No one is here. Let's keep searching the other parks."

Another voice answered, but I couldn't make out the words. Then there was only silence.

I let out the breath I'd been holding and tried to sense where I was and what was below me. I was suspended in some sort of a dark shaft, but I couldn't see or hear anything.

I waited several minutes for Sol to return. Did he really expect me to climb down this dark shaft without any idea where it went or what was at the bottom? My arms began to tire. What if he couldn't make it back by morning? He couldn't possibly expect me to wait in this place with no food or water.

At the thought of water, I realized I could hear something if I listened closely enough. It sounded like running water below.

My stomach seized. Where did this ladder lead?

Cold, shaking, and too scared of being caught to return to the surface, I started down the ladder. The going was slow since each step plunged me into deeper darkness. The sound of running water grew louder. There was definitely a stream of some sort, but I had no way of determining how big it was or how fast.

Please hurry, Sol, I thought, knowing full well that he could be gone for a while. If he was even came back at all. What would I do if he didn't come back? How long would it take for the authorities to track me down? How long before I starved or succumbed to hypothermia?

Had Sol been right about our Harmony implants being untraceable underground? They had been traceable in the Phase Three lab—but the prison had been like an underground village unto itself. My tablet was in my pocket, but I didn't dare pull it out to check for a signal. It might slip from my trembling fingers to the water below.

I started counting the rungs so that if I needed to go back up, I'd have an idea how close I was to the top. The temperature continued to drop the lower I moved. At number 125, I was close enough to the flowing water to feel the moisture in the air. I touched the wall that the ladder was attached to—it was wet stone.

I shivered and continued my descent. On the next step down, my shoe touched water. The stream quickly pushed against my boot, and even through the rubber, I could tell how cold it was. I moved my foot farther down and touched solid ground. The stream rushed over the top of my boot, just enough to send water straight in, soaking my feet immediately.

With no choice but to continue, I lowered my other foot, assessing the strength of the current. It wouldn't be hard to walk in. I stood there for a moment as the water rushed over my legs, soaking my pants, one hand still on the ladder. Then slowly, I felt my way along the damp stone wall. There was a small tunnel that opened on one side, where the water flowed through. A second tunnel opened up from the ladder shaft and appeared to be dry.

I had three choices. Wait in the dry portion for Sol, or follow one of the tunnels? Both sloped downward. The bottom of the shaft seemed to be high point.

I sat down in the dry tunnel, the earth moist and packed beneath me, but not muddy. Pulling the tablet from my pocket, I turned it on. There was one message.

Don't return to the University.

It was from Sol.

I looked at the time of the message—it had been sent when I'd been on the tram leaving the C Level district. I hadn't checked the tablet until now. If I had seen it earlier, what could I have done? Slipped off the tram and tried to blend in with people from the C Level or B Level areas? My science group would have noticed I was missing, and it wouldn't be long before the authorities tracked me down.

There hadn't been any more messages, and the signal was dead. I hoped this meant Sol was right and that my

Harmony implant was also untraceable. Or I could find something to cut it out with. Again.

I took off my wet boots and socks to let them dry a little, although the air was humid. At least I could catch my breath a little. Coming down the massive ladder had sapped my strength.

Rubbing my cold and wet feet, I thought about everything that had happened today: meeting the C Level women, finding out that Chalice had been Banished, running from the authorities, and Sol . . . I pulled my knees up to my chest and wrapped my arms around them, trying to find some warmth.

I closed my eyes against the thick darkness and remembered kissing Sol. It was unlike anything I had imagined, even in the most secret places of my heart. Maybe it was because I was Clinical, but I had connected with Sol in a way that was more than just physical. It had been a communion. And I knew he'd felt it, too.

I was starting to feel much warmer. Not only did I want Sol to come back and tell me his plans, but I wanted his arms around me. Had his heart hammered as hard as mine? Had he felt like he was floating above the ground?

I leaned against the stone wall, resting my cheek on top of my knees. Waiting to be rescued.

CHAPTER 36

I woke to a light shining in my face. It took me a couple of seconds to remember that I was sitting on the floor of an underground tunnel. I jerked back and hit my head the wall.

At first I thought it was a flashlight, and someone was shining it at me. But then I realized it was a light embedded into the wall across from me. As my eyes adjusted, I saw another light farther down the tunnel that I was sitting in.

I exhaled, trying to calm my racing heart, and I realized two things: There were lights in this tunnel . . . and someone had turned them on.

I wasn't alone.

My first thought was that Sol had arrived. I looked around but didn't see anyone. I couldn't hear anything except for the running water. I didn't know if the lights were a good thing or a bad thing.

How long had I slept? Minutes? Hours? I turned on the

tablet again, but there was still no signal, so the time log wasn't accurate.

I slowly stood, stretching my aching body. Walking closer to the water, I peered down the other tunnel where the stream ran its course. It was still pitch dark looking downstream, but with the light from the dry tunnel, I could see that the water was muddy and carried small bits of debris. It didn't look clean enough to drink, but my mouth and throat were so dry that I decided to take a sip anyway. I knelt down and scooped a handful of water. It was cold and gritty. I took a few more swallows.

I moved back to where my socks and shoes were drying out. They were both still damp, so I probably hadn't been asleep more than an hour or two. I walked to the light and sat next to it, hoping to draw some of its heat into my body. Eventually I fell asleep again, leaning against the wall, and by the time I woke up I knew Sol was late.

It must be morning above ground, maybe even midday. Where was he? Had something happened? My stomach turned over with a sharp hunger pain, and my body felt weak. I reached over and patted my socks and shoes—they were mostly dry—as much as they were going to be in a damp tunnel.

I tugged them on and walked back toward the ladder. "Hello?" I called upward.

My own echo made me shiver.

I looked back down the tunnel at the first light. Maybe I could go a little ways to investigate and then come back and see if Sol had arrived. Surely he'd call for me. I walked past the first light to the second and then stopped and listened. Nothing. Looking back toward the bend in the tunnel where I'd slept, I gauged how far I'd come—maybe thirty feet. The tunnel floor sloped downward and turned, but it wasn't dark ahead, so there was probably another light.

Before following the tunnel farther, I turned to look at the shaft with the ladder. It was one way out, that I knew, but would it be one that I could rely on? It emptied back into the professors' neighborhood and the University—two places I couldn't go back to.

I looked down the lighted tunnel again, wondering how many lights I'd have to pass to get somewhere. Anywhere.

As I continued moving, I tried to imagine all sorts of scenarios that I could be walking into. Maybe the tunnel would eventually connect to the Phase Three lab, or some other place where I'd be put through more tests. Or perhaps the lights turned on and off automatically, and I really was alone hundreds of feet below the ground.

What if Sol came, and I was too far away to hear him? What if the authorities discovered the shaft? What if Sol had already been exposed and was being questioned?

The ground was rough and uneven, as were the walls, but every thirty or so feet, there was a light embedded into the rock. Then I heard a soft clicking sound. I paused, listening carefully. I took a few more steps in silence, then heard it again.

I looked up. The ceiling was dark, but I could just make out a metal box with a lens. I took a few more steps, my eyes on the camera.

It moved.

Someone was watching me.

My palms went damp. Should I turn and go back? What would Sol want me to do? He'd just said to wait for him, but had he ever been in this tunnel? Did he know where it led?

My breathing was shallow as I kept walking. The tunnel

curved erratically and then narrowed significantly. I hesitated. I was now quite a ways from the main shaft. Walking around the next bend, I came face to face with a metal door. I looked up to see two cameras pointed at me. There didn't seem to be a hand scanner to open the door so I looked back and forth between the cameras and the door. "Hello?" I said at last.

I took a couple of steps forward and placed my hand on the door. Just as I touched the metal, I thought I heard a voice say "No." Something jolted through me, like a shock from an agitator, and I fell backward, landing on the ground. My whole body tingled. The door had an electric charge in it. I sat up and dizziness washed over me

"Jezebel," a voice said, coming from everywhere at once.

My eyes flew open, and I stared at the door. The voice sounded familiar.

But that was impossible.

The voice was impossible.

The door slid open and three people rushed out, wearing all black. I held up my hands in defense. Two remained standing, while the other knelt down, his golden-brown eyes on me.

My mouth fell open. "Rueben?"

His smile was just as I remembered it, brilliant white against his sun-touched skin.

He tugged me against him with a laugh, and I wrapped my arms around his neck, feeling his vibrant warmth beneath my cold hands. I closed my eyes and breathed in sunshine.

Rueben was alive. He was here.

"You made it," he whispered in my ear. "I knew Sol would get you here safely."

I pulled away. "Sol?" I whispered, my throat raw. I had so many questions. How was everything connected?

Rueben held out his hand. "When I found out you were the Carrier, I knew I couldn't leave you behind. Come inside. You'll be safe with us until Sol arrives."

Rueben knows. Somehow he knows I'm a Carrier. I looked at Rueben's outstretched hand, then up at him. He smiled, and I wanted to smile back, to trust him.

I knew him, yet I didn't know him.

Behind me stretched a dark labyrinth of tunnels a hundred feet below the earth. In front of me was hope, possibly survival. I raised my hand and placed it in Rueben's, and he pulled me effortlessly to my feet.

Hand in hand with Rueben, I stepped through the door, into my future.

Next in the Series:

LAKE TOWN

A SOLSTICE NOVEL
BOOK 2

Acknowledgments

I have many people to thank who helped review and edit this book:

My critique group: Sarah Eden, Robison Wells, Michele Holmes, Jeff Savage, Lu Ann Staheli, and Annette Lyon.

The first round of readers: Tanya Mills, Estee Mills, Julie Wright, Josi Kilpack, Angela Eschler, Loree Allison, GG Vandagriff, and Mindy Holt.

Teen readers: Zach Staheli, Alyssa Holmes, Samantha Lyon, and Kara Moore.

Those who've helped me on this book's journey: Amy Finnegan, Sariah Wilson, and my agent Jane Dystel.

To Claudia McKinney, talented cover artist who worked with me to create the perfect image.

The readers who nominated Solstice through Kindle Scout, and the Kindle Scout editing, production, and marketing teams. And Jaime Theler for proofreading.

The Kindle Press team, especially Megan Mulder for her guidance and direction, and Haley Swan for her excellent editing.

And finally, thank you to my husband and children. You are everything to me.

About the Author

Writing under Jane Redd, Heather B. Moore is the *USA Today* bestselling and award-winning author of more than a dozen historical novels set in ancient Arabia and Mesoamerica. She attended the Cairo American College in Egypt and the Anglican International School in Jerusalem and received her Bachelor of Science degree from Brigham Young University. She writes historical thrillers under the pen name H.B. Moore, and romance and women's fiction under the name Heather B. Moore. It can be confusing, so her kids just call her Mom.

Join H.B. Moore's newsletter list for updates at www.hbmoore.com/contact.

Visit **Jane Redd Books** on Facebook for series updates.

Made in the
USA
Monee, IL